"...At the moment can you consider us entering into an exclusive relationship? To spell it out in plain terms, I'd like us to date only each other. Possibility?"

"A definite possibility," she smiled. "Are you sure you want to date only me? You're a man women love."

"That's exactly what I want. In our profession we're around the opposite sex all the time, and we both know lots of flirting comes with the territory. We're often left with very little time to devote to our personal relationships. I've never been one to date more than one woman at the same time, Kennedy. It doesn't work for me. I don't like being tangled up in romantic webs. Are you up for a serious personal liaison with me, one-on-one?"

This beautiful man was too adorable for words, not to mention genuine. Kennedy just wanted to grab hold of Xavier and never let go of him. The diamondlike sparkle in her eyes was bright, with her pupils afloat in liquid. "I'd love to be romantically involved with you. Deal or no deal?" She mocked his earlier remarks to her.

"Deal." Xavi⬚⬚⬚⬚⬚⬚⬚⬚⬚⬚⬚⬚⬚ the mutual agreeme⬚⬚⬚⬚⬚⬚⬚⬚⬚⬚⬚⬚⬚sionate kiss Kennedy⬚⬚⬚

D1019618

Books by Linda Hudson-Smith

Kimani Romance

Forsaking All Others
Indiscriminate Attraction
Romancing the Runway

LINDA HUDSON-SMITH

was born in Canonsburg, Pennsylvania, and raised in Washington, Pennsylvania. She furthered her educational goals by attending Duff's Business Institute in Pittsburgh.

In 2000, after illness forced her to leave a successful marketing and public relations career, Linda turned to writing as a healing and creative outlet, and became a national bestselling author.

Linda has won several awards, including a Gold Pen Award, numerous *Shades of Romance Magazine* awards, and an African-American Literary Show Award. In addition, she is an *Essence* bestselling author. Linda was nominated for two Emma Awards and a Career Achievement Award by *Romantic Times BOOKreviews*. She is a member of Romance Writers of America and the Black Writers Alliance.

For the past seven years, Hudson-Smith has served as the national spokesperson for the Lupus Foundation of America, and has made Lupus awareness one of her top priorities. She travels around the country delivering inspirational messages of hope. Linda was awarded the key to the city of Crestview, Florida, for her contributions.

A mother of two sons, Linda shares a residence with her husband, Rudy, in League City, Texas. To find out more about this extraordinary author, go to her Web site, www.lindahudsonsmith.com.

Romancing THE RUNWAY

Essence Bestselling Author

LINDA HUDSON-SMITH

KIMANI
ROMANCE

 KIMANI PRESS™

ISBN-13: 978-0-373-86105-7
ISBN-10:　　0-373-86105-2

Recycling programs
for this product may
not exist in your area.

ROMANCING THE RUNWAY

www.kimanipress.com

Printed in U.S.A.

Dear Reader,

I sincerely hope that you enjoyed reading *Romancing the Runway* cover to cover. I'm very interested in hearing your comments and thoughts on this romantic story featuring international supermodels Kennedy Bassett and Xavier De Marco, who find love despite the attempts of other women to turn Xavier's head and make Kennedy feel invisible.

Please enclose a self-addressed, stamped envelope with all your correspondence and mail to: Linda Hudson-Smith, 16516 El Camino Real, Box 174, Houston, Texas 77062. Or you can e-mail your comments to lindahudsonsmith@yahoo.com. You can also visit my Web site and sign my guest book at www.lindahudsonsmith.com.

Linda

This novel is dedicated to Amanda Carter,
Clarence Morrell and Damon Waldon, Sr.:
Your presence in our lives will be sorely missed.

Amanda Carter
Sunrise: November 4, 1912
Sunset: June 19, 2008

Clarence Morrell
Sunrise: March 30, 1930
Sunset: August 2008

Damon Waldon, Sr.
Sunrise: November 22, 1947
Sunset: July 20, 2008

I want to thank all my supporters. Your support and
encouragement means a lot to me. I appreciate having
each of you as first-time and loyal readers.

Hearts in Motion Book Club—Bermuda

The time I spent in your company was special. Each of you
exhibited a warmth and friendliness that touched me deeply.
Thanks for a great time on your beautiful island.

Lillian Grant—Leader
L. Lynette Harvey
Donna Belton
Eulette Mallory
Gabriela Pozo
Loida Ratteray
Sandra U. Stowe
Carol Seymour
Norma Showers
Dasmine Thompson

Ladies of Distinction Book Club—Palatka, Florida

Chapter 1

Xavier De Marco couldn't seem to pull his gaze away from the exotic Kennedy Bassett, the supermodel he'd worked with on a couple of modeling assignments. No matter how many times he'd watched her take the high-fashion runway by storm, Xavier was still overly excited by her performances.

Kennedy looked sensuous and hot as ever. Decked out in leather from head to toe, she wore the heck out of red leather pants, a matching bolero-style jacket and a pair of ankle-length red leather boots. The silk shirt she wore, startlingly white and crisp, showed off a discreet amount of mahogany cleavage. As Kennedy began to slowly and seductively remove the leather jacket, Xavier's breath caught.

This woman had more sex appeal than Xavier thought the law should ever allow. Interestingly enough, despite Kennedy's natural beauty, it was her pureness of heart and selfless spirit he had found attractive. He hadn't gotten to know her all that well, but her kind spirit had shone through during the few times they'd worked together. Kennedy wasn't the least bit demanding on the set, but she would speak up if things weren't going well. She was always polite and considerate of her coworkers, readily accepting directions from those in charge. The cameraman had also mentioned to him that she was a delight to work with. Never once had he known her to be late for a shoot during their campaigns. That in itself was very commendable. The genuine way in which she had interacted with the other models had told him a lot—and it had been enough to let him know she was someone he was eager to learn everything about.

The pride Kennedy felt in her profession was written all over her nearly flawless face and in every magical twist and turn she made. Her tantalizing, high-stepping strut was sure-footed. Modeling the stunning Prada creations with grace and style, she was in total command of every part of her willowy five-foot-eight figure. Kennedy held up her head high, as she flung her long, sable hair back over one shoulder. Suddenly, she cast her smoky hazel eyes upon Xavier.

Possessing an amazing athletic build, all the gorgeous hunk of a man could do was smile brilliantly, showing off a beautiful set of even, pearly white teeth. The butterflies surfing in his stomach belied his confident expression. He was more nervous than he'd ever been over any woman. Since he'd finally gotten up the nerve to re-ask Kennedy out, tonight was the night. After the show closed, they planned to have dinner.

Very much familiar with the runway himself, Xavier De Marco, nationally and internationally renowned, was tall, at 6'3", golden-brown-complexioned and utterly ravishing. His deeply set, bluish-gray eyes, sultry lips and wavy, sandy-brown hair were considered his best assets by many. However, Xavier begged to differ. He thought his unimpeachable character and free-flying spirit were his greatest attributes.

Although Xavier was eager to slip backstage to wait for Kennedy to gather her belongings, he considered it rude to leave before the show was over. He also saw leaving any event early as disrespectful to the other performers. He was a performer, so he knew.

Xavier sat quietly, contemplating the part of the evening he'd later spend with Kennedy. He halfheartedly paid attention to the flurry of activity on the runway, until a thunderous round of applause suddenly broke out. He then sat up straight, giving his full attention to the striking, attention-grabbing model who'd just strolled onto the runway.

As the white-hot Tiaja Rae Montgomery confidently strutted her fine body down the runway, Xavier got a strong urge to find an exit. He'd had more than a few sizzling run-ins with the zesty, 5'9" Tiaja Rae—and he wasn't looking forward to another.

Not so fondly referred to by many as T.R., aka Troublesome Rae, she was gorgeous—with a flirtatious lust jones for Xavier. Mocha complexioned, beautiful and sexy, she had a heart-stopping figure, a dream come true for most men. But Tiaja Rae wasn't remotely the kind of woman Xavier was interested in, not in an intimate way.

Kennedy Bassett was Xavier's ideal woman for romancing the runway.

Although Xavier's eyes gave Tiaja Rae their undivided attention, his mind stayed on Kennedy. This fabulous-looking woman occupied his thoughts quite often, ever since their first meeting. Getting her out of his head seemed impossible.

The very moment the fashion show was over Xavier quietly slipped backstage, where he patiently waited for Kennedy to emerge from the dressing room. As his cell phone vibrated against his waist, he quickly responded, greeting his agent, Kirsten Banks, with an enthusiastic hello. Despite the fact she couldn't see him his broad smile was warm and knock-dead charming.

"I need to meet with you right away," Kirsten said, sounding a tad anxious.

"This evening is booked." Xavier hadn't even taken the time to ponder a response. As far as he was concerned, all his time belonged exclusively to Kennedy. "I can meet you in the morning, early, at your office."

The firm way in which Xavier turned down Kirsten let her know there wasn't any room to negotiate. With that in mind, she settled on his suggested time for the meeting. After wishing Xavier a pleasant evening, Kirsten rang off.

Warm hands massaging Xavier's neck and chest from behind both surprised and startled him. However, the soft fingertips felt good on his flesh, but he was more concerned about who the owner was. If the fingers belonged to Kennedy, though he seriously doubted it, the sexy purring near his ear might've been a real turn-on. It would've also made it difficult for him to keep his manhood from rising to an indecent swelling.

Xavier slowly opened his eyes, cringing inwardly at the sight of the lovely Tiaja Rae, who was right up in his personal space.

Grinning like a Cheshire cat, Tiaja Rae trilled off a robust, throaty laugh. "Spooked you, huh, X?"

Looking strangely at Tiaja Rae, wondering why she always had to be so aggressive, Xavier rapidly moved away from her teasing hands. "Girl, don't you ever stop?"

"If you're honest with yourself, X, you'd go ahead and admit it."

Xavier looked puzzled. "Admit what?"

"My hot little hands feel wonderful to you. You *do* know how to tell the truth, don't you?" Tiaja Rae threw her head back and laughed wickedly, loving his reaction.

As if the moment wasn't awkward and embarrassing enough for Xavier, Kennedy had come out of the dressing room just in time to witness Tiaja Rae's hands all over him. Instead of advancing on her date, Kennedy stood back to see how Xavier would handle her archrival and public enemy number one.

Everyone in the world of high fashion seemed to know about the troubled history with the two models so Kennedy figured he was also aware. *She's so transparent,* Kennedy thought.

Wiggling her fingers in a farewell gesture, Tiaja Rae turned and saw Kennedy watching, then flashed her a dazzling, triumphant smile. She loved to rub Kennedy the wrong way…constantly, at every opportunity. This moment was no exception.

Kennedy sucked in a gust of calming breath. In the next instant she walked over and boldly slipped her arm through Xavier's. There was no way she'd let Tiaja Rae get to her ever again. The silly girl had already tested most of Kennedy's nerves, anyway. "How are you?"

"Fine." *Now that you're here.* Xavier looked relieved. He knew of the rivalry between the two supermodels, which had begun long before he'd ever come to know either of them. According to the rumor mill, theirs was a longtime contention.

Xavier quickly decided not to explain to Kennedy what else Tiaja Rae had been up to, not unless she opened up dialogue on it. Kennedy knew her issues with her nemesis far better than he did, but he hoped she'd one day tell him some of the details. Tonight just wasn't the time to explore anything as negative as a sinister runway rivalry.

As Xavier lightly kissed Kennedy on the cheek, he briefly covered her hand with his. "You were absolutely fantastic on the runway! Then again, what else is new?"

Kennedy's broad smile dazzled. "I felt pretty darn good out there tonight. We always know when it's going good or bad for us. Everything went really well."

"You didn't miss a beat, lady. You immediately worked the crowd into one hell of a frenzy. That red leather outfit made a bold statement. Ready to get out of here?"

Kennedy nodded. "You bet. I'm hungry." Earlier in the day she had been extremely nervous about their first date. She was kind of surprised that she felt this relaxed with him so early on in the evening. "What about you, are you hungry?"

Xavier grinned. "Ravenous. I figured you'd probably be starving, too. I made reservations at a quaint little supper club/piano bar. In no time at all, they'll have you digging in to something real tasty. One of L.A.'s finest."

Kennedy was thrilled she wouldn't have to wait forever at a restaurant to possibly be served only a halfway decent meal.

Even the finest eateries could be disappointing at times, especially when overcrowded. Xavier seemed to have excellent taste overall so she was sure he'd already checked out the place. Kennedy was sure that having a dish like Xavier seated across from her would be a mouthwatering distraction. If he was anywhere near as interesting as he was good-looking, he'd more than likely command her undivided attention.

Kennedy immediately saw that Café Blue was appropriately named. The entire decor was done in various shades of blue. She later learned Blue was the last name of the owner, who was a retired Oakland Raiders football player. Xavier's father, La Monte De Marco, and the owner, Reynard Blue, had been good friends from back in the day. They'd never lost touch, though La Monte resided on the East Coast.

Once Xavier had introduced Reynard and Kennedy, Reynard ushered the couple to the table he had handpicked. The seating arrangement looked out over the Pacific Ocean in Santa Monica. The couple was then given cleverly designed menus: thin navy-blue leather-bound books with light blue parchment paper printed with a darker blue ink.

Soft, romantic music drifted from the overhead speakers, though an accomplished pianist was scheduled to perform within the hour. Kennedy thought it'd be nice to listen to piano music while dining. She'd already fallen for the first-class establishment. The atmosphere was romantic yet not overwhelmingly so for a first date.

Xavier stood. "Excuse me for a couple of moments for a trip to the men's room."

"I'll be right here when you get back." She gave him a sweet smile.

Xavier fought the strong urge to lean down and kiss her, but it was too soon for that. Besides, he'd never been a fast mover when it came to the opposite sex. Taking things at a slower pace was more to his liking. Usually he was into first building a solid friendship, yet he was already sure he wanted more. The kind of torrid thoughts he had about Kennedy on a regular basis couldn't be filed away under "friendship."

As Xavier walked away from her, Kennedy watched after him, loving what she saw. His perfectly rounded derriere had her near panting, which led to her recalling some of the details of their first encounter. *Now that was a night to remember.*

They had met during an intimate photo shoot on a windswept beach in Malibu. The two supermodels had partnered to do a provocative swimwear layout for a high-fashion magazine. Their scantily clad bodies had come into contact quite a bit that day, causing Kennedy's body temperature to rise several degrees above normal. With a body as hard and fine as Xavier's, Kennedy had a hard time keeping her eyes from going too far south and her imagination running wild. The power and sturdiness of his thighs and legs couldn't be ignored. Keeping up her professional demeanor wasn't an easy task, but she'd managed. At the end of the day her nerves had been frayed from the tension of wanting this man in a way she'd never wanted anyone. The time she'd spent working with Xavier was ingrained in her memory. Neither one had denied or validated the chemistry between them, but it was definitely present. In spades.

Shortly before the photo shoot had come too quickly to an end for her, Kennedy had been invited to have dinner with Xavier later in the evening. Regrettably, she'd had to decline because of prior plans. Otherwise, she would've accepted his invitation without the slightest hesitation. Xavier had been a delight to work with. Not only was he enchanting, he had exhibited a beautiful spirit, a rare combination in her opinion.

Kennedy had immediately been wildly attracted to Xavier's high energy. To her, he looked like an African-American version of John F. Kennedy Jr., with a similar style of thick, though sandy, wavy hair. His devastating good looks, long lashes and sexy Boston accent hadn't hurt matters any, but the kind of spirit he possessed was more important to her than anything. It'd seemed to her that their spirits were kindred. Xavier had been a gentleman to everyone he had come into contact with regardless of gender. He was caring and thoughtful toward the entire crew. His willingness to lend a helping hand to others was impressive. Kennedy actually saw quite a few of her own qualities in him, which made her believe he had a good spirit.

According to the fashion gossipmongers, Xavier was well bred and well-rounded and a Boston University graduate with a degree in communications. Both parents were successful physicians. His mother, Adelle, was a general surgeon. His father, La Monte, was an orthopedic surgeon. From what else Kennedy had learned, the older De Marcos resided in an elite neighborhood in Boston, in the same house in which they raised Xavier.

Xavier returned to the table. Soon as he reclaimed his seat, he immediately turned his attention back to his date. "What do you think of the place?"

"I like it. The color scheme is fascinating. All these different hues of blues are actually complementary to each other. I hope the food is as wonderful as the atmosphere. I assume you've eaten here before?"

"The food is spectacular. I've come here with my parents a couple of times. I thought you might like it. It's quiet, a lot like your serene spirit."

Kennedy's breath caught. What a nice thing for him to say. Her spirit *was* a quiet one. She was intrigued with how well he'd already summed up an important part of her character. She loved peace and harmony, detesting conflict in any form or fashion.

"God, you're beautiful," he said just above a whisper, his pulse going berserk. Looking at her was an exhilarating experience. Being in her company was even more awesome.

Kennedy looked perplexed, lowering her lashes. "Sorry, but I'm afraid I didn't catch your last remark."

"It was nothing." While Xavier silently thanked God that she hadn't heard him, his smile was soft and tender. His remark had been totally out of line. Coming on too strong wasn't a good thing, especially at this juncture. Getting to know her better had Xavier all hyped up, but he didn't want to lose her, not when he was this big on winning.

Since it appeared Xavier wasn't going to repeat his remark, Kennedy thought she should let it go, no matter how curious she was. He also looked rather embarrassed.

What had he said to make him blush? She'd surely like to know.

The waiter suddenly arrived, giving them a chance to regroup.

Kennedy instantly settled on the entrée-size Caesar salad, topped with grilled chicken. "Please, put the dressing on the side." Then she asked for water with a wedge of lemon.

As Xavier gave the waiter his order, the deep timbre of his voice caused Kennedy's body to slightly shiver. Grilled Orange Roughy was actually one of her favorite whitefish. Maybe he'd let her sample a bite, she thought, smiling inwardly.

"I like my asparagus crunchy," Xavier explained. "A small garden salad with balsamic vinegar will work nicely for me." He took a last-minute glance at the menu. "Peach iced tea, please. Can you also bring us a small plate of lemon wedges?"

"Absolutely, sir. If that'll be all for you, I'll turn in your order right away."

Xavier nodded. "Our order is complete. Thank you."

Kennedy had a fleeting moment of awkwardness, but she shook it off. She was dining with a perfect gentleman, a very nice, fine one, she quietly assured herself.

The couple carried on a nice conversation as they waited for their meals.

As Xavier was very eager to learn even more about Kennedy, he asked all the pertinent questions, and she happily and truthfully responded to each. He thought that a person's personal background was a great way of learning how they grew up and the value system they'd grown up under. Philadelphia, the city of brotherly love, wasn't too far down the road from Boston.

His eyes gleamed with curiosity. "How was life in Philadelphia?"

"Pretty darn good." Her lovely smile showed off her fondness for the region. "I still love to go home for visits, especially on holidays. My mother, Megan, and my dad, Kennedy, retired educators, wouldn't think of living anywhere else. However, they do love to fly to L.A. a few times a year. If Mom thought she could convince Dad to move west, I think she'd go for it. The cold weather is still pretty daunting for her."

The mention of her parents caused Xavier to think of his. He recalled telling Kennedy a bit about them before, but he went on to do a brief recap. "No one in my family is leaving Boston. Dad is actually an L.A. Lakers fan. Figure out that one."

"There are only Seventy-Sixers fans in my parents' house. Like your father, I'm sort of a turncoat, too. I also love the Lakers. Dad and my brothers, Gregory and Scott, would kill me if they knew how hard I cheer for the hottest team on the West Coast."

Xavier raised an eyebrow. "How bad would it be?"

She shielded her eyes with her hands. "Let's just say I'd probably be disowned."

"I doubt that." Xavier couldn't imagine anyone disowning Kennedy.

Kennedy looked up at the waiter when he reappeared at the table to set down their food orders. Before taking off, he made sure the couple had everything they needed.

Kennedy eyed Xavier's meal with keen interest. "Nice portions. You certainly won't have to go home hungry."

Xavier laughed. "They definitely aren't skimpy with the food, but Mr. Blue may've requested a little something extra special for us. He's a great guy."

Kennedy cleared her throat. "Well, it looks like you can tell him that in person. He's on his way over here," she said, half covering her mouth, speaking lowly.

Before Xavier could even react to her remarks, Reynard had arrived. "Is everything to your liking?" His dark amber gaze encompassed both parties.

"The meals just arrived," Xavier responded, "but I know how you pride yourself on putting it out right. Never been disappointed in anything I've eaten here. Kennedy just mentioned the large portions."

Reynard winked. "We aim to please. You two beautiful young people enjoy your meal. Tell my old bud hello for me whenever you speak with him again."

"I'll do that. Thanks for everything, Mr. Blue."

After Kennedy cut up her salad greens into smaller pieces, she took her first bite. As she savored the tangy taste of the dressing, her eyes closed involuntarily. "Mmm, good."

The dab of dressing left on her lower lip had Xavier desiring to lick it away. Her mouth was full, ripe and juicy, and he couldn't help thinking of what it might be like to kiss her, imagining the tingling sensations he'd probably feel. The image of their lips locked together in a passionate coupling was vivid. Tearing his eyes away from her delectable mouth wasn't easy.

Tinkling music, soft and melodic, suddenly drifted slowly about the room, causing Kennedy to look over to the elevated dais where the shiny black baby grand piano was stationed. The gentleman seated on the stool appeared fairly young, possibly in his early twenties, and was wearing a traditional black tuxedo.

While Kennedy and Xavier continued eating their meals, the soft music played on. She'd been able to recognize a few of the songs even though no lyrics were sung. "Play Misty for Me" had been easy for her to identify. "A House Is Not a Home," a Dionne Warwick song her parents loved. For someone so young, Kennedy thought the pianist sure knew how to play the back-in-the-day classics.

As Kennedy's eyes followed several couples walking to the rear of the piano area, she was surprised yet again. She hadn't noticed the dance floor until now. It looked as if the owner had thought of everything. He had successfully pulled together both a lovely dining spot and a magnificent entertainment venue.

"This place rocks," she told Xavier. "I didn't see the dance floor until now. It seems Mr. Blue is quite talented and a resourceful gentleman. I love it here."

"This supper club is a lifelong dream of his. My father often shares the history of how this place finally came into existence. I'd like to share it with you."

Xavier began to tell Kennedy that Mr. Blue was a favorite grand-nephew to his father's beloved aunt, Lucille Carlton. Blue thought the world of his aunt and had made sure she had at least two box seats for all his home football games. When she'd call and say she had a couple more guests to bring along, he'd make it happen.

When Ms. Lucille died a couple years before Blue's retirement from the NFL, she had left over two million dollars to him. There had been one must-do stipulation in her will: Blue had to use a portion of the money to open the supper club he'd always talked of owning…and he'd had to do it within one year of her death or lose the inheritance.

Kennedy was astonished. "That's such a touching story! I bet he was thrilled no end by his aunt's love and generosity. As a football player, I bet he made lots of money. But had he intended to open the restaurant so soon after retirement?"

"According to my dad, Mr. Blue made excellent money, but not the kind of megamillions athletes make today. He'd planned to build a supper club, but he would've had to take out a small-business loan. The inheritance spared him the grief. He *was* excited."

"I'm sure. His is one great success story. This fabulous place is buzzing with patrons and excitement. What are your plans for after modeling? Or have you made any?"

"My degree in communications will help me land a decent job. I'd actually like to work as a sports commentator or a communication specialist on a show like *Entertainment Tonight*. What are you thinking postmodeling?"

"Acting, but I actually want to get seriously involved in it before my modeling career is over. I've already done a few guest spots on television shows. My degree is in theater arts."

"Looks like we both made sure to prepare for life after modeling. I've been doing this a long time now and I love most everything about it. The international traveling is getting a bit tedious, but I'm not tired enough yet to give it up."

"I know what you mean. I've been places some folks can only dream about. I feel blessed for all the world travel I've done over the years."

"That makes two of us." Noticing that she had laid her fork aside, he wondered if she was through with her meal. "Ready for dessert?"

Kennedy rubbed her stomach. "No room at the inn. What about you? Are you ordering dessert?"

"I never leave here without my sweet potato pie. If you're ready to go, I can order it for takeout."

Kennedy waved off his concern. "I'm in no hurry. If you wait to eat it at home, I won't get a chance to steal a pinch." She laughed at her flirty hint.

Xavier grinned. "I hear you. I'll get the waiter over here right away. Sure you don't want anything else?"

Ashamed that she'd left a fair amount of salad on her plate, she looked down at it. "If I could eat anything else, I'd finish off what I already ordered. In a lot of places salads are supersized these days. I'm not wasteful…and I promise I'll finish what I take out."

"Don't give it another thought." He looked down at his plate and cracked up. "Mama would be proud of me if she saw my dish. It was too good not to eat it all."

The waiter arrived simultaneously with the end of Xavier's comment. He ordered two slices of sweet potato pie, one to eat now and another slice for takeout.

Their intense gazes suddenly caught and locked for several seconds. Kennedy turned her head away. She liked his bluish-gray eyes, loved his dazzling smile and his solid packaging. She felt breathless for a moment. If looking at his tantalizing lips, full, sexy and inviting, took her breath away, what would happen if he tried to kiss her? She'd welcome it and probably grow greedy for more.

Kennedy couldn't get her mind to switch gears. Wondering what might occur when Xavier walked her to her door had her trembling inside.

Xavier reached across the table and closed his hand over Kennedy's. "Think you can find your way back to earth?"

Feeling her color rise, Kennedy tried to laugh off her embarrassment. "Sorry about that. I don't know where my mind skidded off to."

"*You don't?* I know exactly where my mind was in your absence."

She knew he was setting her up, but she still decided to take the bait. "Where?"

His eye color deepened. "Out there on the dance floor, holding you in my arms. Think we can make it happen? I'd love to dance with you." The deepness of his voice was strong and husky, yet intimately passionate.

Dancing was her absolute favorite thing to do. She looked across at the dance floor, where patrons were grooving to the smooth piano tunes. "The feeling is mutual." She scooted her chair back from the table and waited for him to extend his hand.

As Xavier took Kennedy's hand into his, guiding her out onto the dance floor, his smile defied description. The heat emanating from his hands warmed her through and through. The heat grew feverish as he gently pulled her in close to his body, leading her in a seductive slow dance. *A light breeze just might help cool things down,* she thought.

The intense desire Kennedy had to lay her head against Xavier's chest was no match for the common sense busy kicking her in the shins. Her strong attraction to him couldn't be denied. Nor would she try to deny it, but she had to proceed with caution.

Her thoughts flew her back to the beach modeling gig in Malibu, where his fiery hands had explored her anatomy with relaxed ease, touching her like this, caressing her like that. His lips had come within micro inches of hers—and it had been doubly hard not to make the sweetest of introductions. She shivered at the thought of a passionate lip connection.

Kennedy *had* been checking him out the entire day. And she had made it her business to find out if Xavier was in a relationship. She had had her fill of men who thought it was okay to date more than one woman at a time, especially without making them aware of the intent. All of the sources she'd spoken to had been very reliable, which was the main reason she'd accepted his invitation to dinner. According to Xavier De Marco's peers, the man had a stellar reputation.

The many things Kennedy and Xavier soon learned they had in common amazed them. They liked the same music, loved sports—and each possessed a strong desire to see the entire world to experience life in other cultures. Both were champions to the underdog. They were also in just the right profession to have it all.

Xavier realized Kennedy was lost to him again, her mind off to somewhere else, but he was okay with it this time. She was safely in his arms and the night was still very young. "The Look of Love" was playing softly and "Never Can Say Good-bye" had just ended. He hadn't planned to go inside when he took her home, that was, if she even invited him in, but he knew he wanted a host of encore dates.

Kennedy was something special. Xavier's instincts had told him that much. Even though he didn't believe in dogging women, period, he wouldn't ever think of half-stepping with this woman. She deserved his all, his everything, and he was sure she'd come to demand the same from him. He didn't plan on falling short of her expectations.

The quiet ride to her home in the close confines of his convertible Mercedes Benz 350 CLK had her breath catching every few minutes. He smelled so good, so manly. After all their hours together, his light citrus-scented cologne still stirred her senses. As she studied his hands on the steering wheel, she saw that he had tight control, without being uptight. It was like he caressed the wheel, holding it steady and sure. She felt safe.

The radio station Xavier had tuned in to was one of those late-night romance fests, where the DJ had a smooth, silky voice and knew all the right buttons to push to heat things—and bodies—up. Every song was soft and sensuous, sweet, sweltering and sexy.

The more she thought about it, the more she was sure she'd love for Xavier to wrap her up in his arms securely, stroke her limbs tenderly, kiss her hungry mouth passionately and tenderly nibble on her earlobes until her heart thumped wildly.

Laying her head back on the headrest, Kennedy closed her eyes. These were the kinds of provocative moments one savored when becoming lost in the array of intimate possibilities. Xavier was the kind of man Kennedy had often daydreamed about, only to later meet up with him in her bedtime fantasies. Waking up alone was always disappointing.

Taking the keys from Kennedy's hand, Xavier opened the door and handed the heart-shaped ring back to her. "Want me to make sure there's no boogeyman inside?"

The lighthearted teasing from Xavier made Kennedy laugh.

"I'm not scared of any old boogeyman." She flexed her arm muscles. "This girl got muscles. If someone jumps out at me, they'd better be ready for action. I got some serious, kick-butt moves."

"Okay, Miss Tae Kwan Do." His expression suddenly turned sober. "I really enjoyed myself. You're refreshing. Any chance we might do this again?"

"Any chance we might not?" Kennedy shot back. Xavier was impressed by how quickly she'd fired right back. "Or was that just your way of asking me out again?"

He eyed her with intense curiosity. "What if is was? *How* would you respond?"

Laughing, Kennedy shook her head from side to side. "Since you haven't asked me anything specific, I don't know how I'd respond."

He took hold of both her hands. "Will you go out with me again, Kennedy?"

"I'd love to. Nothing would give me more pleasure." She openly flirted.

"What about tomorrow evening? I'd love to cook dinner for you, at my place."

Kennedy appeared impressed. "You can cook?"

"One of the best male chefs around. Dad has major cooking skills and I inherited every last one. Mom is a fantastic cook, but she can't dethrone my father."

"Can't wait to have my taste buds check out your credentials," she teased.

"Just tell me what you want…and I'll prepare it."

"You got a deal." The mischievous, bad-girl side of her took over, as she began thinking up a complicated meal for him to fix. "Beef Wellington is one of my favorites."

Onto her devious mission, Xavier failed at keeping a straight face. "I see you like to get your jokes on, but I *can* do beef Wellington, girl. What time should I pick you up?"

She angled an eyebrow. "What if I just drive myself there around seven?"

"Whatever works better for you. I'll call in the morning with directions."

"Look forward to hearing from you." She grew silent, allowing her gaze to sweep over his handsome face. "I had a really good time, too. You are great company."

Leaning into her, Xavier brushed across her cheek a light, airy kiss. "Tomorrow."

Suddenly a flurry of bright white lights flashed before their eyes. A group of photographers came at the startled couple from every angle. Kennedy's front porch had been invaded. The flashbulbs were darn near blinding, causing them to use their hands as eye shields.

Kennedy and Xavier lived to pose in front of the camera by day, and often by night, loved their jobs as top supermodels, but both hated being completely caught off guard by the ever intrusive paparazzi. *Where had all these men come from?* There had to be at least ten to twelve cameramen. How long had they been following along behind them? It was indeed hard to tell since neither had spotted a single one.

Was this wild scene just the preview of things to come? Kennedy couldn't help wondering what she should expect. They'd been so careful to keep their plans for tonight under wraps. Were they going to continuously be hunted down in the darkness of night like wild game and trapped with nowhere to run? She recalled getting injured a couple of times while trying to flee from flashing bulbs. Kennedy recalled with crystal clarity how she had tripped and fallen to the ground in her frantic escape from the camera-toting paparazzi.

As Xavier did his best to shield Kennedy from the cameramen, he couldn't help wondering if this was the beginning of the end for them. It was tough enough to deal with a new relationship, but these types of wild scenes had proved to be game changers for him in the past. It would take an exceptionally strong woman to suck up this madness, even a professional model like he was.

Chapter 2

Xavier's four-bedroom Santa Monica beach home was exquisitely decorated, yet extremely comfortable. The splendid furnishings ranged from soft leathers to luxurious designer sofas and matching chairs, fashioned in a variety of lavish materials. Although he had explicit ideas for his personal living space, he'd collaborated on the entire decorating process with a professional design studio owned by his dearest friend, Jonathan Alexander, also a close fraternity brother in alpha PSI alpha.

Earth tones and discreet splashes of oranges, yellows and reds, softer variations of the bold colors, were Xavier's choices. User-friendly furnishings had been very important to him. He desired that no one entering his personal space would have to wonder what they could or couldn't use or where they could or couldn't eat, sit or sleep. No stuffy decorum whatsoever had been permitted in any of the rooms.

While Xavier definitely wanted the formal areas in his home to ooze class and finesse, they also had to be heartwarming, relaxing and sociably inviting.

There was even a special room with the young at heart in mind, which included a Sony PlayStation and an Xbox. Xavier loved children. Though he didn't have kids, several of his close friends were family men.

The fabulous loft, cozy with down-home comfort, was also

used as a retreat for deep meditation, where he burned candles and made contact with his inner self. He believed wholeheartedly in communicating with his spirit.

Stretched out on his bed, dressed in silver-gray lounging pajamas, Xavier dialed Kennedy's home number. Hoping he didn't get her voice mail, he laid his head back onto one of six king-size pillows. A bright smile lit up his eyes at the sound of her voice. In the pit of his stomach fiery sensations were already taking over. She had that kind of effect on him. "Good morning, sunshine! Hope I didn't wake you."

"Hardly." She drew in a shaky breath. "Morning, Xavier. By the way, is it okay if I call you X once in a while? I like the shortened version."

"Quite a few people take liberties with my name. X *is* the most popular." He thought about Tiaja Rae calling him by the same name. "X is fine by me. Just remember I'm called that by many folks."

"It slips off the tongue with ease. How're you feeling?"

"Happy I've been blessed with an opportunity to start a brand-new day. Today I'm writing the beginning of a new chapter in my life. Got a pencil and paper handy so I can give you my address?"

"That's a nice and positive way to look at it." She paused, reaching for a pen in her nightstand. "I'm ready. Go ahead and give it to me." Kennedy wrote down the information in her address book. "I've got it. Thanks. I'll see you at seven." Kennedy felt giddy about seeing him again, especially this soon.

"How do you feel about us pairing up with a married couple for dinner? They're good friends of mine. I think you'll like them. Janine and Jonathan Alexander. Janine is a fashion writer. Jonathan, my frat brother, owns a successful interior design business."

"Sounds like fun. I'd love to meet both your friends. Is there a specific dress code for our dinner?"

Xavier chuckled. "I can't believe a fashion diva is asking a question like that. It'll be pretty casual. I love dining outside on the deck. I recently had one of those outdoor entertainment rooms installed. Mine just happens to overlook the Pacific. I'd like you to be comfortable in my space. The offer to pick you up and drive you home still stands."

"I'm pretty familiar with Santa Monica. I think I can find you with the help of my built-in GPS tracking system."

"Good. I'll see you around seven. Have a wonderful day."

"You do the same. Bye, Xavier."

Glad the grocery store wasn't crowded, Xavier went from aisle to aisle quickly, amassing the items he needed for beef Wellington. He chuckled from deep within. He didn't know another person who would've requested the type of meal Kennedy had hit him with. *Whatever you want, I'll prepare,* he recalled saying. *Whatever indeed.* If only she knew his range of culinary capabilities. He was by no means an amateur chef. He'd make sure she was certain of that by evening's end.

"What am I going to wear?" Kennedy shouted. One person should never own this many clothes, she thought, pushing back hanger after hanger on the sturdy racks inside her huge walk-in closet. Many items still had the price tag attached. Designers and fashion houses gave her a fair share of fashionable attire as compliments, yet she still went shopping. Buying new clothes was senseless, especially when she owned a countless wardrobe. But she loved shopping for lingerie.

Casual dinner, Xavier had said. But Kennedy really had no desire to wear jeans. After coupling sharply creased Anne Klein white linen pants with a Nicole Miller lime-green shell and sweater, both with jeweled necklines, she began looking through her clear plastic shoe boxes, stacked by color and style.

Kennedy finally located the perfect pair of Michael Antonio

gold strappy sandals. After removing the stylish items, she set
them atop the armoire. *Perfect,* she thought. Happy that chore
was complete, she left the closet.

Bright and shiny with stainless-steel and smoky-black
appliances and beautiful cherry-wood cabinetry, Xavier's
spacious kitchen was well appointed. Splashes of soft oranges
and reds added a touch of colorful spice to the decor. Bushy
green plants in woven baskets nested on the ledges above the
cabinets, lending a warm touch of mother earth. Fresh fruits
filled a red ceramic bowl centered on the granite island
counter.

Xavier loved to cook in his cheerful kitchen. Ready to get
started on his food preparations, he began to gather up all the
ingredients. Since he'd already made the decision to roast the
tenderloin whole, he pulled pastry puff sheets from the refrigerator.

He had already finely chopped the mushrooms. Shallots
sweated in a small amount of oil, until tender. Both ingredients
were then sautéed in sherry until the liquid totally evaporated.
He seasoned the beef with salt and pepper and coated it with
roasted garlic before adding butter and parsley. Once the tenderloin was rolled up in a pastry puff, he brushed it with egg
wash. Green peppercorn sauce was the last item he prepared.
He would later drizzle the mixture over the roasted meat and
garnish it with dill just before serving.

Once Xavier finished all the cooking preparations, he went
up to the loft, where he'd left the book he was reading, *Reflec-
tions from Earth's Orbit,* written by Winston E. Scott, a retired
Captain, United States Navy. It was a fascinating book. Interestingly enough, this true-life story was written in terms the
average person could understand. Captain Scott was also a
retired African-American NASA astronaut. What Xavier had
read so far was intriguing, demanding him to make more time

to finish it. He loved to read biographies on United States astronauts and other noteworthy Americans.

Parked right outside Xavier's home, Kennedy made a last-minute check on her makeup. Her nose looked a bit shiny so she took out her compact and large makeup brush to dull the shine. After applying another layer of MAC gloss to her full mouth, she pressed her lips together. Hoping Xavier would be pleased with how she looked, she opened the driver's door and slid out from under the leather steering wheel.

After pressing the doorbell, Kennedy stood back to wait for him to greet her. Much to her surprise, a stunning female answered the bell. Her attire was impeccable and every hair on her head appeared in place.

Kennedy couldn't help feeling a little bit nervous. This woman appeared to have it all, even the privilege of answering Xavier's door. Well, she thought, he certainly wouldn't have a woman he was romantically involved with over to his home at the same time he had a date with her. Kennedy chalked her thoughts up to silly nonsense. It wasn't like her to jump to meaningless conclusions and she certainly wasn't the insecure type.

The woman with the bone-straight brunette hair extended her hand. "Hello, I'm Janine. And you must be Kennedy. You're every bit a beautiful as our friend has boasted. Come on in. The guys are outside on the deck. It's a pleasure meeting you."

Kennedy smiled. "Thank you. The feeling is mutual, Janine. I love your outfit." Kennedy truly admired the expensive-looking creamy white pants, paired with a flirty icy-blue and white Chris Han top. "White works beautifully. It makes any outfit pop. I see we both favor it."

"I wear lots of white," Janine said. "Like you said, everything goes with it."

As Kennedy followed Janine through the large house to get outdoors, her eyes darted everywhere, busy taking in some of the finer details of Xavier's living quarters. She liked the spicy color scheme of his decor. From what she could see, the place appeared neat and extremely clean, very well taken care of. The style of the white French doors leading out to the deck was similar to the set installed in her home.

Xavier's smile was wide as he drank in Kennedy. Her sable hair looked salon-fresh, shiny and full of body. He loved the outfit she wore, thinking it fit her to a tee. The lime green looked good against her mahogany flesh. As he began his walk toward her, he couldn't wait to touch her, could barely wait to feel the softness of her skin. Being close to her caused him all sorts of hormonal reactions. Lifting her hand, he pressed a kiss into her palm. "Glad you're here. You look beautiful."

Kennedy blushed. He looked beautiful, too, not to mention sexy. His khaki Loro Piana shorts looked good on his powerful physique. The silk Emporio Armani T-shirt was chocolate. The casual brown leather sandals completed his outfit. As he was freshly shaven, she had a strong urge to laze her hand down the side of his face.

As Xavier reclaimed a gentle hold on Kennedy's hand, he introduced her to Jonathan. "This is Kennedy Bassett, the lady I've been raving about. Kennedy, this is my best friend, Jonathan. I'm assuming you two ladies have already introduced yourselves."

"We have," Janine said. "We actually got straight into the topic of fashion."

Happy the two women had already had a pleasant exchange, Xavier laughed. "I guess that means you guys have already found something in common."

"I'm sure by evening's end we'll find we have lots more in common," Janine said.

"All of us probably have a lot in common," Xavier stated. "The food is done. If you guys are ready to eat, I can put the meal on the table." He was proud of the amazing job he'd done with the gold and white place settings. A professional couldn't have done any better.

After everyone voiced their desires to eat right away, each guest offered to help Xavier bring the dishes out to the deck. Glad for the extra help, he had everyone follow him into the kitchen to grab hold of something.

Inside the kitchen, Xavier guided Kennedy over to the stove, where he pulled down the upper oven to expose his masterpiece. "Beef Wellington," he sang out, "prepared especially for my new friend. Think I can get a proper thank-you?"

Kennedy was stunned by the beautifully browned roast. It looked cooked to perfection. "Depends on what you consider proper." Kennedy eyed him curiously.

He stuck his cheek near her lips. "Do you need more of a hint?"

She kissed his cheek, allowing her lips to linger there for a short spell. "Thank you. I can't wait to taste the fruits of your labor. But can I let you in on something?"

He raised an eyebrow. "What's that?"

She threw her head back and let her laughter trill. "Never in my wildest dreams did I expect you to follow through on my request. Now that you have, I'm going to do my best to do the meal justice. Maybe I can even take home some leftovers."

He winked at her. "Anything your little heart desires."

"Anything, X?"

"Anything! You heard me. Just let me know what it is you want. I'll deliver."

For starters, you. She hoped taking him home with her was on a future menu.

Now that all the food Xavier had prepared earlier was laid out, he ushered Kennedy over to the oval-shaped glass table and pulled out one of the six wrought-iron chairs. Before taking his own seat, he waited for Janine and Jonathan to claim theirs. Xavier then asked Jonathan to pass the blessing. His friend seemed proud to do the honors. Kennedy liked that everyone was familiar with prayer, loved the fact that no one seemed to have a problem giving God His props.

Around the table near complete silence lasted a few minutes, as everyone enjoyed the fabulous meal. Kennedy was so pleased by what he'd done for her. No one had ever cooked her beef Wellington, nor had she ever asked it of anyone.

Kennedy was just being facetious when she'd told Xavier what she'd wanted him to prepare for her. He'd said his father had taught him how to cook this particular entrée—plus many others. He had surely taught his son well. The delicious cut of beef was tender and moist and the pastry puff it had been baked in was flaky and buttery. Kennedy had never eaten food this delectable—and she'd graced a lot of first-class eateries, dining at some of the finest catered events all over the world.

Along with the beef and mushrooms, Xavier had sautéed asparagus and brown rice. The initial sight of the food had caused Kennedy's mouth to water.

The crisp salad greens lying beneath the cherry tomatoes and thin slices of cucumbers, sprayed with an Italian-blend dressing, was a perfect complement to the wonderful meal. Xavier's plate held double portions of everything, except the rice, which he had a bowlful of. He had told Kennedy he was a rice lover, loving it any way it was cooked. Xavier had never had a problem with his weight despite his voracious appetite.

The host reared his chair back slightly. "How *is* everything, Kennedy?"

"It is the best meal I've eaten. Don't you see this huge smile on my face?"

"I get the point. Thanks." Xavier grinned, grateful for the compliment. He looked to Jonathan and Janine for their opinions. Their thoughts were similar to Kennedy's.

Conversation flowed smoothly as the two couples savored a fine French wine. Kennedy learned that Janine was a fashion writer who wrote for a host of fashion magazines and Web sites. She also had a Web site and blog where her readers could write in and give their opinions on her stories. Janine spent a good bit of her work schedule making rounds at popular fashion venues.

As the wife of an interior designer, Janine was there for him, always willing to help out in his business ventures. Many of his wealthier clients were referrals from his bride of four years. He was a fabulous-looking guy who doted on his wife. Kennedy thought they made a lovely couple. Happiness was written all over their glowing faces.

Everyone had finished with their meals, but Xavier noticed that Kennedy was still working on hers. She was a very slow eater. She had informed him of that at Café Blue. She believed eating slow was necessary for proper digestion. Very much into a healthy diet, she also drank plenty of water and got lots of exercise. It wasn't unusual for her to linger over her meal thirty minutes or more. She wasn't a fanatic about controlling her weight, but she did take seriously everything to do with her health and diet.

"Besides your exciting career, what do you do for fun?" Janine asked Kennedy.

"Dancing is my favorite. I include it in my daily exercise routine. I also try to go out dancing at least once or twice a week for fun. Besides, I love to play tennis, the piano and read."

She went out dancing with her girlfriends, Martina Sellers and Bianca Wise, when they were available to hang out. The three women frequented some of the most popular dance clubs around the Los Angeles and Hollywood areas.

To once again make sure Xavier had no doubts about how great the food was, Kennedy rolled her eyes up to the ceiling. "This food is soooo good. If you'll agree, I'd love for you to help me prepare the meal for my upcoming dinner party next week. That is, if you're free to join my guests and me. What do you say?"

Certain that he'd heard her correctly, yet baffled by her request, Xavier widened his eyes. "You're putting me on, right?"

"Of course not! I'm serious. There'll only be six or so of us, total," Kennedy said.

Xavier hunched his broad shoulders. "What'd you have in mind to serve?"

"I'll leave that up to you. After this meal, I definitely trust your judgment."

"Oh, no, I'm not going out like that. If I agree to help cook, you plan the meal."

"We have a few days to decide the menu." Kennedy turned to look at Janine and Jonathan. "I'd feel honored if you'd both come. The group I hang out with is a lot of fun. But I have to warn you, they're lively and very much into playing practical jokes."

"We'd love to come," Janine said, readily accepting the invite for her and Jonathan. Sighing hard, she stretched her arms high above her head. "Can't believe how tired I am. This has been an extremely busy week for me."

Kennedy understood. She was fatigued. Her feet ached, and she planned to soak them once she got back home. But being with Xavier was exhilarating.

Suddenly, Kennedy realized she didn't want to miss out on one moment of their time together, nor did she want to be distracted by any one thing or another. She couldn't sleep in late tomorrow, since she had an early-morning assignment, but this evening she wanted every moment she spent with Xavier to be memorable.

"Why don't you guys go on into the media room and relax while I clear the table? It'll only take me a few minutes to get it all done," Xavier remarked.

Janine got to her feet. "Can't believe you went there. You know how we roll. We always do the cleanup bit together. This evening is no exception."

Jonathan stood up and then kissed his wife gently on the mouth. "Maybe our boy is putting on airs for Kennedy." Everyone laughed. "Let's knock out the cleanup so we can all sit down, relax and listen to some good music," Jonathan suggested.

"Count me in," Kennedy remarked. "We can get everything done in a flash."

Arguing with his friends wouldn't do a bit of good, Xavier knew. He'd been there and had done that enough times to know better. After getting to his feet, he began to clear the table. "Let's do this." He flashed Kennedy a brilliant smile, but all he really wanted to do was lean into her and give her a sweet kiss. He felt like letting go with a low growl, satisfying his desire to act naughty with her.

Smiling back at him sensuously, Kennedy's gaze locked on to Xavier's luscious mouth. *Keep smiling at me like that, and you'll get yourself into a heap of trouble.* Playfully, she swatted his arm, though she would've rather popped him on his sexy backside. Bring it on, big boy, she taunted mentally, gathering up the wineglasses.

Finished with the kitchen duties, the foursome quickly made their way to the lavish media room, furnished with fine Italian leather sofas and several different kinds of chairs designed for comfort. The chocolate-and-gold-veined marble fireplace and beautiful hand-carved mantel were the first items to catch Kennedy's eye. The plush white rug laid out only inches away from the hearth was exquisite. Instantly, her mind conjured up images of their bodies entwined, watching the flames of a roaring fire.

While Xavier's guests took seats, he turned on the CD player he kept stacked with the latest in releases. Big on Mariah Carey and Mary J. Blige, he usually kept at least two discs of each artist on the playlist. He'd learned from Kennedy that she was an Usher and Beyoncé fan. Once she'd accepted his dinner invitation, he had made sure to include a couple of her favorite discs for her listening pleasure.

Jonathan and Janine had a quiet conversation going on between them, one that Kennedy and Xavier weren't privy to.

With the other couple completely into each other, it allowed the host to fully concentrate on entertaining his date.

Xavier extended his arm across the back of the sofa where he and Kennedy were seated. "How was your day?"

"Really busy, but all my days are that way, especially lately. I keep telling myself I'm going to set aside some me-time, but I never seem to do it. You know the type of life we high-fashion models lead. If we're not into one thing, we're into something else. There's always that last-minute call to help someone out because of an unexpected cancelation. I'd love to take a vacation where I can just lie out on the beach and soak up the rays. I love to read, but I don't seem to have much time for that anymore, either."

Xavier nodded. "I know exactly what you're talking about. But only you can make the difference in how you pace your lifestyle."

She looked perplexed. "What do you mean?"

Xavier went on to explain to her that everything to do with a person's life was about choices. He kept a list of the things he wanted to accomplish and he had it in order of importance. As jobs came in, he weighed out each one, deciding to do only those he thought he'd really enjoy or benefit from. He did the same with charitable events.

A newcomer to the profession thought they had to do everything they were asked. As models became seasoned veterans, he told Kennedy they could begin to choose only jobs that held their interest. In fact, they had to learn to choose wisely or face burnout.

Xavier wrapped a tendril of her hair around his finger. "Why take on something you might not enjoy? Favors are just that, favors. You don't have to say yes to everything you're asked to take on. If it's something you really don't want to do, say no."

She eyed him with open curiosity. "Is it really that simple?"

"It's only as simple or as complicated as we make it. We're in a position to make choices. Of course we have to fulfill our contract obligations. But it's normally the noncontractual stuff that steals our free time away. It's great to give support to charities, but we have to limit ourselves to how many events we take on in a given period."

She laid her forefinger against her temple. "Never thought of it that way."

"Then I suggest you start," Xavier said matter-of-factly, smiling softly.

She smiled back. "I think you're right. I often find myself agreeing to do way more things than I have time for. It's hard to turn down people. Tomorrow I'll start working on my list. Thanks for the great advice, Xavier. You've really opened my eyes."

More nervous than he'd ever been around any woman, Xavier sucked in a deep breath, just before kissing Kennedy's forehead. When she didn't object to that bit of intimacy, he dusted her lips with a soft kiss. She smelled so good, so sweet, and the delicate scent of her nearly drove him wild with desire. As Kennedy laid her head against Xavier's shoulder, no one was more surprised than him, surprised and definitely pleased.

Kennedy truly felt safe with Xavier. *Was it because his friends were in the room?* She didn't think so. She didn't like fast-moving and fast-talking men. He didn't seem to be either type. So far, he seemed for real, truly down to earth. Xavier could've asked out any woman in the world, but he'd chosen her. Not once, but twice. Perhaps he'd thought about her as much as she'd reflected on him. Desiring a moment to ponder what might be happening between them, she closed her eyes. Tranquillity washed over her.

Kennedy awakened to glowing candlelight in an otherwise darkened room. She was sprawled out on the leather sofa, and a lightweight blanket had been thrown over her. She looked around the room for a wall clock but couldn't find one. The dial on her watch was too small for her to see without light. Then she spotted the time on the cable box.

3:00 a.m.

Panic rapidly arose within her. *What in the world had happened?* The obvious couldn't be overlooked. *She'd fallen asleep.* Not only had she gone out like a light, she'd done so at the expense of Xavier and his guests. *How rude was that?* What a first impression she must've made on Janine and Jonathan, not to mention her host!

Kennedy had no idea how she was to live down this idiotic act, sure that Xavier was furious with her. The blanket only proved he didn't want her to catch her death. It also showed how considerate he was to her compared to how inconsiderate she'd shown herself to be. *This is awful,* she thought, moving aside the cover and sitting up. As she looked down at her feet, she noticed her sandals had been removed. Then she saw the shoes situated next to the coffee table.

How to get out of Xavier's home without waking him was Kennedy's next thought. Surely he had an alarm system…and it was probably activated. She racked her brain for a solution to her dilemma, but came up totally empty.

The urgency to use the bathroom hit her suddenly. She knew there was a guest bathroom in the hallway, but she'd have to turn on a light. That was risky since it might wake her host. Since she didn't have a choice in the matter, she reached for the switch.

Trying her best to be quiet as possible, Kennedy tiptoed from the room and stepped out into the hallway. Halfway to her destination she ran into something solid, which scared the day-lights out of her, causing her to scream bloody murder.

Strong arms instantly went about her, steadying her on her feet, making sure she didn't fall. "It's okay. It's just me," Xavier whispered, his tone gentle and soothing.

Xavier flicked on a switch and soft lighting suddenly flooded the hallway.

Kennedy looked thoroughly embarrassed. "I'm so sorry for falling asleep on you and your guests like that. Please forgive me." She sounded as if she was about to cry. She'd never done anything so asinine in her adult life—and she felt downright stupid.

As Xavier gave Kennedy a warm hug, he chuckled. "Don't be so hard on yourself. You were obviously tired. That's all there was to it. My friends definitely understood. They work every bit as hard as we do. Janine was worn-out, too."

"Hold that thought," she said. Kennedy was unable to stand still another second, not without dire consequences. "I'll be right back." With that said, she had to run the few steps to the bathroom just to make it in time.

Xavier laughed inwardly. No one was more surprised than him that Kennedy had fallen asleep on him. At first, it had bothered him, simply because he'd thought she might've been bored out of her mind. After he'd gone over the numerous things she'd told him she'd accomplished that week, he'd understood it all had to do with sheer fatigue. And he'd also fed her a huge meal, one big enough to make anyone sleepy.

Janine had also shared with Xavier how tired she felt, which had resulted in her and Jonathan's leaving much earlier than normal. His friends hadn't blamed his date one iota for falling asleep. They had told him he should feel lucky she felt comfortable and safe enough with him to fall asleep in his home. Actually, Janine had seen it as a good omen.

After splashing cold water on her face, Kennedy used one of the fancy guest towels to dry her skin off. She didn't know what she'd say to Xavier, but she knew she had to hurry up and get back out there and face him. Stalling for time wouldn't help matters any. And disappearing into thin air wasn't an option.

Combing her fingers through her hair was the last thing Kennedy did to try and look more presentable. Before stepping back into the hallway, she said a silent prayer. Much to her joy, he wasn't standing out there waiting to escort her back to where she'd left her purse and sandals. Upon spotting Xavier seated in one of the leather recliners, she smiled weakly, wishing she could've mustered up a more convincing one.

Xavier sat up straight in the chair. "I'd like to fix you a cup of coffee. It might help you stay awake if you're thinking of driving home."

She shook her head in the negative. "That's not necessary. I can make it home okay. I think I'm wide-awake now."

"*Think?* That doesn't sound very convincing to me." He looked over at the cable box to check the time. "Look, it's darn near four in the morning. Please accept one of my guest rooms for the next couple of hours or so. You can leave at the crack of dawn if you want to."

"I probably should leave now."

"Why? Are you afraid to stay here alone with me?"

"Of course not! Don't be silly. Is there a reason for me to be afraid?"

"Not a single one. You're perfectly safe here with me. I wouldn't harm a single hair on your beautiful head. You can trust me with your life."

"That sounds promising." Kennedy looked down at her sandals. Then she glanced at the clock again. "I don't know. Maybe I should stay at least until the sun comes up." Her garage had a door leading right into the house, but she thought about what elements might be out there to witness her driving around alone at this hour.

"Leaving at sunrise *is* the best and safest option. Don't you think so?"

"You win. But I'll just stretch back out here on the sofa and use the blanket you covered me with. I don't want to mess up fresh bed linens for a couple hours."

"Nonsense. A bed is more comfortable than any leather couch, no matter how soft it is. Come on. Let me show you where you can lie down until you're ready to leave."

Kennedy knew when she was in a losing battle. And she was

too tired to continue haggling over something Xavier was obviously right about. "The bed it is. Thank you."

The bedroom was lovely and cozy. The comforter on the queen bed was a field of flowers done in white, yellow and lavender. It made her feel as if she was in the middle of a spring day. The white wicker furniture looked new. Three oil paintings, all of them seascapes, graced oyster-white walls. The largest window overlooked the pool and patio, from where the mountain range was in full view. Recessed lighting was soft and glowing.

Kennedy loved the room, knew she'd be more than comfortable there. After she slipped out of her clothes, she put on the long sweatshirt Xavier had provided for her. As she lay there, the earlier vision of her and Xavier entwined suddenly sped into her mind.

The heat emanating from Kennedy's body was no match for any fire burning hotly in a fireplace. As she thought about crashing into Xavier in the hallway, her heart began to pound hard. She looked over at the closed door, knowing his bedroom was right down the hall. The urge to get up and go slide into bed with him was overwhelming. Instead, she grabbed a pillow and shoved it between her knees and let the fantasies begin.

Chapter 3

Kennedy's body had already flown through a flurry of poses. The executions were quick and done with keen precision. Dressed in a black flowing evening gown, long black gloves, her hair pinned up in a beautiful updo with flawless makeup, she was stunning.

Flirting openly with the camera was one of Kennedy's favorite things to do.

"Run your tongue across your lips, Kennedy," cameraman Danny George gently instructed the lead model. "That's good. Now cross your arms up over your head. Hold it. Great!" The shutter went off in rapid succession. "That's a wrap. We're all through here. Thanks for always being so easy to work with. I wish all models were like you."

"Models can be a little temperamental, including me. You've just been lucky not to get me on a bad day. For your sake, I hope you never do. Thanks, Danny. I appreciate how professionally you operate. Hope to see you again soon."

"Take care, Kennedy. You'll definitely see me again. Count on it."

Kennedy rushed back into the dressing room to change into her street clothes. She sat down at the dressing table. Using lots of moisturizing cream, she stripped her face of all the heavy makeup. She then dabbed on a lighter base coat, dusting her face with powder and blush, which left her complexion with a more natural glow.

Xavier had invited her to lunch before she'd left his house earlier. She had happily agreed to meet him right after her shoot since she was often hyperactive after completing a job. Energy to burn. After locating her cell phone, she called his mobile to let him know she was through and could meet him within the hour. He had already picked out a restaurant near her home, one that she happened to be familiar with.

Xavier was already waiting in the parking lot of the Gray Whale. When Kennedy spotted his car, she parked right next to it. He immediately got of out of his automobile so he could open the door for her.

As Kennedy stepped out of her car, Xavier slid his hand down her arm and kissed her forehead. "Hello, there. How'd things go for you at work today?"

"Great." Standing on her tiptoes, she kissed Xavier's cheek and put her arm through his. "Have you ever worked with Danny George?"

"Many times. He's the consummate professional. I like him a lot."

"Me, too. He complimented me today on not being hard to work with. I hated to tell him he just hadn't caught me on a bad day. But I decided to enlighten him." They laughed.

Inside the restaurant Xavier stepped up to the podium and gave his name to the hostess. He hadn't made reservations because he hadn't been sure when Kenney would finish up her job. However, the place didn't look too crowded and only a few people were waiting to be seated. After requesting a window table for two, he joined Kennedy.

Kennedy looked up at Xavier as he drew near. "Think we could sit at the bar until they call your name? I'm thirsty."

"Sure, let's go." Prepared to lead the way, he took her by the hand.

The couple stopped by the podium to tell the hostess their

plans before proceeding to the large bar area, which was practically empty. It was well after the lunch-hour rush.

Kennedy ordered raspberry iced tea and Xavier had a taste for lemonade.

He looked right into her eyes. "What was your session like?"

"Mainly formal wear. I modeled several designer evening gowns for a specialty-wear catalogue. It was a pretty easy gig. Getting in and out of clothes and makeup are the most demanding parts for me. I've pretty much got all the different poses and faces down pat."

"I know. I've been privileged to see you in action. How're you feeling?"

"I'm flying high right now. Everything was so fast paced and exhilarating. In about an hour, I'll start to bomb out."

"I think that goes for all high-fashion models. Men don't have to go through as much as you women, but we have our fair share of demanding jobs. Makeup is still a rough part for me to get through. I can't wait to get it off my face afterward."

"I can see how that'd be hard for any male, since you guys don't normally wear the stuff." Her eyes roved over his face. "You have gorgeous skin. What's your secret?"

"Using a darn good moisturizer. A healthy diet and drinking plenty of water helps, too. This face has never been introduced to a razor, thank goodness. I shave with a light depilatory. For whatever reason, I don't grow a lot of facial hair. Now my chest, that's a different matter altogether," he said, chuckling.

Kennedy recalled with crystal clarity the thick chest hair that eventually tapered off to run down into his shorts. She reined in her torrid thoughts as they began to get out of control. Xavier's last name was then called out, which gave her more time to pull it together. This fine brother had a way of making her imagination go wild.

The couple was then seated at a window table and a waitress was sent right over.

Due to the heavy meal Kennedy had consumed the previous night, she chose a light garden salad with low-calorie dressing, along with a dish of seasonal fruit: strawberries, cantaloupe chunks, blackberries and a dollop of whipped cream. Xavier ordered a grilled chicken entrée, accompanied with his favorite veggie, asparagus.

The couple spoke on a variety of stimulating subjects as they waited for their meals to be delivered. Travel was a favorite pastime for both. Their profession gave them ample opportunity to journey to places they may've never otherwise gotten to. Kennedy and Xavier had already been to many exotic locations.

"How do you feel about us getting away together for a quiet mini-vacation?"

Kennedy couldn't hide her surprise at the question. "I don't know. It all depends on what you have in mind."

"Just some time away from this bustling city. Separate rooms, of course. I thought it'd be nice if we could take a short vacation down to Mexico or possibly up north to the wine country."

Kennedy looked Xavier dead in the eye, as if to test his resolve. When he didn't so much as flinch, she felt relieved, actually liking the idea of getting away for a couple of days and doing absolutely nothing. The idea of being away with him had her heart jumping around. "Separate rooms are a must. Thanks for the invite. I'll have to check my schedule to see what time frames are free. Weekdays are normally best for me."

"I agree. Most of my weekends are crazy. But I'm willing to do whichever I can. Whatever days you come up with, I'll try and match up our calendars."

"We can see if we can work out something. I'll check it out when I get home."

"You'll have no regrets, Kennedy. I promise."

"I trust you to keep your promise. Here comes our food." She had already made a promise to herself to finish all of her meal this time. For a mere second, she thought of offering to pick up the check. Something told her it wasn't a good idea, at least not this soon. Xavier was a man with a lot of pride. She shouldn't risk injuring it.

Xavier eagerly accepted Kennedy's invitation to come into her home. She had said she'd like to show him around if he had time. She had also mentioned they could check her calendar to try and come up with a match, suggesting that he could write down the information to later compare it to his own busy schedule.

The blinding white decor of Kennedy's three-bedroom ranch house took Xavier by surprise. Everything covered in fabric was fashioned in an array of white tones, both softer shades and the more dazzling ones. The dark wood accents relieved the stark whiteness to a small degree, but the rooms still had a white wonderland appearance.

Despite all the flashy whiteness, there wasn't a sterile feel to the place. Kennedy was not the least bit neurotic about her space, either. She made sure her visitors always felt welcome and comfortable in her home. There were no specific rules about where people could eat and drink. Like most folks, she only wanted people to respect her home and not indulge in practices they wouldn't perform inside their own residences. In many ways, both she and Xavier had the same goal in mind for their visitors' total comfort.

It took Kennedy all of ten minutes to give Xavier a full tour since she hadn't spent a lot of time in each room. The master bedroom was as white as the rest of the place, but at least she had pink and lavender designer pillows on her bed. The white comforter was also fringed in a soft shade of pink and a deep violet, with the master bath also done in the same shades. White wood shutters covered all the windows in the house.

Once the couple got into the office, she offered Xavier a seat on an overstuffed chair. Then she rifled through her desk, looking for her calendar, which wasn't where it was normally kept. Kennedy finally spotted it on her computer table.

"Ah, here we go," she said, picking up the large black calendar and an ink pen and writing pad. Walking over to where Xavier was seated, she sat down at his feet and held up the calendar for him to view. "It looks like this month is all filled. Maybe we should look at the next one." She rapidly flipped over the page.

Xavier took the calendar from her hand and flipped it back to the page she'd turned away from. "Take a closer look at what you have written down in the blocks. Maybe there are a few dispensable items."

"If I've already given my word on something, I couldn't back out."

"Just take a look at everything. You'd be surprised at what you can hack away. I thought you'd promised to start prioritizing your time."

Kennedy closely studied the entries, giving each one her undivided attention. She pointed at the second Wednesday of the month. "This event has been canceled. Looks like I forgot to mark it off. Interesting, but the following two days are also free. You could look at your calendar to see how they work for you."

Taking the pen and pad from her hand, he wrote down the dates. "Keep on looking. Maybe you'll spot something else you forgot to cancel."

After more scrutinizing, she didn't see anything else she could hack off, causing her to flip over to the following month. "There are a couple of days in the first week of July. Wow, the Fourth of July is free. It's in the middle of the week, but places are probably going to be pretty crowded then."

"Maybe, maybe not. I'm sure we can find a resort hotel close by to book into." He wrote those dates down, too, before spotting a couple of empty spaces at the end of July. After pointing the dates out to her, he jotted them down also. "Now we have a few things to work with. When I get back home, I'll do the comparisons."

Kennedy smiled brightly. "Assignment completed. Let's go down to the family room and chat awhile. That is, if you have some time to hang out with me."

"I'd like nothing more." As he got to his feet, he handed her back the calendar.

Up front in the family room, Xavier sat as close to Kennedy on the sofa as he thought appropriate. The scent of her perfume drove him wild. The urge to run his fingers through her hair was unbearable. Kissing her thoroughly was his next tingling thought.

Kennedy felt the same kind of vibes as Xavier did. She couldn't count how many times she'd wondered what his kiss might do to her. She had a good idea his mouth would set her entire body on fire. Everything about him turned on her inner flames.

The phone suddenly rang, pulling Kennedy away from her heated thoughts. "Excuse me." Normally she didn't answer calls when she had company, but she was expecting to hear from her best girlfriend, Martina Sellers.

"Hey, Marty, what's up?"

"Everything is cool. A few of us are going out tonight to this new club called Caliente. Knowing how much you like the Latin scene, I thought I'd call to see if you wanted to join Mitchel and me. Bianca is also stopping by for a bit."

"Sounds like fun. What time and where is the club?"

"Around eight-thirty or so, at Redondo Beach. You know nothing really pops off before eight or nine. Get a pen and I'll give you the address."

Using one of the pens and pads she kept next to the phone, Kennedy told Martina she was ready to copy. The beach cities pretty much ran one right after the other. Redondo was on the other side of Manhattan Beach, but it didn't take long to get there. "Okay, Martina, I'll see you guys later. I've got something interesting to tell you."

"Any hints?"

"Not right now. Talk to you when I see you."

Kennedy wasted no time in filling Xavier in on her conversation with Martina, telling him about the new Latin club and how much she loved the music. "Are you busy this evening? I'd love for you to come meet my friends." She cringed, thinking she may've been a tad too forward. *Well, I couldn't possibly know if I didn't ask him.*

"I'm all yours, but I'd better get going. I have a couple of things I should take care of if I'll be hanging out with you and your friends the entire evening." He got to his feet. The desire to kiss her hit him full force again. Instead of giving in to his craving, he took her by the hand. "Walk me out?"

Loving the feel of her hand in his, Kennedy smiled softly. "No problem."

At the front door, Xavier found the nerve to brush his lips against hers. The minor contact shot through him like a major lightning bolt, heating up every part of his body. This was ridiculous, he thought. *How was it possible to feel so much from so little?*

Kennedy was happy Xavier had kissed her, but she was a bit disappointed he hadn't deepened the contact. Still, hope arose in her, causing her heart to float.

"What time should I pick you up?"

"Eight o'clock is good. I promise not to keep you out too late. However, if you prefer, I can always meet you there. Whatever works best for you."

Xavier scowled. "Nonsense! I *prefer* picking you up. Okay with you?"

"Just fine. See you around eight."

Xavier opened the door and stepped outside. Before Kennedy could close the door behind him, he was back inside, gently pulling her into his arms. This time he kissed her the way he'd dreamed of since the first day he'd met her. He kissed her thoroughly, making her moan with sheer pleasure. The intimate contact felt explosive.

Xavier didn't give Kennedy a chance to respond to his spontaneous affection nor stay in range long enough for her to slap his face. He was out the door in a flash, leaving her bewildered and utterly bewitched. As she stared after him, he blew her a kiss.

Sighing deeply, running her fingers across her lips, she wished she could preserve his kiss forever. Maybe she wouldn't have to. Perhaps he wanted more of the same, as she did. She couldn't wait to feel his mouth on hers again.

Xavier hung up the phone after listening to his messages. He could hardly believe the content of the long running commentary his agent had left for him. He had just been offered a guest appearance spot on one of the most popular soap operas on television, *Love, Laughter & Life*. This news was great but totally unexpected.

He'd auditioned a while ago and had been told by Kirsten that the studio planned to use several other professional models for judges in a modeling segment. With that in mind, he thought Kennedy just might be called upon. That'd really be nice, since he definitely wanted to work with her again.

This particular segment of *L,L&L* was featuring a story line about a modeling contest. The producer had thought Xavier would make an excellent celebrity judge. Besides being very easy on the eyes and having a beautiful body, Xavier's warm personality and his popularity among both the older and younger generations had earned him the producer's nod.

He couldn't wait to share his news with Kennedy. The thought of phoning her crossed his mind, but he decided to wait until he picked her up later on. Her facial expression was what he wanted to see most, sure that she'd be overly thrilled for him.

After Xavier washed his hands at the bathroom sink, he went out to the kitchen to get something cold to drink.

Soda in hand, his strides long and deliberate, he made his way into his office, where he pulled from his pocket the paper with the possible vacation dates. After grabbing his calendar, he sat in the leather swivel chair at the desk to compare their schedules. It didn't take him long to find that his agenda was even tighter than hers. Nothing in June worked. July showed that he had the same time frame as she had open at the end of the month. He circled the dates, though he hated that they were so far away.

Still, there'd be plenty for them to do before then. Southern California was a hotbed of all sorts of activities. If nothing else, they could swim and then laze around his pool or the beach. A vacation away wouldn't necessarily bring them closer. If that's what they wanted, they could make it happen by continuing to spend quality time together.

As Xavier thought about their evening, he wondered if Kennedy would mind if he invited Janine and Jonathan along. Janine also had a huge thing for Latin music. But if he wanted to be alone with Kennedy, why was he inviting others to come along?

Well, for one thing, he could hardly consider a club setting as alone. Her friends would be there, too. Maybe they were the same people they were going to cook for next week. If that was the case, breaking the ice before then would be a good thing. Without giving it any more thought, he picked up the phone and dialed his friends.

Out of respect and habit, Xavier stood until Kennedy was seated on the sofa. Now was as good a time as any to share his thrilling news with her. He then thought about waiting until they were at the club, but he quickly dismissed the idea. He wanted it to be a private moment. The timing was perfect right now.

Smiling from ear to ear, Xavier took hold of Kennedy's hand. "I got some great news earlier." He then spilled the beans, giving her all the details his agent had left on his answering machine. He still hadn't talked to Kirsten.

Several seconds passed by and Xavier began to get nervous.

Kennedy hadn't said a word and he couldn't read her thoughts because her expression was blank. He opened his mouth to ask her why she was mum, but he thought better of it. While he didn't quite know what to make of the uncomfortable silence, Xavier didn't want to speculate, either. God forbid he should come to all the wrong conclusions.

All of a sudden, Kennedy laughed and threw her willowy arms around Xavier's neck, nearly toppling him off the sofa. "Congrats," she cried out. "How exciting for you! Oh my gosh, you could end up becoming a soap star. You are going to be on *L,L&L*. That is so cool," she gushed. "Think I can visit the set?"

Xavier laughed at how all of Kennedy's words were tumbling out in rapid succession. "Come up for air, sweetie. Breathe," he joked. "It's okay to inhale and exhale." His laughter continued to ring out, loud and lusty.

Beyond excited for Xavier, Kennedy fell out laughing, too, hugging his neck all the while. "You are the *man!*"

Her reaction made him feel like he'd just been crowned prom king. The expressions he'd barely been able to wait to see on her face were priceless. She hadn't let him down, not in the least. He was just plain relieved, glad the awkward moments between them had passed.

Kennedy stood. "I guess we'd better get going if we're to get to the club on time." Feeling slightly bold, she stood on her tiptoes and kissed him gently on the mouth. "I'm very proud of you. Congratulations!"

Suddenly looking downtrodden, Kennedy turned to face Xavier. "I wasn't going to say anything to you about auditioning for a part on *L,L&L*, but it's deceptive not to. Unlike you, I haven't gotten a nod. My manager, Chase Hudson, hasn't heard anything yet. Since you've been offered a part, I can't help wondering where I stand. The producer seemed to like me. To be quite honest, I'm very disappointed there's been no word."

Xavier's expression was apologetic. "I'm sorry. I hope I didn't hurt your feelings by coming off so enthusiastic."

"My feelings are hurt, but I don't fault you. It would've been nice to have heard something from the producer by now. It's possible they haven't called everyone. Who knows? I'm still happy for you. Please don't think otherwise."

Desperately wanting to taste more of her, Xavier pulled her into him and held her snugly in his arms. His mouth then covered hers in a riveting kiss, one that made her body turn into a mass of jelly. She prayed he couldn't feel the quivering, but she couldn't imagine how he couldn't since it felt like an earthquake was exploding inside her.

As Xavier lifted his head, Kennedy pulled it back down. He wasn't the only one who wanted more of this bursting passion. He had singed her lips with fire and desire and she wanted it to go on and on. Their eyes clashed with fiery heat as they kissed again.

Just as they were about to go out the door, Kennedy told him to go ahead outside. She had forgotten something and promised to be right along. Then she ran into the kitchen and punched in a code on the phone. After giving instructions to the person she'd phoned, she hung up and ran back to the front, where she set the alarm and stepped out.

How Kennedy had managed to have the crystal vase of long-stemmed red roses delivered to the club so quickly had Xavier astounded. It seemed like they'd just left her home, but a glance at his watch had confirmed for him it had been a while. Coupled with the fact that she'd suddenly gone back into the house, he was sure she'd phoned in the florist order then. It was the only time it could've happened. She hadn't been out of his sight before then. He knew of several area florists who did late-evening deliveries.

The congratulations card had been signed "with genuine affection." He liked how she had kindly phrased her feelings for him. Would her fondness for him grow into something more, hopefully something deep and wonderful? Xavier had to wonder.

Seeing Kennedy dancing with her close friend Martina was a thrill a minute for Xavier. Seated at a table near the DJ booth inside the new salsa club Caliente, he simply couldn't get enough of closely observing her. In a totally relaxed mode, she was real, so down-to-earth, and not at all pretentious. She didn't hide who she was behind the glamour and glitter of her profession, nor did she attempt to mask what she felt inside or try and hide her inner thoughts.

Impressing folks wasn't a part of Kennedy's agenda, at least not on a personal level. Wowing the masses was what she did professionally…and she gave the audiences her all, and so much more than that. Who she was inside was what made her a superstar.

Xavier was sorry he hadn't been able to get in touch with Janine and Jonathan. He had left them a detailed message about the club along with the address. Maybe they'd show up later. He knew Janine would go wild for this snazzy new Latin hot spot.

Mitchel Mai, Martina's hunky Vietnamese love interest— both of them were aspiring actors—poked Xavier's shoulder with his forefinger. Once he had Xavier's attention, he lifted his empty wineglass. "I'm heading to the bar. Want anything?"

Xavier shook his head in the negative. "I'm cool for now. Thanks."

No sooner had Mitchel left the table than Kennedy and Martina came back and reclaimed their seats, gabbing and giggling all the way.

Wearing one of the red roses Xavier had plucked from the vase and had shortened for her hair, Kennedy leaned over and kissed him lightly on the mouth. "I missed you out there. Sorry you can't keep up with me on the dance floor."

Xavier chuckled, pursing his lips. "Still got jokes, huh?

Excuse me if I wanted to sit down after ten songs in a row. Fast-paced songs, mind you."

"*Wanted* to sit or *had* to, Xavier? And you sat your tired butt down after three songs, not ten."

"I doubt that. At any rate, the night's just getting started. We'll see whose behind is tired in a couple of hours." He planted a soft kiss in the center of her forehead.

Mitchel came back to the table carrying refills of wine for Martina and himself. The attractive acting couple had moved to Los Angeles from New York City, where they'd been cast in several successful Broadway plays. Trying to land roles on either a television show or a meaty project on the big screen was the couple's current objective.

Mitchel was a good-looking guy, with shocking black hair. He was well over average in height. Heavy into martial arts, he held a black belt in Karate and Tae Kwan Do. Martina had often said he had the kind of body that made her want to rip off his clothes the moment she laid eyes on him. He prided himself on taking good care of himself. Martina loved to go to the gym and watch her sexy guy work out.

Martina and Kennedy had become very close friends, back when Kennedy had also lived in Manhattan. The ladies had met during a television-commercial shoot for a popular shampoo developed for African-American hair textures. They had become instant friends and, because of their limited budgets, roommates. The two women continued to stay in very close contact even after Kennedy had moved west, shortly after Martina had met Mitchel.

Kennedy's interaction with others was interesting and fascinating for Xavier to watch. The exciting way in which Kennedy's lips had passionately conversed with his had already become Xavier's very favorite form of communication with her. The woman had left him gasping for air after their original follow-up kisses. Her guttural laughter had a way of tingling more than just his spine.

As Santana's "Maria Maria" filtered into the room, the music hot and slamming, Kennedy got out of her seat, grabbing Xavier by the hand. "Let's see what you got left."

"I got you as my date…and that's way more than any handful."

Kennedy flashed Xavier a flirtatious smile. As the music rapidly seeped into her soul, prompting her to let her sable hair all the way down, she began to rock and roll her hips in tune with the music. After backing into Xavier in a provocative manner, slowly grinding her curvy hips in a teasing way, she repeatedly brushed herself against him.

Xavier loved Kennedy's fluid movements. She seemed to flow about a room, filling its space with warmth and liquid vibrancy. The girl was an elegant verse in poetry. There was nothing simple about her, yet she was one of the most un-complicated people he'd ever come across. Though soft-spoken and gentle, there was such clarity in everything she said. If he hadn't already fallen hard for her, it was just a matter of time.

Xavier was no slouch on the dance floor and Kennedy was becoming very much aware of it. He knew just how to drop it like it was on fire. He *was* in flames, on fire for her sexy body. As her arms stretched high over her head, he reached up and entwined his fingers with hers. Without missing a single beat, he landed butter-soft kisses at the nape of her neck. Although she was a tall girl, he still had her height beat by several inches.

"Work it, girl. All right now! Love it when you're naughty."

Kennedy threw her head back and laughed. She loved being mischievous. The constantly changing expressions on Xavier's handsome face intrigued her. His bluish-gray eyes looked more gray than blue at the moment. His mesmerizing orbs had the tendency to change to lighter or darker hues depending on his mood or even on what color clothes he wore.

The excitement grew in intensity among the club's patrons when Ricky Martin's "Livin' la Vida Loca" came blasting from the numerous speakers. Shrill wolf whistles, electrifying hand clapping and loud shouting pierced the air. The song had also propelled Martina and Mitchel onto the dance floor. He wasn't as crazy for dancing as she was, but he loved pleasing her. Making Martina smile was one of Mitchel's favorite missions.

As the music slowed down considerably, showcasing the fabulous voice of Christina Aguilera, Xavier's and Kennedy's eyes met in a passionate embrace. As Christina emotionally sang "I Turn To You," one of her extremely popular love ballads, Kennedy and Xavier got real cozy, even daring to kiss in public again.

Xavier loved holding Kennedy close to him like this, delighted in the heavenly way she smelled, thrilled by how she fit so snugly into his arms. "This has been a beautiful night. Thank you for asking me out."

A soft tap on Xavier's shoulder caused him to look behind him. The beautiful lady standing there had her dark bronze body clad in a barely there black dress, one that she wore extremely well. "Hi, Xavier," Brionna Leigh Lewis said, showcasing her perfect white teeth. "How've you been?"

This situation felt downright weird to Xavier, no matter how many times he'd been caught in the same type of trap. He was supposed to be slow dancing with Kennedy, yet this young woman had engaged him in conversation as if they were the only people present. "It's really nice to see you again. Call me. I'd love for us to do lunch."

Brionna turned to face Kennedy. "I'm sorry but I didn't even see you there."

It's impossible for you not to see me, Kennedy thought quietly, smiling nicely.

Xavier felt that now was the perfect time for him to introduce the two ladies, but he really didn't want this little exchange of words to go on much longer. He was ready to return his full attention to his date. Holding on to Kennedy's hand, he introduced them.

Brionna pushed Xavier's hair back from his face. "Xavier and I are old friends. We were roller-skating partners over at the Redondo Pier. I'll let you guys get back to your evening. Call me, X. I'm sure you didn't dare throw away my number."

Xavier smiled but it didn't reach his eyes. "Goodbye, Brionna."

Kennedy knew the man was popular but she was getting to see just how popular he really was. His discomfort over the situation had come through in spades, yet he hadn't been responsible for it. She expected him to have female friends, many of them, but she hoped she didn't have to encounter one of them every time they were out.

A constant trail of women falling all over Xavier wasn't an appealing image for Kennedy. If it continued to happen with frequency, could she continue to ignore it? She wanted Xavier as a friend and a lover. What she didn't want was to inherit petty cat fights with the women who knew him before her. She could handle life's disappointment as well as anyone. Disenchantment in love she could do without. The last thing Kennedy wanted was to share the man she was hot for, the man she was falling in love with.

Chapter 4

Only seconds after Kennedy and Xavier and Martina and Mitchel had reseated themselves back at the table, Bianca and her male friend showed up. Torrance Gardner and Bianca had been getting to know each other, but things had yet to heat up for them.

Bianca, a print-ad model for petite fashion designs, was a pixie beauty with large dark eyes and high cheekbones. Her cinnamon complexion was smooth and even. Torrance, dark complexioned and ruggedly handsome, towered over his date's five-five frame by at least seven inches. He was a television cameraman for a major network.

Kennedy warmly hugged Bianca before introducing her and Torrance to Xavier.

Bianca smiled at Xavier. "I've met you before, when you were gracious enough to judge the petite-modeling competition held in San Pedro last year. It's really nice to see you again."

Xavier's eyes flared with recognition. "I thought you looked familiar. I was actually trying to place you. The pleasure's all mine, Bianca." Xavier then shook hands with Torrance, exchanging brief pleasantries. "Good to meet you, man."

Tiaja Rae suddenly made an unexpected, unimpressive appearance. As usual, she had her five-person entourage with her, two other women and three guys. When feeling somewhat cheeky, Kennedy laughingly referred to the group as the six-pack.

Posing provocatively, with both hands on her hips, Tiaja Rae leveled her gaze onto Xavier. "I'd like to speak to you for a moment, X. Alone, if you don't mind."

"Seeing as I'm with Kennedy and her friends, a private meeting just can't happen. What's on your devious little mind, T.R.?"

Tiaja Rae smirked, seeming as if she loved Xavier's not-so-flattering remarks. "You may wish you'd taken the privacy option, but you can't say I didn't warn you."

Knowing her nemesis's baiting remarks meant big trouble, Kennedy tensed up.

Smiling devilishly, Tiaja Rae extended her hand to Xavier. "I hear that congrats are in order for us."

Looking puzzled, Xavier ignored the outstretched hand. "For what?"

"My manager tells me we're working together on *L,L&L*. We've both been selected as judges for the soap's upcoming modeling segment. *That's* for what, sexy."

Xavier merely shrugged, hiding his displeasure at the news. "Okay!"

"You seem really surprised so I guess you weren't told about it." Tiaja Rae looked right into Kennedy's face. "If you're wondering, you were not selected. First off, you must be a top-ranking model for this gig. You've missed the mark by a wide margin. Wishful thinking, I'm sure. Sorry you've been left out again, Miss Bassett."

"Cut it already," Xavier calmly said to Tiaja Rae. "We've all heard enough."

Xavier saw the frustration on Kennedy's face. Then he saw a mean streak of mischief flash through her eyes. Before he could grab hold of her hand, she had already doused Tiaja Rae with the leftover red wine from a glass nearby.

Kennedy put her hand up to her mouth. "Oops! I guess no one told you you've been selected for a wine bath. Sorry. This is not who I am, but it's who I can become."

Tiaja Rae was so embarrassed that all she could do was run for the bathroom. Her girl puppets quickly followed behind her. Kennedy and Martina slapped palms for high-fives. All the guys cracked up. Then the three males with Tiaja Rae took off running.

Xavier looked at Kennedy in astonishment. "Where did that come from?"

"An ugly place in my heart, a place that obviously doesn't surface enough. We all have protection mechanisms, Xavier. I have simply had enough of Tiaja Rae."

"So I see! She'll probably think twice about waging war with you again," Xavier responded, still astounded by how Kennedy had ruined Tiaja Rae's lovely white shirt.

"She deserved just what she got," Martina chimed in, jerking her head back.

Xavier brushed his knuckles down the side of Kennedy's face. "I knew bad blood existed between you two, but I didn't know to what depth. Are you okay, sweetheart? If it's any comfort to you, I think she deserved it, too. Still, you have to keep your cool."

"Hear, hear," Mitchel shouted, lifting his wineglass in a mock toast. "In this case, I think the girl got off lightly. But you can't let folks push your buttons."

Kennedy looked abashed. "I *know* she had it coming, guys, but already I kind of regret it. I can't let anyone define me. I can already see the tabloid headlines."

Martina looked the club over. "The rag-sheet reporters show up when you least expect them. Paparazzi are crawling all over this place."

"Even if they weren't present, they'd get the scoop anyway. Tiaja Rae will give them a firsthand account. She seeks publicity, soaks it up, negative or positive," Kennedy commented. No sooner had the words left her mouth than flashbulbs started popping.

Xavier stepped in front of Kennedy to shield her from the cameras. "T.R. took too much of our time and now it looks like our evening is over. Let me get you out of here and safely away from these unscrupulous reporters."

Everyone followed behind Xavier. The other women felt heartsick for Kennedy.

Kennedy would rather not go home, but she was determined to stop letting Tiaja Rae make her look like a fool. Leaving with Xavier would help take her mind off the unpleasantness for now, but she knew she had to come up with a way to effectively handle her nemesis and these types of scenarios. She couldn't go around tossing wine on folks whenever she didn't like something.

And for sure, Kennedy vowed to never again refer to him as X, not since Tiaja Rae had called him that.

Xavier came out of the guest bathroom and went into the kitchen, where he found Kennedy rifling through a utility drawer. "What are you looking for?"

"Take-out menu for the Chinese restaurant right up the street, Hunan Star. I've got a serious craving for curry chicken and spring rolls."

"Sounds delicious. Do they deliver?"

"Up until midnight. You want something?" She gave a triumphant yelp, waving the pink menu in the air. "Got it!"

Xavier propped himself up on one of the high-back stools at the breakfast bar. "Sweet and sour chicken is my favorite. Please order me a cheese puff, too."

Loving how polite he was, Kennedy flashed him an adoring smile. "Will do."

As Xavier listened to Kennedy place the food orders, he found it hard to take his eyes off her. She was so femininely soft and pretty and downright sweet—and spicy, too. Just what he liked. Was she just too good to be true? If this was merely a fairytale dream, he didn't ever want to awaken.

Everything about Kennedy seemed so magical. He had dated other supermodels and had eventually sworn off the lot. That is, until he'd met her, his ideal woman, who had never thrown a tantrum, publicly or privately, not until this evening at the club. He had seen a totally different side of her, but he didn't think for a second it was the norm. The sweetness in her wasn't going to one day turn bitter and vile against him.

Xavier clearly understood that Kennedy had been highly provoked. He was actually surprised she hadn't gone off on Tiaja Rae before now. He hoped they could talk about this troubling situation before he went home. He'd really like to know how things had gotten so bad for them. Xavier would like to help her find a way to cope. He didn't like the fact the problem seemed to be controlling Kennedy.

Before joining Xavier at the breakfast bar, Kennedy put the menu away.

Xavier stood until Kennedy was seated. Now was as good a time as any to talk to her about what had happened earlier. To prepare himself, he sucked in a deep breath, exhaling slowly. "If you don't mind me prying, when did all this bad blood start for you and T.R.?"

Kennedy shook her head, looking regretful. "It seems like a lifetime ago. She was already a top model when I first broke into the profession. For one reason or another, she took an immediate dislike to me. I've never understood it. I've tried to find ways to be amicable with her, but she won't have any of it. I'm really sorry about this evening. I know I embarrassed you. More than anything, I shamed myself."

"Don't go getting down on yourself. She asked for what happened at the club." He put his arm around her shoulder and brought her close. "As Mitchel said, and I agree with him wholeheartedly, you can't let anyone push your buttons like that. You're allowing someone else to control you, giving up your power to another human being. The only one who should have any and all control over you is you."

"I already know that. I've never done anything like that

before. The wine was right there at my fingertips and so was she. At the time it seemed an appropriate way to deal with my inner rage. Of course I know better than that."

"Well, to make amends, maybe you can offer to pay her dry-cleaning bill." Xavier laughed, hoping to lighten her mood.

Kennedy rolled her eyes. "Not a snowball's chance in Hades. What is done is done. My work is cut out for me to make darn sure this never happens again. This madness between her and me has already gotten too far out of hand."

"You'll manage. If you can just look at it as giving your power over to another, that should be enough incentive for you not to do it again. The only person you can control is you. I don't blame you for earlier, though. You were pushed to the limit."

Kennedy rested her head against his chest. "Thanks. I needed to hear that, but I was still dead wrong. What I was pushed into was letting her pull my strings. My punishment will come in the form of tabloid headlines. You never know where and when they start photographing you. The reporters could have the whole thing on tape. Next thing we know the whole episode will wind up on TMZ!"

Xavier clearly saw how important it was for Kennedy to take full ownership of her part in the event. It was a good thing. She seemed a bit more content now, like she'd come to terms with her actions. He hoped the fray didn't show up in the rag sheets since she was starting to feel better. It was a good thing, too, because her doorbell was ringing.

Xavier quickly jumped off the stool. "I'll get it. It's probably the food." Before Kennedy could respond one way or the other, he was already on his way out of the room.

After Xavier took delivery of the Chinese food, he gave the guy a decent tip. As he closed the door, he couldn't help thinking of how blessed he was. His life was good. He'd done so many marvelous things in his short tenure on earth, things some folks would never have an opportunity to do. He didn't know what he'd done to deserve such goodness, but he was awfully grateful for each and every blessing the Father doled out.

At this very emotional moment he bowed his head and closed his eyes. Xavier promised God once again that he'd always reach out and help the less fortunate.

Kennedy was humming softly when he reentered the kitchen. Despite how troubled she was by what had occurred earlier, she couldn't help smiling at Xavier. She was proud of him and how he lived his life; the man had been at her side when she'd really needed it…protecting her…and she was grateful to him.

Once Kennedy emptied all the brown bags of the white boxes, she summoned Xavier over to the counter to fix his plate. She'd already pulled out from the pantry a couple of sectional plates.

Kennedy had made a pitcher of mint iced tea yesterday. After pulling it from the fridge, she filled two glasses. She then placed on the table the take-out condiment packets of soy sauce and hot mustard. The Chinese food smelled heavenly. She couldn't wait to eat, but she said a blessing first. Some would think she ate a lot for a woman in her profession, but she knew just how far to go, balancing her intake.

If Kennedy went overboard on her diet, she always made up for it. She never allowed her weight to go over by more than a couple pounds. Because she had the tendency to eat when upset, she was extra careful about her food amounts.

Right after Kennedy took the first mouthful of her curry chicken, she began moaning softly. "Hunan Star's food is still the bomb. They've been in business nearly two years now and haven't fudged an ounce on quality. Many places suck you in with lots of great food when they first open. Soon after they build their clientele base, the taste of the food starts to go to the dogs. I hate it when that happens."

"I know exactly what you mean. When I first started going

to Vic's Seafood House, right there on the Santa Monica pier, I couldn't stop singing its praises. Now I wouldn't even think of feeding their food to my dog."

Kennedy chuckled. "That's interesting, since you don't even own a pooch."

"Figuratively speaking, smarty-pants. You love to mess with me, don't you?"

"Can't argue with you there. But you mess with me aplenty, too."

He nudged her playfully, flashing her that beautiful smile she loved so much. "You had a fabulous time dancing this evening. How're your feet doing?"

Kennedy's eyes lit up at the memories. "I'm afraid dancing is in my soul. I love Latin music and all their exotic styles of dancing. Salsa and mambo being my favorites."

Xavier gazed at her softly. "I sure love to watch your hot dance moves, girl. You give those sexy hips of yours a real workout."

"Great exercise, fantastic benefits. As for my feet, they're kind of still on fire."

"In that case, I'll have to do something about it. Mind if I take special care of your feet? I give a great massage. If you're okay with me tending to your feet, just tell me where I can find a basin and some Epsom salts. That is, if you have both."

Kennedy let Xavier know just where he could find everything in her bathroom.

In the downstairs master bathroom, Xavier looked in the medicine chest and the cabinet beneath the sink to see exactly what kinds of remedies Kennedy had on hand to fulfill his mission. First he filled the portable basin with hot water and added Epsom salts. From the upper glass shelf he retrieved a vial of soothing oil he'd spotted, the kind of liquid substance that heated up the body as soon as it was applied. After removing a couple of fluffy white towels from the linen closet, he carried everything into the family room. He had suggested she go in there to start relaxing.

Once Xavier carefully set down the massage tools on the ceramic tiled floor, he made his way over to the leather recliner Kennedy occupied. Kneeling down, he neatly rolled up her pant legs. Removing her shoes and ankle-high stockings came next. Before immersing her feet in the steamy water, he gently kissed the top of both.

The moment Kennedy's feet hit the soothing water she gasped with pleasure. "Oh, yes," she cooed, "you are my hero. How is it that you can anticipate my needs? And exactly what prompted you to ask me about my feet?"

Xavier chuckled. "I'm observant. You were stepping gingerly as we made it out to the parking lot. I'm also a model. Not that you have to be reminded."

Kennedy nodded with understanding. "I'm glad you're so vigilant."

"Always alert, more so when it comes to you now. People who don't pay close attention to details miss out on so much." Xavier knew that to be a fact.

"I hadn't given it much thought, but you're probably right. Thanks for being so attentive to me. It makes me feel good."

"You're welcome. I like meeting your needs, even when you may not know exactly what you might require at the time."

Kennedy sharply raised an eyebrow, feigning injury. "Was that an insult?"

Xavier shrugged. "Only if you took it as such. Not my intent."

"In that case, I'll just let it slide." Wiggling her toes, she giggled, wrinkling her nose at the same time. "This foot bath is heavenly."

"That's what I was shooting for. I'll massage each of those babies for you after they soak a while longer. I noticed your feet are a little swollen. Do they still hurt?"

"More of a dull ache is happening right now. The pain *has* subsided some."

"Hopefully we can take care of all the aches. Want a magazine to read or should I just turn on the television?"

"Neither. I just want to sit here and look at your gorgeous face. Is that okay?"

"Okay by me, toots." They both laughed at the silly moniker he'd used.

Xavier went right to work on Kennedy's right foot, lifting it from the basin. He dried it off thoroughly, paying special attention to the soft flesh between her toes. As he deeply massaged and manipulated the sole, his tender hands, along with the warming oil, had her foot tingling. Her left foot then received the same loving treatment.

Deciding not to put back on her stockings, because he thought they were responsible for some of the swelling in her ankles, he kissed the tops and the soles of her feet this time.

Xavier seemed to want to keep Kennedy intrigued with him during their budding relationship. It was one of numerous things she positively adored about him. He was such a sweetheart and he seemed to be a really good man. While their future as a couple remained an uncertainty, she felt quite optimistic.

Xavier glanced up at her with concern. "How do your feet feel now?"

She rolled her eyes back. "Divine, simply divine. Thanks again, Xavier."

"Want something hot to drink to further relax you?"

"I actually think it's time for me to call it a night. It's been a long day."

The expression on Xavier's face said he understood, though he'd like nothing better than to stay there until the sun came up. Of course, that wasn't happening.

"I guess I'd better take your subtle hint and hit the bricks. Would it be pushing the envelope to ask to see you again, real soon, like as soon as possible?"

She laughed. "I was actually hoping you'd ask me out again, before I asked you."

Chuckling, Xavier leaned into her for a brief kiss. "I like you. It's nice when I don't have to second-guess. You put it right out there…and in no uncertain terms."

She angled her head to the side. "Isn't it much better that way?"

"Most definitely." He slowly got to his feet. "Anything at all I can do for you before I leave?"

Don't even go there. Kennedy knew if she told Xavier all of what he could do for her, he'd never walk out that front door.

Xavier helped Kennedy out of the recliner. Taking her by the hand, he started toward the front entrance. Her soft hand in his made his fingers tingle. *How could a mere touch send me right into orbit?* He couldn't help thinking of the few passionate kisses they'd shared earlier, kisses that had him craving more intimacy.

Just before Xavier opened the door, he turned to face Kennedy. "Once again, thanks for asking me out. I enjoyed meeting your friends. Bianca is a little powerhouse. Martina is sweet and seems very loyal to you. I believe they both got your back."

"You're right about the ladies. Each friend is a loyal one. They'll be at *your* dinner party, Chef De Marco. Ever since they learned about the beef Wellington, they can't wait to sample your menu. Let's please keep it light though. I've been overeating a bit."

"I'll keep your diet in mind. Speaking of overeating, I don't want to do that, either, but I'm interested in taking in some extra calories, deliciously sweet ones."

Xavier wasted no time in taking Kennedy into his arms and kissing her thoroughly, fully tasting the sweetness of her lips. That one body-singeing kiss led to more of the same. Each subsequent kiss was even more passionate than the previous one. Feeling like he was losing control, Xavier knew it was time to go.

* * *

Since Kennedy didn't want to wash away the soothing oils and lotions from her feet by showering, she had thoroughly washed up her body before donning a short nightgown in white silk. She loved to feel against her skin the caress of sensuously soft fabrics. A mist of lightly scented perfume sprayed on her pulse points was part of her nightly ritual. She loved to smell as good as she looked.

After climbing into bed, despite how tired her body was, Kennedy took time out to journal. The entire day had been rich in experiences and insight, the good and the bad running neck and neck. She had actually learned many valuable things from Xavier and wanted to get them down on paper, often referencing her journal to monitor her growth.

Kennedy had never thought of her numerous negative responses to Tiaja Rae's impetuous tirades as giving up her control to another. She definitely saw it differently now. Her nemesis *had* been controlling her, just as Xavier had suggested. It was plain to see now that he had pointed it out to her. The thought of being controlled was *extremely* unsettling.

Working on that very aspect of her character had to take precedence over everything else, Kennedy quickly decided. She didn't want to be seen as someone people could rule over. It was interesting what you could learn about yourself from someone else, especially from a person who was looking deeply in on the situation for the first time.

Realizing she hadn't checked her messages for quite some time, Kennedy pushed in the auto-dial button. Once she'd turned on the speaker feature, she grabbed her trusty pen and pad. After writing down each message, she either hit the save or erase codes.

At the end of the last message, Kennedy threw her head back and laughed, hardly able to believe what she'd just heard. According to her manager, she'd been invited to do a guest appearance on *The Lacy Donavan Show,* a popular talk show forum. Lacy was a mega-successful retired supermodel—people all around the world knew and loved her. She was beautiful, bright and multitalented.

Kennedy tuned in to Lacy's show whenever she had time; she really liked what was happening with it. It looked as if Lacy had already silenced her core of doubters, the ones who thought a model couldn't be substantial.

As another call beeped in, Kennedy switched over to the second line.

Hearing Xavier's voice was an immediate turn-on for her. "You're home?" she asked.

"Just walked in, hoping you weren't asleep yet. I had no control over making this call. My fingers just took over. Did I wake you?"

Kennedy giggled softly at his flattering remarks. "You didn't. I'd been doing some journaling before listening to my phone messages. It's all good. I've got some really great news to share with you. Interested?"

"In everything that has anything to do with you," he whispered huskily.

Breathless at his sweet and sincere response, Kennedy wiped away the tears at the corners of her eyes. That he was interested in everything about her made her feel so special. Little did he know that she was every bit as interested in him. "You're going to be on *L,L&L* and I just learned I've been invited to make an appearance on *The Lacy Donavan Show.* How is that for wonderful news?"

"Congratulations! You're on your way to becoming a television star. I heard the joy in your voice. You sound really excited about the invite."

"Way beyond that. There are so many models she could've chosen."

"But she chose you. Hope I get to see the show you're on. What time will it air?"

"Eleven a.m. It's an hour long." Kennedy thought hard about

what she wanted to say next, hoping it wasn't inappropriate of her. "If you're free that day, maybe you could come down to the television studio during the taping. You know, for moral support."

So touched by Kennedy's generous request, Xavier had to take in a deep breath. "If I can make it, I'll be there to support you, in any way I can. Please know that."

Kennedy's hand dropped down over her heart. "I do know. Thanks."

"Look, I'm ringing off now, Kennedy. I'm back in control of myself."

"Good. We should never let anyone or anything have control over us," she teased.

Xavier appreciated what she'd said, understanding exactly what she'd meant by it.

"Sounds like you got it down pat, girl. Talk to you tomorrow." There was a pregnant pause. "Kennedy," he breathed softly, "sleep tight and have pleasant dreams."

Xavier was on cloud nine when he cradled the telephone. All he could do was sit there on the side of the bed, thinking of Kennedy, his mind involved in a total recall of every sweet kiss and tender caress they'd shared. No one had ever made him tremble like he did before, during and after kissing her. She had the softest and the sweetest lips ever.

Whether Kennedy knew it or not, she had already gotten her hooks deep into him, Xavier mused. Laughing softly, he recalled the old O Jays megahit which talked about how a woman had gotten her hooks into a man. Or Usher singing about being caught up. Xavier knew how the brothers felt now. He didn't think he could break free of Kennedy, either, nor did he want to.

Kennedy wiped her eyes and said a brief prayer, thanking God for bringing Xavier back into her life. Although it had only been a few weeks since their first date, if he was the one God had handpicked for her, she asked Him to show her a significant sign. She didn't just want a man. She wanted a good man, a spiritual brother, one who would respect, love and cherish her. Kennedy wanted to get back exactly what she was more than capable of doling out to God's choice for her.

Seated at the conference table in her manager's office, Kennedy gave Chase a hard look. "And just how long have you known this?"

Chase nervously drummed his fingers on the desktop. "Only yesterday, I swear. The producer of *L,L&L* called me just as I was leaving the office. I had a doctor's appointment and was running late. That's why I called you so early this morning."

Kennedy was shocked now. Had Chase informed her of this in time, she might've been prepared for Tiaja Rae's comments at the club. She really hadn't taken it seriously until the phone call this morning. "What reason did he give for not casting me?"

Sorry for the pain she appeared to be in, knowing the truth would cause even more hurt, Chase pressed his lips together. "Tiaja Rae Montgomery landed the judging spot. The guy didn't come right out and say it, but he sort of hinted at being pressured. We both know this isn't the first time this has happened to us." He looked down at the floor and then back up at her. "I'm really sorry."

Kennedy was crushed. Knowing she should be used to this happening by now, she squared her shoulders, as if trying to slough it off. "When is this going to stop?"

The horror-stricken look in Kennedy's eyes made Chase feel terrible for his client. "I've done some snooping around and it seems that Miss Montgomery has a good friend working on the show. Whether this has anything to do with you not being chosen, I don't know. There are some folks who think it has everything to do with it."

Angry as hell now, Kennedy jumped up from the chair. "This should be unbelievable but it isn't. As it is, she's top banana. What's her beef with me? Had I known she was auditioning, I may not have put myself through this kind of torture. I get lots of jobs, but I wanted this one badly. You have no idea how badly."

Chase shrugged. "It's plain rivalry. She sees you as the one who can dethrone her. She's afraid you'll take her crown."

"Plain bull is what it is. I'm sick of this. I can't help but wonder if it's all worth it." She shook her head. "But if she thinks I'm a quitter, she'd better think again. I won't let her win, not with these dirty tactics."

With that said Kennedy walked over and gave Chase a hug. She then hurried out the door. Before she could make it to the elevator, she broke down. Tiaja Rae had done her in once again. Although she was in tears, she no longer felt awful about the wine bath her nemesis had been so deserving of. If she had it to do over again, she wouldn't hesitate in the least.

All week long Kennedy's food intake was moderate. She'd mainly feasted on raw veggies and fresh fruits and chicken or fish. For desserts, she'd had sugar-free Jell-O or vanilla pudding and also fat-free flavored yogurts. She'd kept her body hydrated with plenty of water while using other sugar-free liquids only moderately. While she eyed all the special food trays lined up on her granite island counter, she was definitely glad she'd cut back on her eating prior to this social event.

As Kennedy examined the delicious-looking foods Xavier had prepared for the dinner party, she had a hard time not reaching for a taste of this or a pinch of that. Her mother still had an occasion to run her daughter out of the kitchen when Kennedy would come into the room talking about "taste-testing time." Kennedy loved to sample.

The meat entrées include braised lamb chops and tender roasted breasts of chicken. Sautéed asparagus, ginger-lemon carrots, a steamed vegetable medley and a ten-layer salad completed the vegetable menu. Rice pilaf was the only starch she was serving. Xavier had ordered from the bakery two sugarless apple pies. Skinny Cow vanilla ice cream was also available to turn the dessert into pie à la mode if desired.

Xavier had allowed Kennedy to hang out in the kitchen with him while he'd worked, but she'd been forbidden to lift a single finger. He'd only needed her there to tell him where to locate things, so as to not waste precious time on search missions.

Needing a few things he'd forgotten, Xavier had run out to the local grocer's. He still had to get dressed when he got back, having brought along with him a change of clothing. Kennedy had thought he'd sounded so adorable but unsure of his request when he'd called her to ask if she'd mind him showering there after preparing the meal.

Kennedy saw Xavier's absence as the perfect opportunity for her to get dressed; she had already showered. Her guests were due to arrive within the next forty-five minutes…and she didn't think her fluffy white bathrobe would go over very well.

Sticking close by Kennedy's side, his arm loosely about her waist, Xavier was the perfect cohost. He had insisted on their greeting the guests together at the door, which she had thought was downright charming.

Janine and Jonathan had been the first couple to arrive. The doorbell pealed nonstop after that, up until the last guests had arrived, which were Bianca and Torrance. A total of four couples were present once Martina and Mitchel had made an appearance.

Bianca held up a dainty lamb chop, directing her attention to Xavier. "What seasonings did you use on these delectable delicacies? That's if you don't mind sharing."

"Not a problem. Just mix All Seasonings, curry powder and

garlic salt with olive oil. Then brush it on both sides of the chops. I also use the same recipe on a whole leg of lamb, just a lot more of it. It's best when you can marinate it several hours or overnight."

"The curry is jamming. I thought that's what I tasted," Bianca said. "Very well done, Xavier, utterly divine. And tender, too. Ever consider becoming a chef?"

Xavier chuckled. "I already consider myself one. I can hang with the best."

Mitchel reared his head back. "That's a lot of confidence I just heard coming from my brother. Rightfully so, I must say. Everything I've tasted so far is delicious. The mixed-vegetable medley tastes fantastic. I'm a terrible cook." He nudged Martina. "Was I right to warn him, babe?"

"Yeah, you were." Smiling impishly, she rolled her eyes back. "Like I'd ever let you cook for Xavier at our place. None of you ever have to worry about that."

Kennedy cracked up. "I don't want to embarrass you, Mitchel, but please let me tell them about my one and only experience with your cooking."

Mitchel shrugged. "Go ahead and get a good laugh at my expense. I don't mind."

Kennedy turned her bottom lip down, as a sad gesture of sympathy for Mitchel. "Then I won't share."

"No, go ahead," Mitchel insisted. "I can take it like a man. I *am* the man."

Everyone laughed at the way Mitchel executed a King Kong move onto his chest.

Kennedy then told how Mitchel had offered to fix oatmeal for her one morning, when she'd been running late for an assignment. According to her, it hadn't been fit for human consumption. First off, he hadn't used enough water to boil it in, causing it to scorch slightly. Then he'd loaded it with sugar and butter to try and hide the burned taste. The group howled, including

Mitchel. He couldn't help laughing at Kennedy's telltale expression.

Torrance looked over at Bianca. "Can you cook?"

Bianca looked back at him with indignation. "Why? Is it a requirement?"

Torrance's surprise at her surly comeback was obvious. "I don't know."

"What's that supposed to mean? It is one or it isn't." Bianca chucked back.

"A requirement for what?" Torrance asked, looking a tad perplexed.

Kennedy thought Torrance had cleverly turned the floor back over to Bianca. It in fact looked to her as if he may've put her friend on the spot. She could see that everyone, including herself, was dying to hear Bianca's response.

"Do the women you date have to know how to cook?" Bianca asked pointedly.

"Of course not. That's absurd," Torrance replied, scowling hard.

"Then why'd you ask the question in the first place?" Bianca fired off at him.

Licking his lips, Torrance ran his hands through his hair. "I guess 'cause it just popped into my mind. The subject *was* cooking, wasn't it?"

"Okay, okay," Mitchel said, trying to calm down the natives, "I'm not trying to get in the middle here, but it seems to me the initial question called for a yes or no answer, Bianca. But you went all over the map with it. *Can* you cook or *can't* you?"

Seeing this wasn't getting her anywhere or anything but embarrassed, Bianca was only too happy to bring to a halt what she'd started. "I *can* cook. But you can bet your sweet booties I won't be cooking for either of you," she muttered lowly, speaking directly to Torrance and Mitchel. When Bianca began laughing, everyone else followed suit.

"Hey, what do you all think about your girl being on *The Lacy Donavan Show?*" Xavier asked the others. Putting his arm around Kennedy, he squeezed her shoulders. If there'd ever been a time to change a subject, right now had been perfect timing. Kennedy smiled at Xavier, loving his ability to lead and to take charge of quelling a controversy.

Glad he was at her side, Kennedy smiled at Xavier. "Thanks for the heartfelt sentiments, guys. I'm excited about being invited to appear on the show." Her lack of excitement came through loud and clear, and Kennedy knew it. "I just hope it doesn't get too personal." That it would get very personal was one of her biggest fears.

Kennedy actually dreaded the topics that might be covered by the host. The agenda items would be discussed with her before airtime but not in any great detail. She could only pray that Tiaja Rae's name wasn't mentioned. If her name did come up, she hoped she could hide her deep disdain. Airing their feud on television wasn't something she was keen on. Some things were better left unspoken.

Chapter 5

Despite the countless audiences Kennedy appeared in front of, she was extremely nervous while seated on a comfortable sofa in a private room on the set of *The Lacy Donavan Show.* Lacy was a newly retired supermodel who had recently landed a much-sought-after talk-show-host contract on a major television network.

Kennedy picked up the crystal pitcher of ice water and filled one of the matching goblets. As she sipped on the refreshing liquid, she halfheartedly watched the show on the large plasma television. The celebrity Lacy was currently interviewing was an actress starring in a feature film, one scheduled to open in a week.

While Kennedy quietly pondered the list of interview questions the producer had gone over with her earlier, she dreaded responding to the more personal ones. A person's romantic liaisons were really nobody else's business and the one she shared with Xavier was so very new. What they did in their private lives wasn't something she wanted to speak on, especially in such a public forum. She'd told the producer that as delicately as possible.

The couple had seen so many relationships go up in flames after they'd foolishly spent too much time in front of a television camera discussing personal issues. Kennedy fervently prayed that Lacy would tread lightly in the areas of her personal life.

The door to the room suddenly popped open, causing Kennedy to look up with a start. Seeing Xavier standing there caused her heart to race. That trademark smile of his, dazzlingly white and sexy, had a way of emotionally filling her to the brim. Every time he smiled at her like that she felt this incredible rush of heady adrenaline course right through her. Her full lips curved up to offer a return smile. "Hey, you!"

Thrilled to see Kennedy, Xavier winked at her. "Hey, you, right back!"

Xavier's long legs carried him across the room with ease, his stride deliberate. He took Kennedy into his arms. His desire to kiss her breathless was the only thing he'd had on his mind all morning. Out to accomplish his mission, he fully covered her sweet mouth with his. As he felt his own breath swept away, his heart danced on his tongue.

Xavier held Kennedy at arm's length. "You looked so surprised to see me."

"I was. I really didn't think you'd make it."

His eyes scolded her lightly. "I told you I'd do all within my power to get here before you went on. I knew how much you wanted the support."

Gently caressing his face with one hand, her fingertips grazing his lips with the other one, Kennedy momentarily lowered her lashes. "I know you did. You're here with me now…and I couldn't be happier about it. Thanks, Xavier."

"I'd do just about anything for you, K.B. You know that, don't you?"

Kennedy's heart rate sped up even more. He'd never used only her initials before. She liked it, loved the way his lips had caressed the new nickname. "I *do* know it. And I promise not to take you for granted…"

A soft knock came on the door before it swung open wide. A young black male stuck his head halfway inside. He held up five fingers. "You're on in five minutes, Miss Bassett. I'll be back to escort you to the set."

Once the door closed shut, Xavier began to tenderly but firmly massage Kennedy's shoulders, feeling her tension. "It's almost showtime. Relax, girl. You'll do just fine."

Lacy Donavan, stunning, tall, curvaceous, caramel-brown complexioned, beamed from head to toe as she warmly welcomed Kennedy to her show. Once the two women were comfortably seated, Lacy gave her audiences quite a bit of pertinent information about the celebrity supermodel.

Lacy crossed her legs. "When did you first start thinking about becoming a model, Kennedy?"

"Ooh, I'd have to say around six or seven. My desires started very early."

"Wow! What a big thought for such a little person. Why a fashion model?"

Kennedy laughed. "I loved playing dress-up…and I was a big ham. If there was a camera anywhere around, I always found a way to get my picture taken. Experimenting with my mother's makeup also started at an early age. I thought models were so cool."

"Sounds to me like you were *really* into the modeling thing. Did your parents ever try to talk you out of pursuing your dream of becoming a fashion diva?"

Kennedy shook her head. "Not in the least. I have very supportive parents. Mom and Dad's only demands were that I go to college and excel in my academics. A good education was always the big push around our house. I'm grateful for that, too, because education is extremely important." Kennedy mentioned her degree in performing arts.

"I know what you mean. As models, we should always prepare for life after we retire from the runway. Education *is* the key, no matter how clichéd it might sound. What's your favorite charity, Kennedy?"

"I have so many. However, I'm a huge supporter of CLWC,

Children Living with Cancer. I'm also the national spokesper-son for the vital organization."

A thundering round of applause broke out, pleasing Ken-nedy greatly.

"That's marvelous! Can you please tell us a little bit about CLWC?"

"I'd be happy to, Lacy."

Kennedy shared with the audience and the viewers some background information on how the nonprofit organization came into being, besides reciting its mission statement. She was also able to share recent statistics regarding the number of children living with cancer. Similar to the Make a Wish Foun-dation, CLWC also helped to turn ailing children's wildest dreams into happy realities.

"Thanks so much for sharing your passion for CLWC with all of us. If anyone would like to make a donation to CLWC, the information on how to do so will be posted on our Web site, *www.lacy.d.television.net.*"

A fleeting sparkle of pure devilment flashed in Lacy's eyes. "Rumor has it that you're dating fellow supermodel Xavier De Marco, one of the most gorgeous men on planet Earth. Care to dish up the dirt, Kennedy?"

Dish up the dirt! Although Kennedy had known this line of questioning was coming her way she still felt uneasy. "Xavier and I *have* been spending quality time together. As friends and colleagues in the same industry, we enjoy many of the same social activities, as well as each other's company."

"You make it all sound like nothing more than a casual friend-ship, but I think we all know better than that. Don't we, audience?"

Cheering, halfhearted clapping and then loud gasps came from the audience.

When Kennedy realized the audience was looking at some-thing behind her, she wondered if the producer had brought out Xavier to join her on the set. The slight turn of her head revealed a large plasma screen. A closer look at the screen had her feeling sick inside. Seated atop the same carousel horse, their lips extremely close together, yet not touching, Xavier and Tiaja Rae's bold images were there for the television world to see.

Lacy's producers certainly hadn't made Kennedy privy to this kind of scenario. They had to have known she would've objected to a scene like that. It wasn't fair to either her or Xavier. For now, though, she knew she had to ride out this major humiliation.

The commercial break helped Kennedy tremendously to regain her composure.

As she nervously licked lips that now felt bone-dry, she tried to imagine why anyone had thought it necessary to splash all over the screen a picture of her boyfriend in an intimate embrace with her number one enemy. Was it a modeling pose? Xavier *had* worked with Tiaja Rae on numerous modeling assignments…and she knew they'd work on many, many more.

Smiling sympathetically at Kennedy, Lacy came over to where she sat.

Despite Kennedy's twanging nerves, she forced herself to smile back.

"I'm sorry, Kennedy, for this unfortunate incident. I clearly saw your discomfort. It wasn't our intent to embarrass you. It appears that the photographs somehow got mixed up. With you and Xavier as the newest, hottest supercouple in the world of fashion, we just thought we'd have a bit of fun by showing you off. Everyone loves you both."

The notification of it being time to go back on the air kept Kennedy from responding. It was just as well. The things she had on her mind to say might only make it worse. Some things were best left unsaid. And, in all fairness to Lacy, it could've been an accident. However, it was a hard sell since she and Tiaja Rae looked nothing alike.

The rest of the interview only took up another ten to twelve minutes; it seemed like a lifetime to Kennedy. They talked of her desire to act in a feature film or a soap opera, which led up to her being asked about her feelings on being left out of the modeling judging contest on *L,L&L* Kennedy thought it was a fair enough question.

"The directors have a right to choose guests as they see fit. I would've loved the job, but it wasn't offered," Kennedy responded truthfully. "I'm happy for all the others."

Despite the earlier incident with the photos, the long rivalry between her and Tiaja Rae was brought up next. As ugly as it was, it was just another topic Kennedy had to grind through to save her professional face. And she did save her decorum, admirably so.

There was no rivalry, not as far as Kennedy was concerned.

One person had to covet what the other one had for a competition to exist.

Tiaja Rae had absolutely nothing Kennedy desired or needed or couldn't have.

Kennedy discreetly gritted her teeth as Lacy once again profusely apologized for earlier. As far as Kennedy was concerned, the incident was over. She had no desire to keep rehashing it. It certainly wasn't going to change anything. However, if it *had* been done on purpose, she'd like to have only one question answered.

Why was it so easy to apologize for something versus just not doing it at all?

Kennedy hoped there wouldn't be any major fallout from the show's ignorant blunder. She knew this type of stuff was the Hollywood way; rag-sheet heaven. Like her, everyone had to get over it already. It was done.

Xavier took Kennedy into his arms the second she was ushered back to the private room. He had opted to watch the interview in peace and quiet. During the interview, he hated that she'd been thrown off-kilter because of the unexpected photographs. Still, he thought she'd handled it all very well. Xavier didn't think viewers saw her discomfort. He only saw it because of his emotional involvement with her.

Xavier realized how very emotionally involved he was with her. "I'm so sorry, babe."

"No." Kennedy looked up at Xavier. "Don't ever apologize for someone else's insensitivity. This is not our fault and we have to refuse to own it. I can't help wondering if Tiaja Rae had something to do with embarrassing us like that."

Xavier frowned. "I really hope you're wrong about that one. As for being embarrassed, I wasn't. It was only a modeling assignment, period. End of story."

Kennedy sighed. "You're right. I'm dead wrong. And Lacy would never stoop to that level. She's always been kind and fair to me." She kissed him tenderly on the mouth, deciding she had made too much of the incident "End of story," she repeated, planning to call Lacy later and thank her again for inviting her as a guest. She'd already sent the talk-show host a huge basket of wildflowers right after the invite had been accepted.

Xavier kissed her again. "Let's blow this joint."

The ride to Xavier's place was taking longer than usual due to the always-to-be-expected L.A. traffic jams. Since she still seemed upset he offered his place as refuge. She accepted. With Kennedy following along behind him in her car, he was still somewhat troubled by the talk-show incident. The picture of him and Tiaja Rae was a racy one. Still, it had been nothing more than a working arrangement, one that had called for an intimate, sexy shoot.

Xavier let loose with a mild expletive when Kennedy got caught by the yellow traffic light he had just sailed through. She'd never make it, not without running the red light. There were only a couple more miles to go before they reached his home. Xavier felt he needed to pull over and chill out to make sure they got there in one piece. He did just that.

* * *

Xavier yawned as he and Kennedy came through the kitchen door leading from his garage. "A nap is high on my list of things to do," he said. "I am so tired. Guess I've been out late too many nights over the past few weeks. Girl, you're a bad influence on me."

"Not so. We are not typical Hollywood folk. How we've survived this crazy town is a mystery to me. The nightlife alone is a known killer. And I once thought New York was the toughest place I'd ever live through. My initial modeling days in the Big Apple were very scary. I was so young then. It's not so frightening to me now. I came to love Manhattan."

"We've done great, kid. Your native Philly is also a tough city to grow up in."

"Some of the suburbs of Philly weren't all that tough. As a longtime teacher and a principal, my parents were able to carve out a pretty decent living for us. I loved growing up in Philadelphia. My parents made sure I stayed grounded and received a good education. Kennedy and Megan Bassett are proud of my brothers and me. And we're equally proud of them."

"I know you are. And you've done a lot for them to be proud of you for." Xavier sat down at the kitchen table. "Did you have any apple pie left over?"

"Darn near all of it. But the sugarless pies you brought over were eaten. My neighbor Ms. Hannah just doesn't understand why I can't eat all those sweet sins she brings over to my place. And I don't have the heart to hurt her feelings."

"That's what happens when you're so helpful and sweet to your elderly neighbors. Just Ms. Hannah's way of showing you how much she appreciates all you do for her. Stop fretting over it. I'm willing to take the delicious sins off your hands."

"I wish I'd known that earlier. You would've already had it in your possession."

Xavier walked over to Kennedy and pulled her to her feet

and into his strong arms. His lips grazed hers ever so slightly. "Mind if we lie down for a bit? I'm pretty strong at keeping my hormones in check. Deal or no deal?"

"Deal! But let's not shake on it!" She laughed with a wink.

Upstairs in the master bedroom, after handing Kennedy a pair of his dark, lightweight lounging pants and a plain gray T-shirt, Xavier pulled back the white down comforter on his king-size, four-poster bed. A flick of his finger turned on the remote-controlled, double-sided gas fireplace, which could also be viewed and enjoyed from the good-sized but cozy sitting area adjacent to the bedroom. He then went into the master bathroom, where the walk-in closet was, to change into something more comfortable.

Just the thought of lying in bed with him had her heart pumping wild. To make the atmosphere even more romantic, she walked around the room and lit the jasmine-scented candles nestled in crystal diamond-cut, swan-shaped votive candleholders. These special gifts from her to him were situated on the nightstands. She'd given them to him as a professional gift after working a photo shoot together.

Kennedy changed into the too-large lounging attire and then slid into the center of the bed. It was the same spot she occupied in her own bed at home or in hotel rooms and in guest rooms of family and friends. It just happened to be her favorite spot to sleep.

A couple of seconds after Kennedy began searching for the television remote, she suddenly realized there wasn't a television set in the bedroom. *What was that all about?* She had to wonder, but not for long, since she planned to ask him when he returned.

The very subject of her thoughts came through the door and walked across the room, quiet as a mouse, agile as a gazelle. Xavier inhaled deeply of the heady jasmine scent before climbing into bed with Kennedy, where he curled up behind her, pulling her back against his warm body. Moaning gently, he dropped kisses into her thick mane of hair.

Kennedy lifted her head and angled it just enough to look back at him. "What's up with the television? Where is it?"

Xavier pointed toward the sitting room right off the bedroom. "Television is a no-no inside my bedroom. That's my special rule. That's why we watch it from in there."

"What? You're kidding! I can't live without turning on the plasma set in my bedroom, especially at bedtime." She thought his no-television rule was a bit eccentric, hoping he didn't expect her to change the rules in her bedroom. That wasn't happening.

Xavier softly kissed her temple. "The bedroom should be used for total relaxation, sleep—and also as the sacred place where a man and woman express their deepest forms of love, both spiritual and physical. When I lie down in bed with you, I want you to have all my attention…and vice versa," he explained. "However, I have no objections to listening to soft music in the bedroom."

Kennedy had never heard anything so sweetly inspiring from a man. The words had come from his mouth but had arisen right out of his spirit. He had touched her deep inside her heart, way down in a place where she didn't think she'd ever been caressed before.

Eccentric? Hardly. The man possessed a powerful soul, one full of sensitivity.

While Kennedy and Xavier had not yet come together physically, each was very particular about whom they surrendered their physical selves to. He pretty much felt the same as she did on one-night stands and meaningless physical contact: extremely uninterested. Although curling up together in each other's beds would always be a risky proposition both adults knew exactly what they wanted: each other.

Content in allowing this relationship to progress naturally, Kennedy and Xavier were ever mindful of physical lust vs.

spiritual love. Temptation was always lurking about, something each was highly aware of. Giving in to the lure was always a very real possibility, but they were happy and content to bask in each other's undivided attention.

Thinking that she had to be the luckiest woman in the world, Kennedy entwined her fingers with Xavier's, right where his hands encircled her waist. "Is it okay if we just lie here quietly for a few minutes? I want only our spirits to talk."

Sucking in a deep breath helped Xavier get through the emotion erupting within. Kennedy often said things that caused his sentiment to give way. He loved the way she so easily but poetically expressed herself. Instead of responding to her verbally, he laid his head upon her shoulder. They lay there quietly.

Listening to Kennedy's even breathing was a special first-time experience for Xavier. It sounded like new music to his ears. He was thrilled to see her looking so vulnerable. Studying her soft features brought a sense of calm to him.

Xavier wondered if she had gotten past the incident at the television studio. The only way for him to find out was to ask, he surmised, thinking they'd been quiet long enough.

Xavier dropped a soft kiss behind Kennedy's ear, his finger-tips gently outlining her jaw. "Are you feeling any better about what happened on the talk show?"

Turning up on her side, Kennedy laid her head against his chest. "I've come to terms with it. Although I'd like to know if it was done purposely, I don't see what difference it'd make now. It can't be changed. Like I said earlier, I've given Lacy the benefit of the doubt. I've already called her to show my grati-tude."

"Glad to hear that. It's not good to harbor bad feelings. I'm really hoping it wasn't done intentionally, but we may never know." The phone rang. His first thought was not to answer it. He then decided he should at least look at the caller ID. Seeing Janine and Jonathan's home number, he decided to return the call later.

"Aren't you going to get that?" For a brief moment she wondered if the caller was another woman. *What would that matter?* She didn't have exclusive rights to him and his time. However, she hoped they'd eventually consider a monogamous relationship.

Looking deeply into her eyes, his fingertips returned to her face, this time touching her cheeks and outlining her lips. "Are you dating anyone else?"

Laughing inwardly, Kennedy had to wonder if Xavier had read her mind despite the fact that such a thing was impossible. "Only you. At the moment."

At the moment? Xavier snapped his head back, suppressing a groan. "Does that mean you're planning on it?"

Looking sweetly innocent, Kennedy batted her eyelashes. "I didn't say that."

He looked perplexed. "Then what are you saying?"

"I'm not dating anyone else. I answered your question honestly the first time."

"Yeah, you did. I just didn't get the 'at the moment' part. At the moment can you consider us entering into an exclusive relationship? To spell it out in plain terns, I'd like us to date only each other. Possibility?"

"A definite possibility." She smiled. "Are you sure you want to date only me? You're a man women love."

"That's exactly what I want. As models, we both know we're around the opposite sex more often than not, and we both know lots of flirting comes with the territory, as well as a lot of demands on our time. Very little time to devote to our personal relationships. I've never been one to date more than one woman at the same time. It doesn't work for me. And I don't like being tangled up in romantic webs. Are you up for some serious one-on-one with me?"

This beautiful man was too adorable for words, not to mention genuine. Kennedy just wanted to grab hold of Xavier and never let go of him. The diamondlike sparkle in her eyes was bright, with her pupils afloat in liquid. "I'd love to be romantically involved with you. Deal or no deal?" She mocked his earlier remarks to her.

"Deal." Xavier wasted no time in sealing the mutual agreement with an astonishing kiss, a passionate kiss Kennedy would not soon forget.

Like always, one delicious kiss led to a flurry of others. His lips undulating over hers was mind-blowing as he rapidly turned her body into a scorching firestorm. He had a way of seducing her lips with featherweight kisses before allowing the pressure to increase to the point of deep, deep intensity.

Kennedy weaved her hands through Xavier's wavy hair, crushing it with the pads of her fingers. Her soft moans became more frequent as her physical desire for him increased tenfold. In the next few seconds, fearful of things getting out of control, she rolled away from him, positioning herself flat on her back. Her breasts rapidly rose and fell with each labored breath she took.

Catching her breath wasn't easy, but Kennedy did her best to steady her ragged breathing. Things had started to get out of hand. It didn't matter much to her who had managed to regain control, but their ardent desires had to be reined in instantly. It was too soon to make love.

Keeping a close eye on Kennedy, Xavier drew her back into his arms. The look of panic on her face had him a little worried. He looked down into her face. "Are you having doubts about us lying here together?"

Snuggling up closer to Xavier, Kennedy kissed him tenderly on the chin. "No doubts, but someone has to remain in control. It started to look as if we were both goners."

Laughing, Xavier shook his head. "Nah, I wasn't there yet. Close, but not quite. Do you trust me to keep you safe?"

"I trust me to keep me safe. This isn't about being safe, and we both know it. This is about a physical desire so strong it's frightening. You know what I'm talking about?"

Xavier nodded. "I think I do. It's hard but we *are* in control. If and when the time comes to take our relationship to the next level, we'll handle it the right way."

Not ashamed to confess his feelings about them, Xavier went on to say that his physical desire for her was always strong. He wanted her every time he was with her, but it wasn't all about sex for him. "We just recently decided to date only each other. Everything is moving at exactly the right pace, slow and easy. Let's sit back and continue to let our relationship develop naturally."

Kennedy's eyes revealed her admiration for him. Since she was the one who'd pulled away, she took full responsibility for nearly losing it. Xavier was sizzling hot. What flesh-and-blood woman could lie in bed next to him without getting hot and bothered? He made her feel all sorts of spine-tingling sensations, many that were foreign to her.

As Kennedy's eyes slowly drooped, Xavier grew very still, closely watching over her. She was beautiful, soft and feminine, but she also exhibited an abundance of strength. He seemed to lose himself in her effervescent presence each time they got together. Her sense of humor was energizing. He hadn't laughed this much in a long time. Kennedy's vast intellect allowed them to get into some conversations that could go completely over the average person's head. He could go on and on in his thoughts of her since she was that interesting a person. Now that she was asleep he wanted to do the same. Laying his head as close to hers as he could get without disturbing her, he closed his eyes.

Kennedy had dozed off to soft jazz filtering from the wall-mounted speakers. She awakened to the same sweet melodies. Darkness had already fallen, but the glowing candlelight was adequate for her to see by. As she looked around the room,

Xavier was nowhere to be found. Needing to use the bathroom, she quickly slipped out of bed and dashed into the adjoining room. After washing her hands and drying them off, she went back into the bedroom to slip into her own clothing.

It was time to go home, Kennedy reckoned, but if she had her way she'd spend the entire night right there in Xavier's bed, where she had felt safe and secure. He had taken very good care of her, had been very gentle and gentlemanly. The night couldn't have gone any better. If there were more times like this in their future, she'd welcome each one.

By the time Kennedy had fully dressed and was slipping into her shoes, Xavier sauntered into the room, tossing her a smile that made her heart swoon.

He frowned slightly. "Why are you dressed?"

Wrinkling her nose, she shrugged her shoulders. "It's time for me to go home. All good things eventually come to an end. We both know that."

"This beautiful night doesn't have to end. It's been great. Will you spend the night with me if I sleep in one of the guest rooms?"

"What would be the point? I'd be in your bed and you'd be elsewhere. Temptation will track us down and do its best to send us fleeing into each other's arms."

He grinned. "That's not such a bad thing, is it?"

"I guess not. I'm going home, Xavier. There'll be other times. Okay?"

"I give up. You win. I'm a sucker for those beautiful, expressive eyes of yours. And for you."

Suddenly, feeling a bit chilled, Kennedy shivered. She had a tendency to feel that way after she and Xavier parted company. The evening temperatures in the beach cities could get pretty cool, but she knew that the outdoor temp had nothing to do with her chill. However, she had a lot of warm memories to ponder to keep her from missing him so much. *Well,* she thought, *we'll be back in each other's company before you know it.*

Until then, you have plenty of things to do to fill the hours, she thought.

The moment Kennedy slipped into bed she reached for the phone. After dialing the first few digits of Xavier's home number, she almost changed her mind. She finished dialing, recalling how sincere he was in requesting her to call back to say she'd made it home safely. When his answering machine picked up, she looked confused. It was late and she couldn't help wondering where he was. He'd said he was going back to bed, but he'd lay awake until she'd called. Perhaps the sandman had been too much for him to resist.

Once Kennedy left a message for Xavier, telling him she was safe and sound in her own bed, she put the speaker on to listen for her messages. The third one left on the machine was regarding a modeling job, a layout for a travel magazine. The content of the message from her manager intrigued her and she couldn't wait to return the call first thing in the morning, hoping the offer was still on the table. Her mind was clicking on all cylinders by the time the messages ended.

At the first dusting of daylight, Kennedy thought about changing the linens on her bed, the one task she needed to tackle right away. Her assignments had kept her on the go, causing her to neglect her intimate spaces in the house.

Thinking of all her upcoming assignments had Kennedy wanting to recheck her calendar. She hoped she wasn't scheduled to travel out of the state, but Las Vegas had been periodically ringing on and off in her head.

Check out the calendar, clean up the bedroom and then get the rest of your day under way, Kennedy pondered. The things she had to do were firmly planted in her mind. Smiling brightly, she made her way to the linen closet inside the master bathroom.

It didn't take Kennedy long to strip the bed and put on clean linens. She then did the laundry.

While the clothes were being washed she went into the family room and clicked on the television to CNN. She quickly took a seat as a special report out of downtown Charleston, South Carolina, caught her ear. It seemed that the owner of the K. Morgan Boutique had fallen through the catwalk as she'd come out to thank the attendees and participants. Rather than waiting to be rescued, she had crawled out on her own. Shortly after the rescue team had arrived, *they'd* had fallen through the catwalk, as well. It had been a comedy of errors but fortunately no one had been seriously hurt.

Kennedy flinched as she recalled Miss USA falling down during the evening-gown portion of the Miss Universe Pageant. Experience—or the lack of it—was not without its share of pain. She had come close to falling a few times during different modeling assignments, but she'd been fortunate enough to have recovered nicely each time. The thought of falling had often been in the back of her mind, especially early on in her career. Then she'd learned not to think about it at all.

Right after Kennedy turned on the computer to check her e-mail account, she saw on her home page that she was part of the headlines. She clicked on the icon to read the full story, the picture of her dousing Tiaja Rae with wine in Technicolor. Reading the story didn't make her feel any better. Although no one had interviewed her about the incident it was reported that Xavier De Marco was at the very center of the women's hot tempers.

Coverage of these episodes made Kennedy feel even worse. Xavier had never been intimately involved with the other model, but the press had determined it to be the case. He was now being cited as the main contention between her and Tiaja Rae, when their problems had begun long before. Briefly, Kennedy considered calling a halt to her love affair with Xavier.

Was it worth this trouble? She prided her successful, steady career on her good reputation. All this gossip may jeopardize it. And that was the last thing she wanted for her life.

Chapter 6

It wasn't hard for Kennedy to believe how quickly and drastically things could change in her line of work. Last-minute jobs came with the territory. If someone had told her she would be in Ocho Rios, Jamaica, on this beautiful morning, lying in a huge canopied bed, she wouldn't have believed them if she were in any other profession. That Xavier had flown to Jamaica with her was a bit harder to take in.

The late-evening phone call to Kennedy from her manager, Chase Hudson, had revealed an amazing offer for her to do a photo shoot at an elite, first-class Jamaican resort. The model who had been scheduled for the travel magazine layout had suddenly taken ill and a replacement model was needed. Kennedy had been highly recommended by the ill West Indian model herself, Lorna Tokay. The two supermodels of color had worked together on numerous assignments and had hit it off beautifully.

Out of the blue Kennedy had asked Chase to make a special request to the magazine editor for Xavier to do the layout with her. Suggestions and ideas were exchanged all the time among industry professionals so it wasn't such an unusual appeal.

Needless to say, Kennedy was thrilled when the suggestion was instantly embraced by the editor, who had thought it was an awesome idea, as well as a lucrative one for all parties involved. The modeling duo had been quickly approved by the "powers that be," as time had been of the essence. It had only taken them ten days to work out all the details. During the wait, Kennedy and Xavier had spent lots of quality time together.

This was an ideal situation for the couple to find themselves in. He was so glad she'd inquired about their working together. It was so ironic. His agent, Kirsten, was actually working on a similar situation for them to pose together in a layout for a major fashion design house. By working together, they'd also get to take advantage of sharing in even more time together.

Some models might shy away from working with their significant others, but not these two. Kennedy and Xavier were excited about looking for new challenges and dynamic ways to reinvent themselves. They had even discussed the pros and cons of indulging in such a delicate proposition before making the decision to move forward. It could prove risky for the couple's personal relationship, but both were very secure within. The potential for them to succeed in these ventures was even greater.

With the idea of achieving success in mind, before ever boarding the aircraft to Jamaica, Kennedy and Xavier had already begun setting up specific boundaries for their working relationship, simply because they wanted to maintain a professional decorum. Things had been heating up between the couple, but Kennedy wasn't quite ready to take the ultimate step in their love affair. Not just yet, but soon. Very soon.

Hearing a light knock on the door, Kennedy looked at the bedside clock. It wasn't even 7:00 a.m., yet it seemed maid service was already there to clean the room. Kennedy recalled not putting out the Do Not Disturb sign last night.

"Be right there," Kennedy yelled, trying to grab her bathrobe. After spotting it at the foot of the bed, she smiled, hurrying to slip into the silk garment so she could get the door. Wasn't it too early for housekeeping?

"Room service," Xavier sang out, wearing a huge grin on his

face, his hands wrapped around a large plastic tray. "Is a light breakfast okay with you?"

The fluffy croissant and lemon and cherry Danishes looked mouthwatering and the freshly brewed coffee smelled heavenly. Two boiled eggs, chunks of fresh fruit, strawberries and clusters of red and white grapes made it a bit more than a light meal.

"Leave it to you to think of something so sweet." Smiling broadly, she backed away from the door. "Come on in."

Once Xavier was inside the suite, Kennedy picked up the Do Not Disturb sign and inserted it in the slot on the door, risking the room not getting cleaned until later.

Xavier set down the tray on the round table and then pulled out a chair for Kennedy to be seated. She quickly excused herself for a moment to go wash her face and hands and brush her teeth, apologizing to him for the necessary delay.

"How'd you sleep last night, K.B.?" he yelled out to her.

"Just fine," she said, stepping back into the room. "The bed's dangerously comfortable. How'd you do?" She walked across the room and sat down at the table.

"I fell unconscious the moment my head hit the pillow." He unfolded a napkin and placed it in his lap. "We had an unusually late-night flight. I'm glad we've been given twenty-four hours to hang out and enjoy Ocho Rios before and after the shoot."

"Oh, yeah, I can't wait to hit the beach to laze out. With the ocean just outside the doors of this hotel, paradise is at the tip of our toes, literally."

Xavier looked over at the clock. "What time do you antici-pate getting outside?"

"As soon as breakfast is over, but I plan to shower before getting my tan on."

"You're not getting into the water?"

"Sure, but only as far out as my deck chair will stay lodged in the sand. Hair and makeup is already a lengthy process without me getting my locks wet and gritty."

"Thank goodness that only applies to you women." Laughing, he made a mock gesture of shaking out his wavy hair. Xavier then held up his Danish to Kennedy's mouth. "Taste it. It's delicious."

Although Kennedy preferred to taste Xavier's lips, she took a small bite of the fluffy, fruit-filled pastry. "Mmm, that *is* good."

As the couple fell into an amicable silence, Kennedy basked in the serene decor of the posh suite housed in the Paradise Bay Resort. The atmosphere was surreal, the suite lavishly furnished and luxuriously comfortable. Much like the decor in Kennedy's house, white in various shades was the prevailing color, including the stark white bedding and the creamy white barrel chairs and matching sofa. The carpeting was a soft shade of ecru and the ceramic tiles a gleaming white. The other furnishings were a striking, contrasting black, to include coffee and end tables, an entertainment center, dinette set, ergo desk and high-back leather chair.

The large black-and-white-polka-dot framed mirror was a favorite accent for her.

Kennedy was also thrilled and uplifted by her budding romance with Xavier. The opportunity to see their love blossoming right before her eyes, in one of the most romantic spots on earth, was both encouraging and exciting to her. This modeling assignment couldn't have come at a better time in the relationship. Other chances for them to work together seemed promising, more so if this campaign proved successful.

Kennedy turned to Xavier and placed a moist kiss upon his succulent lips. "I'm glad we could do this together."

Xavier kissed the tip of Kennedy's nose, feeling blessed to have her as his exclusive love interest. "Me, too. This trip is a blessing. We'll leave here a much stronger, closer couple."

As soon as Kennedy and Xavier had finished their meals, he had gone back to his suite to change into his swimwear. They'd made plans to meet up in the hotel lobby.

Ready to take on the sweet challenges of the day, hoping there wouldn't be any not-so-sweet ones, Kennedy dried off her body after an invigorating steamy shower. She wished she had been able to lie in bed a bit longer, but no woman in her right mind would ever turn away from their door the fine-as-the-priciest-wine Xavier.

Late last night Kennedy had unpacked all her clothes and had already put them neatly away. From the chest of drawers she chose a royal-blue bikini to complement her fabulous figure and skin tone. The sheer cover-up was done in the same royal hue but trimmed in white. A pair of cute white and royal blue leather sandals and a large-brimmed straw hat with a wide white band rounded out her sunny but cool beach-day look.

After Kennedy stuffed her white straw satchel with a couple of large and fluffy beach towels she was all ready for a few hours under the Jamaican sun—and more than ready to be in the company of the sexiest man alive.

The knock on the door had Kennedy scurrying across the room. This time it *was* housekeeping rapping away. The timing was perfect. She stepped aside to let the housekeeper through. Kennedy was out the door in seconds.

This is going to be a great day. I can feel it.

Kennedy was stretched out in the chaise lounge which had been pulled a short distance out into the surf. Xavier was seated right next to her in the sand in the shallow waters. With his knees drawn up, his hands cupped his kneecaps.

The tropical weather was absolutely gorgeous on this day. The five-star resort had so much to offer, especially in the way of recreation or just plain relaxation.

Besides the breakfast, lunch and dinner buffets offered daily at the resort, there were five fine, reservation-only restaurants for the couple to choose from for the dinner hour. The property also housed two first-class nightclubs and a magnificent casino.

A fitness center and spa could be found inside the hotel, as well as a beauty salon and barbershop. Pricy clothing and novelty gift shops were other amenities.

Four nights and three days was enough time for Kennedy and Xavier to get their groove on after the workday. She loved reggae music. The resort offered steel bands every single night inside the large pavilion located on the west end of the property.

Kennedy reached down and lightly splashed Xavier with the beautiful, clear-as-glass turquoise water. "Mind rubbing more sunblock on me?"

Xavier wrung his hands together in eager anticipation, smiling flirtatiously. "I'd love to. Nothing gives me more pleasure than holding you, touching you, kissing you."

To cool the heat she felt from his words, Kennedy fanned herself. She then dug into her straw satchel for the sunblock. As she handed him the bronze-colored tube, their hands touched, causing their eyes to connect in a warm embrace. He loved how she looked at him.

Kennedy's lashes lowered at the same time Xavier's hands tenderly massaged into her skin the silky lotion. "Is this a little taste of paradise or what?"

"I don't think we've seen the half of it yet, K.B. I've heard of Dunn's River Falls. That's where the first shooting will take place. Friends have told me it's breathtaking."

"If it's anything like the pictures I viewed over the Internet, breathtaking might be an understatement. This modeling job should be a breeze for us."

"Let's hope so. The weather can be totally unpredictable this time of year, raining and gusting winds without a moment's notice. I guess we should just think positive."

"Well, I don't think it'll be all that bad if we're forced to stay an extra day or two due to inclement weather. I know I won't be mad at anybody."

Xavier grinned. "I get your drift." He rested his hand on her thigh. "Sure you don't want to try your hand at snorkeling or scuba diving?"

Kennedy looked skeptical. "I still don't know. My hair…"

"That'll be taken care of. It's not something you have to worry about."

"I guess you're right. I should at least try out one or the other."

Xavier could hardly believe his ears. He was thrilled. "That's my girl!"

"Let's make it snorkeling so I don't have to go too deep into the water."

"Whatever you're most comfortable with. When we're done here, I'll go to the concierge's desk and make the arrangements. All I want to do now is kiss your tempting lips." His tongue caressed his own lips, his eyes settling hotly on her luscious mouth.

Xavier got up and stretched out on the chaise with Kennedy. After taking her into his arms, he nibbled gently on her ear. Loving the soft feel and sweet taste of her, he moaned softly. As he turned up on his side, facing her, she tossed her leg across his hip. The contact with his hard body made her shiver with longing. Indulging in each other's staggering passion, they embraced tenderly, kissing and hugging and whispering sweet comments to one another.

The sky was blue and the clouds were as white as newly fallen snow. The sun was high as it spilled its dazzling rays onto the white sugary beach. In the distance, sailboats, gleaming white, drifted lazily atop the calm turquoise waters. Swimmers in colorful gear cut through the waters with ease. Powerful jet skis churned up the surf until it became white with froth. Kennedy saw Ocho Rios, Jamaica, as a replica of the Garden of Eden. The natural beauty of the festive yet serene place nearly brought her to tears.

Now that Kennedy had agreed to go snorkeling with him, Xavier thought it was time for her to get all wet. Because she looked so cute and sexy in her blue bikini, he had a moment of reluctance. Like her, he also had a mischievous streak, one that he had a hard time containing at the moment. Using his weight and one leg for leverage, he tipped over the chaise lounge, dumping both of them into the calm waters.

As Kennedy screeched loudly in protest of Xavier's impish antics, tiny colorful fish swam about their bodies, causing her to gasp in awe. Now that she was completely engrossed and enchanted with the harmless sea life, he grabbed her around the waist and dragged her further out into the warm-as-bath Caribbean waters.

Peals of laughter rent the air as the couple frolicked about in the sea. As if they were the only two people occupying this island paradise, they found it easy to slip further into what seemed like a fantasy, enjoying the sweet here and now. Passionate feelings were abundant between Kennedy and Xavier. Life was good. Both were eager for things to get even more romantic between them. Though they'd have a hard time imagining it any better than this, they both knew it could escalate to unattained heights.

Once Kennedy pulled her hat down far enough to shade her face, she closed her eyes. She hoped she hadn't made a big mistake by agreeing to go snorkeling. To back out on Xavier now would make her feel stupid. He seemed so eager to get going. She figured it shouldn't be too hard to learn the water sport. Kennedy definitely knew how to swim.

The reluctance on Kennedy's part really had been all about her hair, but it had already gotten wringing wet. The photo shoot would take much longer to get through now that her hair had to be given the full treatment. Her tresses were thick, long and unmanageable, making it more difficult for a stylist other than her regular one to tackle. She didn't like anyone to go to any extra trouble on her behalf even though the cosmetologists were contracted to tend to her hair and makeup. It was too late for her to renege now. Xavier had already gone back inside the hotel to finalize the arrangements.

Grin and bear it, she pondered, trying to convince herself it would be a lot of fun. Being with him was really all that mattered. Xavier would take excellent care of her.

As Kennedy's mind slipped back to the night she and Xavier had gone dancing at Caliente, she felt yet another deep twinge of regret over how she had behaved so badly during her unpleasant interaction with Tiaja Rae. Her mother and father would've been appalled at her errant behavior. Despite feelings of remorse, her lips curved in a half smile, as she recalled the shocked look on Tiaja Rae's beautiful face over the wine bath.

Tiaja Rae should feel lucky. The wineglass could've been filled to the brim.

Before now Kennedy hadn't allowed herself to entertain thoughts on how she felt about Xavier and her rabid nemesis working together on *L,L&L*. She didn't like it, not one iota, but she'd never think of asking him to turn down the assignment. No doubt in her mind that Tiaja Rae would go after Xavier. The woman had no scruples whatsoever.

Tiaja Rae was insanely jealous of Kennedy, but she'd never admit it to anyone.

Although Kennedy believed Xavier could and would probably thwart the hot advances of the she-devil, she didn't like seeing him put in that position. Temptation was a powerful entity for any man to reckon with. Just the thought of them working together in such close proximity had her stomach feeling queasy. God forbid that he might give in to man's natural lust for the flesh. If he did, their relationship would abruptly end.

No, Kennedy thought, Xavier wouldn't do that to her. She had to give him way more credit. She didn't believe he'd ever intentionally hurt her. He had expressed to her numerous times his dislike for dishonesty and cheating in relationships. Because he'd been cheated on, he had firsthand knowledge of how excruciatingly painful it was.

Nikki Simmons, a woman Xavier had believed in wholeheartedly, had put it on him pretty badly. She had been an average-looking woman, with a mind-blowing figure. Her seeming compassion was what had drawn him to her. It had only taken a month for him to learn she was merciless. A guy she had met through Xavier, a cameraman acquaintance of his, had turned Nikki out one evening, after they'd run into each other at a nightclub.

Xavier had gotten through it all because he hadn't been in love with Nikki, yet the betrayal had still devastated him. She hadn't even been the one to confess the affair. Joel Cox, the cameraman, had come clean with Xavier, but only after Joel had found out Nikki was involved with yet another man, a good friend of his. This scenario for Joel had turned out to be a clear-cut case of what goes around comes around, according to Xavier.

Kennedy found comfort in learning that Xavier hadn't been in love with Nikki.

Seeing Xavier running across the sand caused her heart to go berserk. His skin, now a golden bronze, was shimmering from the heavy sheen of suntan oil. His muscles appeared to ripple with every stride he took. His sexy black swim trunks were a perfect fit on his strong, lithe body. He looked like a bronze statue, powerful and sturdy.

Kennedy felt herself blush as she thought of Xavier's manhood thrusting deep inside her, making her body yearn for his deliciously intimate touch.

How many times had her body craved his since their very first kiss?

Wishing they didn't have separate rooms, Kennedy eagerly anticipated making love with him for the first time, laughing softly at her incendiary thoughts. Just because they had different rooms didn't mean they couldn't spend time together in the same one, she concluded. Since this evening was the last of their leisure time on the island until after the shoot, Kennedy decided she should make it a special one. They had played hard today and would probably do so tonight. Still, they'd work well together in the morning.

The snorkeling lesson had been a breeze for Kennedy. She had gotten it down pat in just a short while. She didn't have to wear an awkward oxygen tank on her back to snorkel. That would've been scary for her. She figured she had watched too many movies featuring serious scuba mishaps to be comfortable trying it out. There was a risk in most everything people did, but some things were riskier than others.

Xavier was proud of how well Kennedy was doing as they maneuvered the water.

The colorful sea life was spectacular and the number of different species was astounding. The Jamaican party boat that had taken them out to the reef bobbed up and down on the water. Still aboard the craft were those passengers who hadn't been interested in snorkeling. The vividly colored fish and array of plants Kennedy spotted not that far below the surface were awe-inspiring. She'd never seen this kind of natural beauty, with all its amazing enchantment. Her eyes thirstily drank in her paradiselike surroundings.

Surprising to Kennedy, the atmosphere was romantically charged. Every now and then Xavier would take her hand, kiss her palm and entwine their legs. At times he swam right over top of her, close enough for her to feel his body hovering above. He pointed out so many things of beauty to her, those she might've otherwise missed. She loved the fact that he wanted her to enjoy snorkeling as much as he did. Xavier loved to bask in nature just as much as Kennedy did.

* * *

Back aboard the party boat, Kennedy and Xavier enjoyed an ice-cold rum concoction called a blue lagoon. The drink was very tasty, but they knew to practice moderation. The sweet taste could be deceiving. Jamaican rums were very strong.

The reggae music was lively and funky, as the crew of the party boat put on a dance routine fit for royalty. Kennedy wished she had the same kind of tight control over the muscles in her derriere that the dancers appeared to have. If she could move her butt like that, she'd never have a sagging one. These ladies were doing lots of serious rump shaking, which had many of the men looking on in a trancelike state.

The look on Xavier's face spoke to his amusement, but Kennedy could tell that he was definitely enjoying both mesmerizing shows. Twinkling lights danced in his eyes as they followed the soulful, rapid-fire movements of the dancers. Reggae was one of his favorite styles of music so she was sure he was right in his element.

Watching the expressions on Kennedy's face was far more enchanting to Xavier than the seductive routines the dancers indulged in. Clearly, she was enjoying herself tremendously. Every time Xavier looked at Kennedy his heart swelled with his feelings for her. He liked seeing her happy and animated. At the moment, she was both. Her joy made her eyes sparkle. The wild expressions of her lovely body were indeed lively.

Because it was one of Kennedy's favorite indulgences, she loved to relive in her mind all the dates she'd had with Xavier, especially the special dining ins and outs they'd had before leaving for Jamaica.

As Kennedy's mind spun back to a few days ago when Xavier had called to ask her to accompany him to a cocktail party, her eyes stayed on him. The date had been an after-five, dressy affair. She loved to dress up and had chosen an exquisite metallic silver Giorgio Armani cocktail number. She had modeled the classy dress in a celebrity fashion show. Afterward, the dress had been presented to her as a thank-you gift.

The party had been lots of fun, but it hadn't been entirely painless. Kennedy had lost count of the beautiful women who'd come on to Xavier in just a matter of minutes. A couple of guys had hit on him, too. She'd been surprised by how well he'd handled himself with the men, showing his affable side.

Kennedy and Xavier's personal after-party was the highlight of the date. He had hired a limousine for the entire evening—and the couple had later been driven into downtown L.A. to the Bona Venture Hotel, where'd they'd enjoyed a spectacular view from inside the top floor's revolving restaurant.

While sipping on cool Cosmopolitans, Xavier had once again let Kennedy know exactly what type of man he was and also what he was looking for in a personal relationship. The couple pretty much wanted and expected the same things from a romantic liaison. Each was happy to know they were still of one accord.

At the end of the evening, before they'd gotten out of the limo, he'd done something quite unique by presenting her with a dozen roses, which normally occurred at the beginning of a date. At the door of her home, he had yet again sincerely expressed his desire to continue seeing her. She had been thrilled silly and would've been bitterly disappointed had he not ever called again. Xavier's kisses to the back of Kennedy's hand were a provocative gesture that hooked her instantly.

When the party boat crew members asked all the tourists to join them in a dance, Kennedy and Xavier were the first ones to step up. As a line dance was taught patiently by the crew, Kennedy closely observed every step they made. The dance was actually a newer version of the electric slide, Xavier soon realized. Executing the exhilarating dance steps to reggae music was so much fun for everyone.

As Xavier came up behind Kennedy and circled her waist, laughing, she threw her head back against his broad chest.

While moving to the fast-paced, funky beats, the couple managed to keep in perfect step with one another, happily learning the updated routine.

Seated on one of the barrel chairs in Kennedy's suite, Xavier watched over his exhausted lady as she slept. The girl had conked out on him rather quickly. Only five minutes ago they'd been conversing lively with each other, making plans for later on in the evening. They'd planned to make an early night of it because of the early-morning wakeup call. It seemed to him as if the day's activities had already been too much for her.

After getting up from the chair, Xavier walked over to the desk, where he picked up a pen and wrote Kennedy a very legible note on a hotel notepad, asking her to call him later. He graciously planned to give her a rain check if she was too tired to go out.

Xavier thought that room service and a movie was a nice alternative to having dinner out in one of the resort's finer restaurants, and perhaps more dancing. Some slow dancing in private. Although he had no idea when they'd revisit Jamaica again, Kennedy getting the proper rest before undertaking a major modeling assignment was paramount.

After Xavier drew a heart at the bottom of the notepad, initialing the center of it, he quietly left the suite. Glad that the door to the room would lock automatically, confident about her safety, he stepped out into the hallway. Even though they'd been together for hours and hours on end Xavier could hardly wait to see her again. It was nice being in exotic Jamaica with the beautiful Kennedy Bassett.

Xavier thought it felt even better being with Kennedy every waking moment.

Chapter 7

The early-morning temperatures were hotter and muggier than the photography crew had anticipated. Those weather conditions could make for a very difficult shoot. The one thing Kennedy and Xavier were grateful for was the cooling, cascading waters at Dunn's River Falls, where the first photo shoot was taking place.

The scant designer swimwear Kennedy and Xavier were clad in kept them from becoming too overheated. The spraying mists from the falls also helped keep them cool. Her worries about her hair had all been for naught since getting it drenched by the falls was one of the desired photographs for the layout. However, her hair would require full salon treatment for the formal-wear session to take place later on.

Seductive posing with the man of her dreams wasn't a bit difficult for Kennedy now that she was romantically involved with Xavier. There were no pretenses here. She wanted Xavier. And he wanted her. When the photographer called for him to press his body firmly against hers, she actually felt how much he desired her. If he was embarrassed by the hardening of his sex, there were no visible signs on Xavier's face.

A basic black, halter-style swimsuit revealing ample cleavage would've been considered average had it not been on Kennedy's bombshell figure. On her firm physique the swimwear looked like a million bucks. The stylish low-slung swim trunks worn by Xavier screamed out his sex appeal, his well-defined manhood outlined in a daring way.

As the striking modeling duo stood face-to-face, their expressions sultry, eye contact flirtatious, the smiling photographer clicked away at the camera's shutter with the speed of lightning. In the next pose, with Xavier's hands posted on Kennedy's hips, his full lips came close enough to her luscious, berry-glossed mouth for her to feel his breath fanning hers, yet their lips never touched. The pose was hot and provocative.

Fully stretched out against the rocks, water from the falls cascading over his sexy body, Xavier tenderly held Kennedy in his strong arms. With one side of her face pressed against his broad, hairy chest, his lips moved upward and came to rest on top of her head.

Walker Harrison, the photographer, held up his hand to garner attention. "Lift your head and look up into Xavier's eyes, Kennedy. Now give him a hint of a smile, an encouraging one. Let him know you're hot for him. That's it. Nice, very nice. Now place your hand on his chest. Splay your fingers. Good. Hold that pose, guys. Yes, yes, great."

Walker took two dozen or so more shots of the couple as he softly voiced his commands to the giddy Kennedy and Xavier to attain the most perfect, leap-off-the-pages poses he desired for the magazine layout. Walker saw this issue as a blow-out bestseller.

The resort's sweeping, ceramic-tiled terrace offered a breath-taking, panoramic vista of the Caribbean Sea. Kennedy and Xavier had a spectacular view of the palatial paradise from the restaurant they'd chosen, where flowers blossomed everywhere.

Kennedy felt like she had stepped into a picture postcard. She had no problem imagining Xavier and her living out the rest of their lives on this island. The atmosphere evoked the wildest in emotions, yet she felt completely at peace here.

Xavier was just plain impressed with the entire vacation resort. He hadn't felt totally relaxed in a long while because of his busy schedule. If he wasn't modeling, he was involved in celebrity appearances or charity events of some sort. There were days when there weren't enough hours to do it all. Today, he was in a beautiful place, with an even more beautiful woman at his side. A man should be very reluctant to ask for more.

The large display of delectable buffet foods was arranged nicely, beautifully presented, yet Kennedy and Xavier had opted to order from the large lunch menu.

Xavier looked up at the waiter and nodded. "Thanks for the entrée suggestion. We'd love to try the lamb kebobs. We'll both have steamed broccoli for sides."

Setric, the waiter, looked down at Kennedy. "Anything more for you?"

Loving Setric's thick Jamaican accent, Kennedy smiled up at the handsome, extremely well-built waiter, wondering if he was a surfer. If she wasn't in love with Xavier, she would definitely give Setric more than a mere a glance of interest. She couldn't imagine any woman not wanting to hang out around the island with him.

"I'd like to change the dressing for my salad," Kennedy mentioned. "I'll have the vinaigrette rather than the Caesar. Is that okay?"

"Not a problem, madam. Can I get anything else for either of you?"

Kennedy and Xavier both declined. They had all they wanted—and needed.

Just as the waiter walked away from the table, a tall, willowy lady leaned over Xavier from behind his chair and kissed both his cheeks. "I couldn't believe my eyes when I glanced over here." The stunningly attractive, caramel-complexioned lady's accent was British. She pointed out where she'd been sitting.

There was a man seated there also. "How have you been, my darling?" The lady was quite gushy.

Without waiting for Xavier's response, Serita Devlin came around from behind his seat and kissed him full on the mouth, totally disregarding Kennedy's presence. She quickly pulled a chair away from a nearby table and sat down uninvited.

Looking totally uncomfortable, Xavier smiled weakly. He was concerned for Kennedy. "Serita, this is my beautiful girlfriend, Kennedy Bassett. Kennedy, Serita Devlin, an old friend of mine from London."

Kennedy forced to her lips one of her nicer smiles. "Nice to meet you, Serita."

"Charmed, I'm sure," Serita said curtly, without bothering to look at Kennedy.

Serita seemed to only have eyes for Xavier. Kennedy felt invisible, especially after the lady purposely turned her chair around so her back was to Xavier's date.

Serita's amber eyes hotly roved Xavier's anatomy. "I see you're still fine as hell...and on all fronts. What are you doing here in Jamaica?"

"At the moment, I'm trying to have a cozy lunch with my girlfriend before it's time to get back to work. Maybe we can catch up at a more convenient time, Serita. This *was* a table for two," he said jokingly, though his expression showed he was dead serious.

Serita didn't seem the least bit daunted by his right-to-the-point remark. "Dinner, for *two, you and me,* say around seven. Is that convenient enough for you?"

"I'm afraid *we,* as in *Xavier and me,* already have plans for dinner, Serita. In fact, every minute of every hour of our time left on the island is booked solid. Sorry if that's inconvenient." Kennedy's smile dripped with sugar, as she bit back the remaining acid.

Serita whipped her head around and glared hard at Kennedy.

"You should be sorry, since I wasn't addressing you, *Mz.*" Serita instantly turned her attention back to Xavier, smiling beautifully, as if nothing was amiss. "As I was saying…"

"No, no, your say is over, Serita. Please excuse yourself," Xavier said curtly.

Grinning wickedly, Serita jumped to her feet. "I think you already know how persistent I can be, Xavier De Marco. We *will* see each other later. That's a given. As for you, *little mizz thing,* you should learn to stay out of *grown folks'* business."

Kennedy decided not to add anymore fuel to the fire. A flippant response from her would only keep this horrific situation from being over. Instead, she just watched in silence as Serita once again took liberty with Xavier's lips. The lady then sashayed away.

Kennedy felt a rush of sympathy for the poor man seated at Serita's table. It seemed as if he didn't stand a chance with the woman who held very little regard for the feelings of others. It was such a shame, too. Serita was an extremely attractive woman, one with a stupendous figure, yet another female who desired Xavier over her dignity.

Kennedy positively understood why women got all excited and hot and bothered by Xavier. He was definitely a hottie. Although she didn't like all the attention women gave him, especially the bold ones like Tiaja Rae and Serita, she vowed to deal with it. Xavier needed a confident woman, not one who bowed down to petty jealousies. She wasn't insecure and she wasn't going to change who she was to satisfy anyone.

Xavier reached over and covered Kennedy's hand with his. "I'm so sorry things like this keep happening. Please forgive this latest rude intrusion."

"You have to stop apologizing for these ill-mannered women. I don't see you at fault here, Xavier. I just wish so many women weren't attracted to you, but I'm actually flattered that they all want what I have."

Xavier grinned. "And what might that be?"

Smiling flirtatiously, Kennedy ran her thumb across his lower lip. "Your undivided attention and your sweet affection. Like you don't already know that."

He grinned "I'm cold busted, babe. I know exactly what you have in me."

Xavier was impressed that Kennedy wasn't faulting him for the way women came on to him. Actually, he'd seen worse behavior from ladies than any she'd witnessed. He was careful not to encourage the brazen advances, but he didn't know how to stop it. He had dated Serita for less than a month when he just couldn't deal with her anymore.

Nothing physical had occurred between Xavier and Serita because she'd become too demanding and confrontational right from the very beginning. He planned to tell Kennedy about the relatively short relationship, but not until after they'd left paradise. He wanted the rest of their stay in Jamaica to be beautiful and trouble-free.

The couple was relieved to see the waiter only inches away from their table. Both had worked up a voracious appetite.

Xavier consulted his wristwatch. "We can't linger over lunch now, but there's time to digest it. I don't see how they can make you any more beautiful than you are, but we've got to get you to hair and makeup in time for the next session."

Kennedy moaned. "I hate the thought of it, but that's what we're here for."

Xavier laughed. "And we're actually getting paid for hanging out in one of the most beautiful places in the world."

Kennedy couldn't agree with him more.

The siren-red floor-length gown Kennedy's body was seductively wrapped up in was nothing short of exquisite. Her long hair, shiny from the high-gloss sheen, had been curled all over and pinned up in a sophisticated style. A few loose tendrils hung at her nape and on each side of her face.

Loaned out by a noted jeweler on the island, a three-carat pear-shaped diamond pendant graced her elegant neck. Matching diamonds dangled from her delicate ears. On her left wrist she wore a thick diamond cuff. Clear, pliable vinyl was the material used to fashion the dainty shoes, making them look like glass slippers.

As Kennedy was all dressed up like Cinderella on the night of the grand ball, Xavier could easily portray the handsome prince. His white jacketed tuxedo had been custom-designed, fitting his fabulous body perfectly. His shirt, white and crisp, looked as if it had been tailored right on his anatomy. A red silk bow tie and cummerbund were striking accents. His black patent leather shoes appeared spit shined.

The handsome couple looked model perfect.

For the romantic backdrop a full orchestra had been commissioned for the magazine layout. The orchestra pit had been erected right on the sand, under several lighted palm trees. Raised just above the music pit, a dance floor, shimmering with tiny lights, had also been laid out atop the sand. Each musician, male and female alike, was dressed in black tuxedos. Like Xavier's formal wear, the tuxedo accents were red, only a darker shade than his.

The ambience couldn't be more perfect, as there was a full moon overhead, with brilliant stars flitting happily about the purple velvety skies.

As Xavier slowly guided Kennedy over the dance floor, she gazed up into his eyes, looking at him with adoration. The look of love was etched upon her lovely face, as she appeared to float in a dream world where he was the featured star.

Xavier looked as if he'd been rendered spellbound, his eyes softly conversing with Kennedy in the universal language of love. How he truly felt about her was written upon his handsome face. His feelings for her ruled his heart and soul. His spirit reveled in his deep, abiding love for one Kennedy Bassett.

* * *

Wearing an eye-catching white silk kimono-style dress, with a thigh-high split, Kennedy was quite the seductress. The brightly multicolored peacock embroidered on the back of the body-clinging sheath was strikingly beautiful. She had bought the spectacular dress in Tokyo while on a modeling trip. Backless red and white linen heels made a nice contrast to the soft whiteness of the silk material.

While Kennedy waited for Xavier to make his appearance, she went about the suite lighting all the candles. At her request, the housekeeping staff had earlier set the lovely table, dressed in the hotel's finest linens, crystal and china.

A bottle of fine champagne was chilling in a silver ice bucket. She planned to serve later the Brut Yellow Label in celebration of wrapping up a successful photo shoot. The three-course meal featuring petite filet mignons would be delivered by room service at 7:00 p.m. Xavier was due for dinner at six-thirty, a mere half an hour away.

After stacking the CD player with a selection of soft romantic ballads the hotel had provided, Kennedy popped into the bathroom to do a last-minute check on her attire in the full-length mirror. Freshening up her makeup a bit and adding a few more mists of the alluring scent she wore wouldn't hurt matters any, she decided. Xavier always complimented her on the array of enchanting fragrances she chose to tantalize each of her pulse points with.

Excitement stirred in Kennedy's perky breasts as provocative thoughts whirled around in her head about the evening that she could hardly wait to spend with Xavier. Thoughts of making love to him for the first time ever had her body yearning for the feel of him deep inside her.

The crisply starched burgundy-and-navy-blue-striped shirt Xavier wore accented his broad chest and the navy dress slacks defined his muscular thighs well. He looked good in anything he wore, but Kennedy was looking forward to seeing him naked.

Genuinely surprised by the surprise dinner Kennedy had planned for their evening, Xavier brought her to him and planted a thrilling kiss on her sweet mouth. "What did I do to deserve all this finery?"

Kennedy hunched her shoulders. "It's what we both did. These photos are probably some of our best work. This celebration is all about *us*."

"Nice thought. I'm starving. What's on the menu?"

"You have about twenty minutes to wait, mon," she joked. "We're at the mercy of room service. I requested a seven o'clock delivery time. What about a glass of wine?"

Xavier rubbed his abdomen. "Not on an empty stomach. Lunch is long gone, babe." His eyes suddenly zeroed in on the bowl of green apples.

Guessing at what Xavier was probably thinking, Kennedy dashed across the room, positioning her body in front of the table. "Please don't ruin your appetite. Dinner will be here soon. Be patient a little longer."

The thought to move Kennedy aside and grab for an apple only fleetingly crossed Xavier's mind. He didn't have the heart to spoil her special dinner plans, though the fruit wouldn't have had any negative effects on his appetite whatsoever. "In that case, I'll just have to feast off your delectable lips." With that said, he kissed her passionately.

As a hard knock thudded against the door, Kennedy pulled away from Xavier.

"Dinner's here," she announced jovially. "And right on time, since it seems you were about to devour me."

"That's an understatement. I'll just have to save you for dessert."

"I'll be a willing participant." Kennedy blew him a kiss on her way to the door.

Stepping aside, Kennedy allowed the room-service waiter to

roll the portable table inside the suite. The delectable scents drifting up her nose caused her mouth to water. She hoped everything tasted as good as it smelled. She was sure that it'd be delicious. All of their previous meals had been cooked to perfection. Kennedy expected this dinner to be just another divine culinary experience.

Soon after the waiter poured ice water and chilled wine into the crystal glasses, he set on the dining table the silver-domed plates and then placed the salads there also. The waiter had left the covered desserts on ice on the nearby coffee bar. Just as the waiter was about to vacate the premises, Xavier politely asked him to pop the cork on the champagne bottle.

The minute the very grateful waiter took his leave, having earned a hefty tip from him, Xavier walked across the room and pulled out the chair for Kennedy. He waited until she was seated before seating himself.

In the flickering candlelight the couple made small talk and indulged in moaning expressively as they happily dined on generous portions of tender filet mignon, zesty and flavorful vegetables and fresh mushrooms sautéed in wine and butter. Every now and then they took a sip of the wine, smiling across the table at each other.

Kennedy and Xavier talked a little about the earlier photo shoots and spoke of how happy they were to have had this opportunity to work together yet again, something they hoped to do a lot more of. They were very comfortable with each other.

Kennedy looked over at the bar, where the desserts had been placed by the waiter. Remembering what Xavier had said about having her for dessert, she smiled. The chocolate mousse cake probably tasted a lot better than she did, but she was sure he would say otherwise. He loved to nibble on her ear, whispering to her how sweet she was to him. His charm was always readily available, but she thought he was very sincere in the flattering remarks he often made.

Xavier stretched out his hand for her to take. "What about a walk on the beach?"

Kennedy gently squeezed Xavier's fingers. "It's a beautiful evening. I think I'd like that." She had other things on her mind, but the evening shouldn't be rushed.

"Good." He winked at her. "I haven't forgotten about having you for my dessert. I plan to wait until we get back, though I can hardly wait to taste you again."

Xavier's desire to kiss Kennedy was so strong, but he knew if he took possession of her mouth they'd never leave the suite. Their relationship wasn't about the physical aspects and he didn't ever want to give her that impression. He valued her in every way.

Kennedy recovered the empty plates with the silver domes and pushed them to the center of the table. She then stored the untouched cake in the compact refrigerator. Before leaving the suite with Xavier, she thought it best to take a bathroom break. Deciding he should do the same, he left to go to his own living quarters, telling her he'd be right back.

The warm trade winds blew gently about the island, slightly kicking up the sand around the path Kennedy and Xavier strolled upon, hand in hand. She had made a last-minute decision to change into flat walking shoes and comfortable clothing, very glad that she had done so. The white silk dress would probably be soaked through and through by now, as the Jamaican evening was extremely humid.

The atmosphere was romantic on this breathtakingly colorful island. Large waves slapped against the shoreline, leaving behind mounds of white foam. Reggae music could be heard coming from the pavilion, where various steel bands performed nightly.

Walking along the white sanded beach with the one he loved was both exciting and kind of sentimental to Xavier. The moon had long ago made its grand entrance into the heavens and the stars appeared brighter than ever, making him desire Kennedy in the worst way. His manhood was ramrod stiff and there was nothing he could do about it.

Stopping dead in his tracks, Xavier wrapped his arms around Kennedy and gave her a deep, soul-stirring kiss. Then his lips tenderly caressed her face, neck and ears. "I wish we didn't have to leave here. I love this island," he whispered to her.

Kennedy looked up into Xavier's eyes. "We'll have to make plans to come back again. I love here it, too."

Xavier gave Kennedy another passionate kiss. "On our one-year anniversary."

"What?" Kennedy had been completely taken off stride by the remark.

"We can come back here and celebrate our one-year anniversary." He then cited the actual date of their first date.

Kennedy was impressed that Xavier remembered the exact date. "Gosh, that would be so nice. I'll mark my calendar."

"Be sure to do that," Xavier whispered softly.

This time Kennedy was the aggressor, as she sealed their anniversary pact with a staggering kiss. Xavier wasn't the only one who knew how to get the blood boiling. She also knew that he wanted her, desperately—and she wanted him every bit as much.

Xavier tightened his hold on her. "It is past time for dessert," he whispered onto her lips, "but the reggae music is steadily drawing me in. Up for a little dancing?"

Kennedy threw her head back and laughed. "My favorite pastime! Of course."

The couple picked up speed, as they quickly made their way to the pavilion.

The funky rhythms entered Kennedy's soul as soon as she stepped onto the dance floor. As she closed her eyes, her hips began gyrating wildly to the thundering music. Twisting and turning in every which way possible, Kennedy lost herself to the cadence.

Xavier just stood there, watching Kennedy. She was mesmerizing, enchanting, and he couldn't get enough of her insidious charm. Stepping up behind her, he pulled her back against him, matching the hypnotic movements of her rocking hips. Reaching back, she wound her arms around his neck, without missing a beat. The bumping and grinding going on between them was anything but subtle.

The music suddenly slowed down. Without missing another beat, Kennedy quickly turned around and seductively pressed her body into Xavier's. Locking his hands into her hair, he kissed her until both were breathless. Searing his lips onto her forehead, he closed his eyes and brought her in even closer to him. Swaying in tune with the music, Kennedy and Xavier continued dancing slow, knowingly heating up each other's bodies to fever pitch.

Without any warning, Kennedy wiggled free of Xavier's relaxed embrace, running up the beach toward the hotel. He chased after her, catching up to her before she reached the entry. What she'd love to do was drop down to the ground and let him have his way with her. Getting arrested and thrown in a Jamaican jail wasn't the least bit funny. She wanted to make it to her suite so he could do with her as he pleased. Making love to him heavy on her mind, Kennedy made a mad dash for the elevators.

Knowing she'd never make it into the bathroom, let alone into the shower, Kennedy surrendered to Xavier's overheated advances right in the middle of the living room floor. She moaned as their mouths connected in a series of fiery kisses.

Taking time to enjoy the delicious sights of what was beneath each article of clothing he removed, Xavier slowly stripped her out of her dress and undergarments. His hands trembled hard as they made an art form of removing the white lacy bikinis.

Now that Xavier had unclothed Kennedy's body bare, she silenced all her thoughts. She was too hot to care about anything but having him inside her. As she laid her face against his broad chest, she closed her eyes, ready for whatever delicious erotica he had in mind.

Xavier made fast work of stripping out of his own clothing, thoughts of making wild, passionate love to Kennedy running rampant through his head. There were so many delectable things he wanted to do with her and for her. He was in no doubt about what he'd receive in return, sure that she was every bit as hot and sweet as he'd imagined.

After settling Kennedy's nude body onto his lap, the sweetest of foreplay began.

As his hands tenderly roved her nudity, she relaxed, allowing him to take her to whatever destiny he had in mind. His tongue circling the tip of her nipples caused her to squirm about. As gentle fingers unhurriedly parted her intimate flower, the flames of her desire burned deep inside her, making her want him more and more, more than she'd ever thought possible.

What came next was almost more than Kennedy could bear. His tongue was everywhere and she couldn't stop writhing and moaning, though she desperately wanted to. She was losing control fast, but it felt wonderful. It was easy to surrender her body to the man she loved. For in the absence of love, none of this would've been possible.

In the next instant their nude bodies were all tangled up in the most delicious coming together. She moaned with passion at the first probing but gentle thrust—and the next deeper one caused her to bite down on her lower lip to keep from screaming out his name. The island was paradise, but they had just lifted off, heaven-bound.

The tender grinding of Xavier's hips against Kennedy's had her twisting her fingers up in his thick hair, tugging on it with gentle force. Xavier's plunging thrusts had now grown intense. He had already built up quite a mighty head of steam, whispering wild, sexy things into her ear, following up his words by provocative actions.

Making love to Xavier was even better than their sexual couplings in Kennedy's dreams. Lying beneath him felt so natural to her, so right. It was like she'd written this sexy script from one of her numerous highly combustible dreams. Bare skin meeting bare skin caused the heat to intensify between them. She felt like her body was ready to explode. Kennedy was in no way ready for this beautiful encounter to end. If she had her way, they'd make love to each other all night long.

Xavier looked down at her and smiled. "You're everything I dreamed you'd be. You have no idea how good you make me feel."

Kennedy smiled knowingly. "You want to bet?" she whispered. "If you're feeling anything close to what I'm experiencing, you're no longer on this planet." Lifting up her head to meet his, she kissed him passionately. "Think you can take me higher?"

Taking her challenging comment to heart, Xavier grinned broadly. "Let me show you just how high we can climb."

"Take me there," she breathed huskily. "You make me feel so beautiful."

Xavier kissed her deeply, his tongue exciting hers. "You are beautiful, all over, and you're every bit as sweet."

Lowering his head, his tender but hungry mouth began to take liberties with her entire body. Without giving her the least bit of mercy, his tongue slowly drove her into a heated frenzy, exploring every inch of her nudity, tasting this extraordinary woman he was sure he never wanted to find himself without.

In one fluid motion, Xavier turned on his back and drew Kennedy on top of him. With her straddling his body, his fingers kneaded her full breasts and then reached down to gently tease her inner core. Taking her higher and higher, closer and closer to the climactic finale, he put his whole heart and soul into making sure he took her there, just as she'd so sweetly requested.

Tossing her head back and forth, Kennedy moved over Xavier

with near reckless abandon, as though she couldn't get enough of him. Loving the feeling of being in control, she leaned her head forward and laved one of his nipples and then the other.

As his sweat mingled with hers, her hands roved his finely hewn body. His flesh felt like moist, hot silk, turning her on even more. She kissed him hungrily. Moving up and down and then in circular motions. The feel of his erection deep inside her had her heart racing and her body quivering.

Just as smoothly as Xavier had changed positions before, he rolled Kennedy over onto her back and then covered her body like a second skin.

As Kennedy did her best to keep up with Xavier's barely controlled movements, thrust for thrust, grind for grind, she did her best to match his every mind-reeling stroke. Then her body began to shake uncontrollably, causing her to hold on to him for dear life. The wild bucking continued on and on, as she fought hard to hang in there for the grand finale. As Xavier's body began to shake in the same way as hers, she let herself go.

As Xavier dried off Kennedy's body with a bath sheet, pleasuring her with his mouth and hands, she felt it was such a shame they'd soon be leaving their island paradise. Still, she was grateful for the leisure time the magazine editor had so graciously allotted them. Even though they had a late-afternoon flight, they had to catch the shuttle bus early enough to get them back to Montego Bay in time for their departure.

Kennedy had heard from one of the hotel employees that the travel time from Montego Bay to Ocho Rios had been cut nearly in half now that the newly built road from one island to the other was finished. She hadn't kept up with the drive down because there had been too much beauty to behold.

When they had stopped at a café in the middle of nowhere, she knew she was getting a taste of the real Jamaica versus the luxurious resort they'd been booked into. The unbelievably delicious and infamous jerk chicken was to die for. Kennedy had high hopes of the bus driver making the same pit stop on the way back to the airport. She could already taste the spicy meat.

Kennedy reminded herself of Xavier's suggestion to come back to Ocho Rios for their first anniversary. Thrilled by the idea of their returning, she loved how sentimental he was with her. Knowing they'd come again made her feel better about the departure.

Now, Xavier held up Kennedy's fluffy white robe as she slipped into it. Before tying the belt snugly around her waist, he lowered the collar down over her shoulder. As he kissed her creamy flesh, he deeply inhaled the baby oil and perfume-scented powder he had massaged into her body.

Xavier held Kennedy at arm's length. "I know we set boundaries for our stay here, but I'd love for us to spend the rest of the night together."

Although Kennedy already had the answer to Xavier's query, she chewed on her lower lip, as if she was deeply pondering his request. Then her smile came slow and sweet. "Looks like you beat me to the punch. I was hoping for the same."

Xavier lifted Kennedy off her feet and carried her into the bedroom, where he pulled back the bedding and laid her down gently on the mattress. As he climbed in and cuddled up next to her, Xavier had an all-night rendezvous in mind, *a night to remember.*

Chapter 8

"I told you we'd see each other again, didn't I?" Serita asked Xavier, sending Kennedy a glaring "I told you so" glance. "I just didn't say when."

There were times when Xavier felt that if he didn't have so much bad luck he wouldn't have any luck at all. *What were the odds that I'd end up on the same shuttle bus with Serita?* Kennedy was seated next to the window and he was on the aisle. On the very opposite aisle seat of the same shuttle bus sat Serita, looking smug and cantankerous.

Xavier moaned under his breath. "Yeah, you warned me, all right."

"*Warning?* Is that how you saw it? You didn't see it like that when we were hanging out together, when you were sleeping in my bed."

There was no use in Xavier challenging Serita's last statement despite the fact it was a bold-faced lie, a lie told to hurt his credibility with Kennedy. He hadn't gone to bed with Serita, hadn't come close to it. She'd shown him who she was long before reaching that stage. Had he gotten physically involved with Serita it would've been the biggest mistake he could've ever made. Being possessed by someone and having them obsess over him weren't the ideal ingredients for a great personal relationship.

As Xavier looked over at Kennedy and shrugged his shoulders, he saw the uneasy look on her face. He hoped she knew he'd spare her this uncomfortable situation if he could. Since all the seats on the bus were taken, they couldn't move to another area. Besides, he wouldn't want to give that kind of satisfaction to Serita.

Serita reached across the aisle and attempted to grab hold of Xavier's hand. He had seen it coming and had rapidly moved his arm out of reach.

Serita's laughter was filled with ridicule. "I remember when you were happy to have my hands all over you…and vice versa. How soon we forget! Oh, by the way, did I tell you that I'm living in L.A.? Yeah, for an entire year, a temporary job move. I'm sure we'll get together when we're back home and settled in. I'll look forward to it."

Xavier could see that Serita was actually enjoying this gloomy little confrontation. "Don't count on it, Serita, 'cause it's just not happening."

"Oh, it'll happen. I just happen to be working as a guest producer on *L,L&L*, the modeling segment. You know all about that gig, don't you? Who do you think referred you to the show's executive producer? I hope you don't think you got it on your own. That would be such a shame if you did." She turned down her lower lip in a mocking pout. "Tsk, tsk, one should never bite the hand desiring to feed it."

Kennedy leaned over Xavier. "Don't you ever shut up?" She hated her outburst as soon as it'd left her mouth. She'd given Serita exactly what she'd hoped for. Kennedy mentally cursed her stupid blunder, wishing she hadn't let this woman get to her.

"Bad, bad temper! Anger management just might help out," Serita scoffed.

Xavier rubbed Kennedy's shoulders to help calm her down. He felt her trembling, wishing this wasn't happening. Tiaja Rae's and now Serita's verbal attacks were a lot for any woman to take.

Even though Xavier had plenty he could say back to Serita, he thought it best to say nothing. They still had a good distance to go before reaching Montego Bay airport. Then her remarks about the temporary move to L.A. suddenly rang loudly in his ears. He prayed hard that they weren't on the same flight. It would be disastrous.

Concerned with how quiet Kennedy had been since she'd had words with Serita, he'd tried to engage her in conversation several times, but her responses had been rather terse. It was a long flight back to L.A., and the thought of having to endure this kind of silence set his teeth on edge.

Serita *was* on the same plane with Xavier and Kennedy, which only made things worse. She was seated right across from him, pretty much the same seating arrangements as on the bus. Serita and Xavier occupied aisle seats but weren't right across from each other because the first class seats angled. Kennedy sat on the window seat and the middle seat between her and Xavier was empty.

Xavier moved over to the middle seat and laid his head on Kennedy's shoulder. "Hi," he whispered. "I miss you. Please talk to me, babe."

Kennedy gently placed her hand on the side of Xavier's face. "I miss you, too. We can talk. I'm feeling better now."

Xavier smiled. "Happy to hear it. Do you want a glass of wine or something else to drink?"

"I'm fine right now. I'll wait until the flight attendants offer beverage service."

Kennedy didn't want to purposely fling her relationship with Xavier in Serita's face. But the loud-mouthed woman couldn't seem to keep her eyes off him. She didn't know what kind of personal relationship had existed between them, but she wouldn't dare ask him. He'd offer up the information if he wanted her to know.

Kennedy wasn't at all the clingy, desperate type. She understood perfectly that a person couldn't make a heart love someone it didn't want to love. Since Xavier wasn't involved with Serita now, it was obvious someone hadn't wanted a long-term situation. If whatever they'd had had worked, they wouldn't have separated. Kennedy believed there might've been a romantic relationship between the two, but she wasn't interested in spending any more time speculating.

Kennedy didn't like the rudeness of any of the women or the untimely interruptions. She loved being in the company of Xavier, but she didn't like these confrontations. They were happening too frequently. It was one thing for it to happen at home, but to have it occur in another part of the world was downright unsettling. Xavier couldn't help how good-looking he was. That definitely was no fault of his.

In spite of not wanting to contemplate it one way or the other, Kennedy had to wonder if it'd always be like this when she was with Xavier. Would the women attracted to him come at her from every corner of the globe? She wasn't jealous, but she was terribly annoyed by the drama she'd thus far endured.

Xavier looked at Kennedy with curiosity. "I thought we were going to talk."

"I apologize." She lifted his hand and kissed the tip of each of his fingers. "I was busy reliving last evening."

As an erotic scene from their wild, passionate lovemaking flashed across Xavier's mind, he grinned, sighing with deep satisfaction. "Which part of the evening?"

"Before you nudged me, I had been thinking about the program we watched."

"Oh, I see," he said rather blandly, eyeing her with skepticism.

"You sound disappointed. What did you *think* I was thinking of?" She knew the answer to her question, but she wanted to hear what he had to say. "Well?"

"I'm sure you already know, but I'll indulge you anyway. It's something I haven't been able to stop thinking about. I thought you were thinking about our lovemaking escapades, the one before and all of those times after the show."

"All of those! Aren't we exaggerating a tad?"

"No, *we're* not. We made love four times after our first rendezvous, if we count the wild session from early this morning, just before I left to go pack."

Kennedy groaned. "Who's counting, anyway?"

"I'm not. Reminiscing is what I call it, babe. Sweet, sweet memories."

The sudden appearance of one of the female flight attendants thwarted Kennedy's next remark. Instead, she looked at Xavier and laughed.

The flight attendant offered chicken or beef meal choices.

"Chicken for me," said Kennedy. "Thanks."

"I'll have the same as the lady. I'd also like a glass of Chardonnay."

"Me, too," Kennedy chimed in. "I need to relax. I'm feeling a little uptight."

"I can tell. You look the part. And that should also *tell* you something about your man." Serita rudely put in her two cents. "If your man can't relax you, who can?"

Chuckling softly, Kennedy shook her head from side to side. "Lady, this is an *A* and *B* conversation. Please *C* your way out."

Xavier howled at Kennedy's remark, which earned him a dagger-sharp scowl from Serita. The murderous look didn't stop his laughter.

Serita clapped her hands. "So the silly little girl's got jokes. I'll give you that one." As if to dismiss the couple, Serita picked up the in-flight magazine and opened it.

Kennedy nudged Xavier, giggling lowly over what had just occurred. "Maybe she won't bother us the rest of the flight," she whispered.

"Fat chance," Serita said candidly, without bothering to look their way.

Glad for whatever length of reprieve Serita might give them, Xavier and Kennedy exchanged knowing glances, their eyes twinkling with mischievous thoughts.

Xavier took the lid off Kennedy's food to let the steam out before he prepared his own container for consumption. The portions were a pretty good size, considering what most airlines served. The soft moaning sounds coming from his companion had him guessing the food was also tasty.

"Is it that good, Kennedy?"

Kennedy nodded. "The chicken is very tender and flavorful. I like it."

Xavier took in a mouthful of saffron rice. "Mmm, not bad." He poured the packet of dressing on her salad and then took care of his own.

"Thanks." Kennedy loved all the special attention Xavier gave her.

Kennedy often received a lot of envious stares when they were together, and she knew why. She might be envious of any woman who had the same kind of man. At times, she could hardly believe how considerate he was of her.

One of Tyler Perry's films was the entertainment offered, and they were sure they'd enjoy it. Shortly after the trays had been picked up, Kennedy had fallen off to sleep. Xavier took this time to study her lovely features, unable to keep himself from staring at her.

Xavier walked back to the front door inside Kennedy's place. Though he wasn't ready to depart, he thought he should. If she asked him to spend the night with her, he would, but it didn't seem as if it was her intent. As much as he'd like to stay over, he had a lot of work to catch up on at home. He had checked his e-mail while away, but not any of his phone messages. Xavier had the tendency to lose track of just about everything when he was with Kennedy.

Kennedy stood on her tiptoes and kissed Xavier good-night. "I'm going to miss you. If I find it hard to sleep, can I call you?"

"You'd better. I'll miss you, too, baby, but I hope you have a good night's rest. Let's get all settled in and see what happens."

"Great idea." She reluctantly opened the door for him to exit.

Xavier leaned into Kennedy and gave her another kiss. "Later."

Kennedy stared hard at the closed door. He was gone. Their good times were over for now. Things always ended way too soon for her. She loved having him around because he brightened things up considerably. She recalled what it was like when he wasn't in her life. It wasn't that her life had been dull. Xavier just made it more exciting.

Why hadn't she asked Xavier to spend the night? Kennedy had to wonder what had made her hold back. Perhaps it would've been too presumptuous of her.

One more night wouldn't have hurt anything, but Xavier hadn't bothered to ask about staying over, either. It would've been a nice extension to their mini work vacation. She had no idea when they'd get to work together again, but she hoped it would be real soon. He was such a lot of fun to work and hang out with.

Sighing hard, full of regret at a missed opportunity to spend more time with the man she loved, Kennedy strolled into the bedroom, where Xavier had taken her bags. She hated unpacking, but it had to be done. She lifted the larger bag and hoisted it up on the bed and opened it up.

As Kennedy pulled out her bathrobe from the top of the disorderly heap, Xavier's manly scent hit her full force. The smell was from the citrus cologne he'd splashed on before he'd cuddled up against her the entire night, after they'd showered together. She couldn't help smiling.

* * *

Missing Kennedy like crazy ate away at Xavier's resolve. He had hoped she would've called by now to tell him she was lonely for him. He was desperately lonesome for her. How had he gotten himself so whipped by this beautiful creature—and in such a short time? The girl had whisked his breath away and he still hadn't caught up with it.

For the umpteenth time Xavier reached for the phone to call Kennedy, only to abort his intent once again. He'd been tossing and turning since he'd first gotten into bed over an hour ago. The way he was acting was downright ludicrous. If she knew what was going on with him, she'd think he'd lost his mind over her. And he had.

Their sensuous nights in Jamaica had Xavier wondering what it'd be like to spend every night of the rest of his life with Kennedy. It wouldn't be romance and candlelight all the time, but he'd spend every day of his life trying to enhance her joy. He'd give her his all, and then some.

The sudden buzz of the phone caused Xavier to nearly jump out of his skin. His heart thumped hard against his rib cage as he peered over at the caller ID. Suppressing the urge to laugh with glee, he snatched up the receiver. "Are you as lonesome for me as I am for you?" Xavier asked Kennedy.

"Every bit as much. I know it's late, but please come back or let me come there."

"I'm on my way as soon as I grab a change of clothes and slip on a coat. I've got pajama bottoms on and a T-shirt. That's the way I intend to ride. See you in a few minutes, babe."

"Just be careful, Xavier. I need you in one piece. I've got mad love on my mind."

The flickering candlelight and the soft, colorful flames burning in the fireplace in Kennedy's bedroom cast an amazing, romantic aura about the intimate space. Soft love ballads only added to the electrifying ambience. No better mood than this could be set.

Kennedy deeply inhaled the smell of Xavier's fiery passion. The scent was exciting and sexy, making her crave him like crazy. She was way past hungry for the taste and feel of him. Dressed in a pure white teddy, fashioned in a stunning combination of lace and silk, she looked gorgeous and alluring.

Kennedy trapped Xavier's eyes in her melting gaze. "Look at me, all of me," her expression suggested. Her eyes let him know she was dying to be touched by him, desired to have him sample her tempting flesh, needed him to rock her world for however long their bodies could withstand it. Although she hadn't breathed a word of her desires, he knew. The heated desire for him was right there in her misty eyes.

This emotional and physical coming together between Kennedy and Xavier was not to be rushed. This eagerly anticipated journey into ecstasy would be slow, mystical, demanding and tantalizing. Last but not least, it was utterly fulfilling. She wanted to taste him in places she hadn't yet dared to venture. She was confident that her flirtatious mouth was capable of making him scream out her name.

Xavier's heart rate was out of his control, his breath tangled. Kennedy could easily tell it was all he could do to keep from gasping for air. If he thought she had already taken his breath away in Jamaica, he was in for a heck of a sensuous awakening. This time he'd have to chase after his breath hard if he wanted to catch up to it.

Kennedy's eyes made direct contact with Xavier's bulging crotch, his bare, hardened flesh still hidden beneath the silk of his pajama bottoms. Putting a finger to her temple, she licked her lips provocatively. "Take them off for me," she whispered softly. "Please undress for me."

Kennedy had spoken so softly Xavier had just barely heard her. *Forget what he had or hadn't heard.* Paying close attention to the language of her body would lead him to the pathway of her every desire.

Xavier undressed, obeying Kennedy's request. The T-shirt and pajama bottoms were the only items he wore. After lifting up his buttocks, he easily slid the silk bottoms down over his thighs and feet. The one and only thing he wore now was a silly little smile.

Xavier stifled his laughter over Kennedy's shocked expression. His manhood wasn't the only thing bulging. Her eyes were nearly out of their sockets. For the sake of safety, he always kept a condom or two in his wallet, which was lying on the nightstand. Keeping his eyes trained on her, he leaned over and picked up the swatch of leather and removed the gold foil packet. Smiling flirtatiously, Xavier held up the condom.

Keeping her eyes engaged with his, Kennedy reached for the packet. That bold move surprised Xavier. Once she tore the foil open with her teeth, she handed it back to him. She'd only help him put on the circle of safety if he asked her to.

This was an interesting form of foreplay. Nonetheless, Xavier loved every minute of the seduction. He raised an eyebrow. "Want to do the honors?"

Kennedy stuck her hand out and Xavier handed the packet back. As her breath grew shallow, she slowly scooted closer to him. She had never done anything like this before, but she didn't need to be a rocket scientist to manage. The uncertainty flashing in her eyes had Xavier patiently showing her what to do to get it right.

Once the condom was snugly in place, she laughed gently, shaking her head from side to side. That one erotic adventure had actually heightened her sexual desire. Kennedy believed the intimate experience had brought them even closer.

Xavier brought Kennedy to him, running his fingers through her hair. He kissed her over and over again, until he felt her go limp with relaxation. As his mouth lowered, manipulating her breasts, her hands entwined in his hair. Her nipples were already erect but grew tauter as his tongue flicked away. The streak of electrical currents shooting wildly through her body felt awesome.

Xavier positioned Kennedy on top of him. As he stroked her hair, she blew into his ear, gently flicking her tongue around the outer portion. His manhood felt ready to burst. The throbbing was painful, but he could endure. They had a ways to go yet. Foreplay was a strong suit for him, but not nearly his strongest. He prided himself on his expert lovemaking techniques. However, bringing the utmost pleasure to his partner was what mattered most to him.

Kennedy lifted her head and looked down into Xavier's eyes. "I love you. I want you, all of you."

Xavier's breath caught. As if he hadn't known how she already felt before this very moment, he was deeply touched by her confession of love. Kennedy knew that he loved her, too, deeply, completely. His mind and body had revealed that to her in Jamaica. He was darn near out of his head with his desire for her. He had always taken the lead in lovemaking sessions, had always enjoyed doing so.

This time was different.

Not only would Xavier let Kennedy lead, he was content to do so. The foreplay would go on for as long as she wanted. Whatever she decided to do with his body, he'd be okay with it. He could barely believe that this beautiful, sexually vulnerable woman had already taken him as her lover in Jamaica. She wanted him again and he wanted to love her back just as much.

Did it get any better than this? They each thought so.

Using the tip of her fingernails, Kennedy lazed a line from Xavier's chest to his stomach. His body trembled lightly beneath her erotic touch. Lowering her head, she flicked at the inside of his navel with her tongue. Her mouth then traveled upward again, suckling each of his taut nipples. As she pressed her lips against his, she slowly slipped her tongue past his teeth.

Running his fingers through her hair was all he could do to hold back. Kennedy had a wicked tongue and he loved how it heated up his flesh.

The contractions of her intimate inner muscles began to come in waves. She was so excited, but it was way too soon for her to come unglued. He was putty in her hands right now. His sex was already stiff but she wanted to continue teasing and tantalizing him. The expressions of ecstasy on his face revealed to her what he was feeling. He desired her body in every way, just as she did his.

Kennedy enjoyed straddling Xavier, resting back on her haunches, eyeing him intently. As she leaned forward, he raised his head and gently captured her lower lip between his teeth. Slowly, she moved in closer and closer, until his manhood came into contact with the hot, moist flesh at the entry of her womanhood. Her intimate treasure burned feverishly for him, her hands tenderly sliding up and down the hardened shaft, making him squirm all over the place.

Taking the ultimate step, she lowered herself down onto his sex, fusing them together as one. Making him want her more and more, she touched him all over, slowing her caressing, deliberate strokes. The slower pace of her hands grew in urgency, as she continued stoking the blazing flames of their combined passions. Before she lost control to the rhythms of their turbulent movements, she rolled off Xavier and lay on her back.

Kennedy gasped with wantonness. "Make love to me, Xavier. Make me love you back."

Slowly, teasingly, tauntingly, Xavier continued to work Kennedy into a further state of euphoric passion, her mind, soul and body loving his tender ways. Hands caressed, teeth nipped, fingers entwined and manipulated, lips undulated, as thrusting hips ground together. As his lips found and tasted her creamy throat, she squirmed beneath him, feeling the burning intensity of his touch right down to the ends of her toes.

Kennedy's hands tenderly squeezed his buttocks. The frenzied throbbing of his hardened flesh further excited her, her nails raking his back. Contemplating their coming together in uncontrollable ecstasy had her totally off-kilter, very close to breathless.

The moment Xavier entered Kennedy with infinite tenderness she held her breath. In the next second she gave herself up to the sweetness engulfing her. The couple still heard the soft music above the loud thundering of their heartbeats. Xavier made an art form of grinding his hips into Kennedy's to match the passionate rhythm of the seductive tune. Higher and higher they rose, rising above infinity. Serenity mingled with wild pleasures, creating a perfectly arousing balance, exalting bliss.

As heaven continually rose up to meet them, tossing them high above the ether, Kennedy and Xavier exulted in riding the deliciously tumultuous waves of pure ecstasy. He felt her body vibrating beneath his. In response to her fiery vibrations, he increased the intensity of their sweet lovemaking, keeping the thrusts tender but deep. Satisfying her meant everything to him. Meeting Kennedy's needs came first.

As the couple joyously reached the pinnacle of fervent passion, continuing on to the crescendo of fulfillment, sweat streamed, pulses raced feverishly, bodies shuddered uncontrollably. Breathlessly, each screamed out the other's name.

Xavier rolled away but quickly brought his trembling body to rest right next to Kennedy. Completely speechless, all he could do was look at her, his eyes misty and still aglow with passion. He hoped he had once again satisfied her physically and emotionally. The floating liquid around her orbs concerned him, only because she looked ready to cry. He hoped she hadn't felt any pain.

The telltale flush of Kennedy's mahogany skin had Xavier smiling inwardly. Her lips were swollen from his kisses. He thought the condition of her skin and mouth was a good sign, but he wished she would smile to reassure him.

Unable to converse with Xavier at the moment, Kennedy reached for his hand, hoping to communicate with him through her touch, the language of her eyes and the art of her expressions. She felt so at peace. There were no warring factions at work.

As a trickle of water escaped from the corners of Kennedy's eyes, she smiled to let Xavier know her emotions were joyous ones, not sorrowful. Her body was still vibrating, making her desperately want him again and again.

Xavier had utterly fulfilled Kennedy, just as he had done in Jamaica. She smiled smugly when she thought of the extremely wildly sensitive areas on her anatomy, some of which she hadn't known existed, let alone ever experienced arousal there. She wouldn't initiate a second lovemaking session. It was all up to him now. She wasn't sure if the bold decision to call him to come and make love to her was attractive to Xavier, although he certainly hadn't rejected the notion.

Kennedy squeezed Xavier's fingers, hoping she could speak coherently. "I never dreamed I could feel more beautiful than I did our first time. Yet you've heightened those feelings, Xavier." Feeling there was too much space between them, she drew closer to him, nestling her head onto his chest.

"You *are* beautiful, in every way." Xavier kissed Kennedy on the forehead. His manhood instantly readied itself for takeoff again. He shouldn't have risked kissing her, not in his physical state. This was what happened every time he got close to her. He was still naked as a jaybird so he couldn't hide his arousal or stop its throbbing.

Xavier filled his fingers with sable hair. "Could I possibly interest you in seconds?" He looked down at his erection. "I guess I don't have to say how much I want you again. It should be pretty obvious."

After glancing down at Xavier's "obvious," Kennedy giggled. Stifling the round of laughter threatening to break free, she kissed him gently on the mouth. "I wasn't sure if you'd ask for an encore, but I'm thrilled you did."

As Xavier carefully rolled on top of Kennedy, his smile revealed how thrilled he was. "If I ever forget to tell you I love you, I love you."

Kennedy blushed sweetly. Color swept softly, gently into her cheeks. Even his sexy voice caused her color to rise. She loved hearing him say he loved her. How many times had she wondered what love had to do with anything? She now knew love had something to do with everything. "I love you, too."

Kennedy was happily exhausted. Worn-out from Xavier's titillating seconds and thirds, she could barely stand beneath the pulsating shower. Her legs felt so wobbly, her mind unstable, most of her energy depleted. She had left Xavier in her bed, sound asleep. Perhaps she had worn him out, too. Just the thought was a great boost to her confidence. The thought of him knocked out cold brought on a huge smile.

Xavier had looked so peaceful when she'd crept out of bed, careful not to wake him. She had to wonder if he was too tired to drive home. They'd only spent the entire night together in the same bed in Jamaica. Although they'd done a lot of cuddling, it had never gone this far or throughout the night. The trip to Jamaica had changed everything. Before then, they'd only shared unspoken boundaries.

Would these two nights of continuous lovemaking change their relationship? She hoped so.

Xavier opened the glass shower door and stepped inside. Immediately, he reached for Kennedy. He couldn't recall how many times he'd conjured up erotic images of them showering together again. Reality was always the real deal. She was in his arms and he was in hers, locked in a tight embrace.

"I missed you. When I reached for you, you were gone. As I lay there wondering where you were, I heard the running water." He kissed her deeply, passionately. "And here I am. Couldn't resist joining you."

Wondering if their intimacy would lead to more lovemaking, Kennedy smiled, kissing Xavier back. She was still exhausted, but his exhilarating presence had already begun to rejuvenate her. "I missed you, too, glad you're here."

Xavier's lips grazed Kennedy's mouth. "As young as we are, we've already achieved a lot. There aren't many things we can't afford to get for ourselves." He pointed at his heart. "This is all I can offer you. It's the only thing I have of priceless value. My heart is yours, Kennedy, every square inch of it. Can I trust you with my most treasured possession, without reservation?"

Crossing her heart with her forefinger, Kennedy looked up into Xavier's teary eyes. "Yes," she breathed, "yes. And I entrust my heart to you, completely."

Chapter 9

Breakfast served in bed to Kennedy by Xavier the next morning consisted of fresh fruits: sweet slices of cantaloupe, pineapple chunks, plump blackberries and sliced strawberries. He also served her hot green tea. He intended to stay with her awhile, up until it was time for him to go by his agent's office to discuss upcoming bookings.

Mercedes Benz often used Xavier in their print ads and he'd even done several commercials for them. According to Kirsten, the huge corporation was throwing a charity benefit fashion show in a couple of weeks and wanted to make sure he was included as one of the male models. Mercedes was a good company to do business with, paying extremely well.

The next morning, his head resting against the backboard, Xavier was seated upright in bed next to Kennedy. "Besides the charity event, the other modeling assignment is also in Orlando," he told her.

Unimpressed with the destination, Kennedy simply nodded. She liked the city, but it wasn't one of her favorite haunts. "Orlando can be pretty exciting, but once you've done all the theme parks it is just another busy metropolis."

Xavier scratched the center of his head. "Will you consider going to Orlando with me? I know I'll be working, but we'll get some time together. The charity event should be nice. When

I'm on the other booking, you can shop and also get in some good rest."

Kennedy was definitely thrilled by the offer, but she doubted she had enough free time to go to Florida, unless it was on a modeling assignment. The departure and return flight across the country would take up a lot of time. She thought about the dates she'd checked off on her calendar for the mini getaway, but Jamaica had taken care of that. The Orlando trip couldn't even be considered until she knew the exact dates of his travel.

Kennedy placed her hand on Xavier's arm. "I love being with you, but the timing has to be just right. Once you know your travel dates, I'll check my calendar. Do you know how long you'll be gone?"

"A week or possibly more. Kirsten *did* mention an approximate time frame."

Kennedy frowned. "I already know I can't do that kind of time. I'll be lucky to get a couple days in a row. That's a long way to travel for a short time. At any rate, I'll see what's up after you know when you're leaving."

He leaned over and kissed her forehead. "Don't fret. If it's meant to happen for us, it will. If not, we'll communicate by e-mail and phone."

She kissed him back. "I think I'll take your advice."

Kennedy got out of bed and reached for her robe, draping it around her nudity. As much as she'd like to lie there and do absolutely nothing, she had lots of chores to tend to. Anytime she went away she had to make up for the lost time.

"Where are you going, lady?"

She looked back at Xavier. "To handle my business, mon."

"What business?"

"Chores, lots of them."

Naked, he leaped out of bed. "I'll help you."

Kennedy cracked up. Was this too sensuous or what? Did he plan to work around her house in the buff? Just the thought of it caused a stirring deep in her feminine secrets. Her mouth turned down in a frown when he reached for the pajama bottoms. She hoped against hope that he wouldn't put on his T-shirt, too.

"Show me what's on your list of chores. I'll do the heavy stuff. I just need you to show me which products you use on what."

Xavier wouldn't get any form of protest from Kennedy. She wasn't the domestic type, yet she didn't think her household tasks warranted a housekeeper, either. Even with her financial success. It kept her grounded. Her parents had taught her to take care of her own bedroom and to help with the other important chores around their lovely, modest home. Accepting responsibility for herself had been instilled in her at a young age.

Once Kennedy fulfilled Xavier's request, she watched as he effortlessly hauled the vacuum cleaner down the hallway, cheerfully ready to help her clean up her house. She saw his desire and willingness to assist her in the household chores as a special quality. Her dad always helped her mom around the house—and did so even to this day.

Kennedy didn't know how the time had gotten away from them so quickly, but they had accomplished quite a bit. The house was now sparkling clean and all the laundry had been washed, dried, folded and put away. While the couple had worked together so harmoniously time had marched right on by.

Out in the kitchen Kennedy was busy preparing lunch for her and Xavier. He was off taking a shower since he planned to take off right after eating.

After filling a bowl with a mixture of crisp field greens and carrot shavings, Kennedy rolled up several thick slices of smoked turkey. After cutting them crosswise, she laid them on top of the lettuce. The white American cheese was cut in wedges and the tomatoes were thinly sliced. Both items were placed around the edges of the salad bowls.

Kennedy also kept lots of other fresh salad fixings refrigerated in small Tupperware containers: black olives, dill pickle slices, red onion and banana peppers. She added each of these ingredients to the salads. Her friends teased her about copying her preparation techniques from Subway, which she thought was a pretty good system.

Chilled cranberry and orange juices were poured into separate glass pitchers. Neither of them indulged in a lot of bread so she didn't serve any. Every now and then Kennedy might eat a bagel or a slice of toast, but that didn't occur often.

As Kennedy's mind strayed backward in time, to when she and Xavier were on the flight back to California from Jamaica, she again thought of how she'd have to learn to deal with the women who were attracted to him. Although she received her fair share of stares, flirtatious smiles and appreciative glances, he was downright gawked at and openly and verbally flirted with by the opposite sex.

The looks wouldn't bother her as much if the women didn't always make some sort of remark to him. *Darn, you're fine.* How many times had she heard that phrase since they'd been dating? Every single time they went out in public.

Then there was Serita.

Interestingly enough, Serita hadn't bothered them too much after the first ugly encounter. She'd had a sassy thing or two to say periodically, but she hadn't been nearly as overbearing as earlier. Downstairs in baggage claim she had also behaved herself, yet before exiting the area she had warned Xavier to always look over his shoulder. The last words Serita had said to him were she'd see him on the set of *L,L&L*.

Last but not least, Serita had blown both Kennedy and Xavier a farewell kiss.

As Kennedy thought about all these things, she surprisingly

found herself laughing. *How many women would love to have my problem? Which was what? Do I really have a problem?* She had a fabulous-looking man who had said he loved her. Not only had he confessed his love for her, he had shown his feelings through his actions. Even before the moment the words had left his mouth she had felt loved by Xavier.

Now, even before Xavier leaned over and kissed the side of her neck, Kennedy had felt his presence. She had also smelled his alluring cologne. Freshly showered, he was dressed in a pair of jeans and shirt designed by Sean John.

Looking as fine as ever, Xavier dropped down at the kitchen table. "I'm ready for that salad. Can I help put the food on the table?"

"Thanks, but I've got it. Just relax. Cranberry or orange juice for you?"

"The cranberry juice works for me. Do you want me to pour you some?"

"I'm drinking green tea the entire week, cold, hot, luke-warm, however."

"In that case, I'll be happy to polish off the juices."

Smiling at the newspaper Kennedy had set next to his place setting, Xavier was pleased she'd anticipated another of his desires. He loved to read the paper, though he normally did it first thing in the morning or late in the evening. He liked the fact she took time to observe his habits. He felt like they'd grown to know each other very well from their initial date. It actually felt like he'd known her all his life.

Kennedy placed one of the chilled salads in front of Xavier and one at her own place setting. She went back for the drinks. The moment after she took a seat Xavier said a blessing. After thanking God for the food, he thanked Him for bringing Kennedy into his life, citing how blessed he was to have her.

Kennedy's heart began hammering away at his emotional comments.

"Amen," they said simultaneously.

Picking up her fork, Kennedy looked over at Xavier and smiled. "I hope you know I feel the same as you. My life is even more wonderful because of your presence."

"Not to come off cocky, but I *do* know. How you are with me lets me remain confident. We've had a great start. Time is rapidly moving on us, girl…and I'm glad we're not in danger of it running out. My life has been great with you in it."

Kennedy blushed. "Mine, too, Xavier. We're good together."

"You got that right. Very good." Xavier took his first bite of the crisp salad. "I feel like I'm eating a Subway salad."

Kennedy laughed. "You, too, huh? My friends tease me about patterning my salads after the way Subway does theirs. It makes it easier when you keep the ingredients cut up and stored in airtight containers."

"It's great. No complaints." He nearly downed the glass of cranberry juice in one gulp. Since she'd left the pitchers out on the table, he refilled his glass. "I notice you're not as fanatical about eating. I've seen some ladies' eating habits that scared me. What do you attribute to staying in good shape?"

"Consistent exercise…and I have an amazing metabolism. When I was younger, I ate like a horse but never gained any weight. Mom says it'll catch up with me one day, like after babies. She's had three kids and is not much over her pre-baby weight."

Xavier leveled soft eyes on her. "Do you want babies some-day?"

"I do, hopefully by thirty-five. I used to want them while I was really young, but I have far too much to accomplish, too many goals to achieve before settling down into motherhood. What about you? Are you interested in being a daddy one day?"

Xavier smiled. "Absolutely." If Xavier had his way, they'd start on babies now. Yet he was smart enough to know they had a ways to go before the prospect of marriage was discussed.

However, deep in his heart, he already felt she was the right one for him, the one he wanted to share the rest of his life with.

There were some things a man just knew, some things he just felt.

Xavier couldn't wait for the time when a condom wouldn't be necessary. He couldn't wait to feel Kennedy's sheer nudity and have her feel his. "So, what are you doing to keep the babies at bay until you're ready for motherhood?"

Kennedy closed one eye and peered over at him through the other. "Is that your way of asking if I'm on birth control? If so, it's a little late for that, isn't it? We did use condoms, remember?"

"I didn't think I was being clandestine. That wasn't my intent."

She smiled gently. "I guess not. I'm protected, for as much as any of these contraceptives are foolproof. I'm also on the Pill. Abstinence is the only fail-safe method of birth control."

"You're right. And if you wanted abstinence, I'd do my best to oblige you."

Kennedy jerked her head back. "For sure? That's very interesting. After all the passionate love we've made, you could just put a halt to it like that?"

Xavier nodded. "If that's what you wanted."

"But it really wouldn't be what you wanted," she remarked.

"I want what you want in this relationship. Kennedy, I respect you. I respected you before and after we made love. I'm a man, not a fickle boy masquerading."

Xavier's comments were felt deeply by Kennedy. He *was* a man, in every sense of the word. She could compare him to a lot of guys who had masqueraded as men. Since he was incomparable, she couldn't even go there. So far, Xavier had proved himself one of a kind. Being with him was beyond anything she'd ever imagined.

The couple continued to talk, learning more and more about each other's likes and dislikes. He was surprised to find out Kennedy was fearful of roller coasters, Ferris wheels and other high, fast-moving amusement rides, yet she loved to visit theme parks.

Kennedy actually imagined Xavier playing basketball, as he enthused about one of his favorite sports and pastimes. She could envision his bare chest, rippling muscles and sweat trickling from his beautiful body. He told her he occasionally got involved with weekend pickup games down at Venice Beach. Martial arts were the top favorite for him and he promised to teach her a few self-defense moves.

Much like Kennedy, Xavier loved to read. He admitted to being as absorbent as a sponge when it came to knowledge, believing it was power. He loved anything to do with computers and had taken a Web-design course from a community college.

"I have my own Web site," she announced. "KennedyBassett.com. You should check it out. It is really something. Martina designed it."

"Have you been to my site yet?" Xavier queried.

She blew on the tips of her fingers. "It *is* hot! I imagine you get thousands of hits a day. Do you get lots of e-mail?"

"Too much for me to read in one sitting. After my manager goes through it, I do my best to answer it all, but I'm sure one or two fall through the cracks. My fans are so important to me."

"Popular man with the ladies. That's for sure."

He narrowed his eyes. "Are there times when my popularity gets to you?"

"To be honest, yes, it does. It's just the overbearing women that make me cringe, especially the bolder, brassier ones like Tiaja Rae and Serita."

Xavier chuckled. "They *are* that. They're beautiful until they open their mouths. Then it's on and over. Hopefully they'll mature one day soon. They're both shock jocks."

Kennedy nodded. "Hadn't thought about it like that, but I think you're right. Catching you off guard is to their advantage.

It gives a person little chance to come back at them because of the shock. I'll keep that in mind for future situations."

"Hope there won't be any, but I'm not foolish enough to believe that."

Xavier got out of his seat and began clearing the table. He hated to leave Kennedy, but he had important business matters to discuss with his representation. He also had to get home and get organized, go through the mail, unpack, etc.

As much as Xavier wished he could've extended their vacation, he had to accept that it was over. Jamaica would only be realized in his thoughts and dreams until they returned to their island paradise upon their first-year anniversary. As sure as he was breathing, he felt positive they'd make it to the one-year mark…and far beyond.

Loneliness didn't get a chance to settle in on Kennedy. Shortly after Xavier had left her home Bianca showed up there bearing gifts. She'd been out shopping and had picked up a couple of lingerie items for Kennedy. It was commonplace between them. Both were givers. A pair of silk shortie-pajamas in pink and a satin chemise in red had caught her eye. Since the items looked like something Kennedy would wear, she'd purchased them. Kennedy often liked to pick up various niceties for her friends, too.

Sipping on a cup of hot apple-cinnamon tea, Bianca had her feet propped upon the leather hassock in Kennedy's family room. Dressed in navy capri hip-hugging pants and a gray-and-navy-striped top, she looked cool and stylish. Her feet were shod in stylish navy FitFlop sandals.

Bianca drummed her fingers on her thighs. "I'm so bummed out."

Kennedy raised concerned eyebrows at her friend's comment. "What's wrong?"

"Torrance is talking about moving to New York. He's

thinking of changing networks. I don't think he's even considered me in his decision."

"Have you two gotten close enough for that? I haven't been able to tell. You haven't said a lot about it, either. How much does the possible move bother you?"

"I'm perturbed because he has yet to ask me how I feel. What I feel is dispensable. He's not much of a romantic, either. We're not clicking like I'd hoped." She sighed heavily. "Maybe we're just not meant to be. And, at times, he can be such an irritable drama king."

Kennedy cracked up. "The King and Queen of Drama sounds like a great title for a fiction book. Maybe it could even be a television sitcom."

"I like the name and the idea." Tears suddenly welled in Bianca's eyes. "You know something, I'm not too happy. I feel total discontent with this relationship. We've not been together that long, but Mr. Gardner still hasn't mentioned what his intent toward me is. Not once. Shouldn't I be concerned about that? I'm probably making too much of this whole thing, huh?"

Catching her lower lip between her teeth, Kennedy gently chewed on it. It had surprised her to hear Bianca's grievances. She had no idea her friend had problems in her relationship with Torrance. Bianca seemed terribly on edge over the matter.

Kennedy sighed. "How long have you felt this way?"

Bianca shrugged. "I don't know. It comes to mind on occasion. It's not that I want to get into a full-blown relationship right away, but it'd be nice to know if the guy is even interested in me that way. We've been dating over two months. It's something we should've discussed by now. Don't you think so?"

"Don't know. Any imminent plans to bring it up to him?"

Forming a steeple with her hands, Bianca blew against the sides of her fingers. "I want to discuss it, but I'm not sure it's even appropriate. He's into getting his career off the ground. In fact, that's all he thinks and talks about lately. At the moment, I'm not sure our relationship is really important to him."

"He's not a selfish guy, is he?"

Making direct eye contact with Kennedy, Bianca gave the pointed question some thought. "There are times when he can be a bit self-centered."

"So where does that leave you?"

"Alone, especially if he heads to New York."

"Care to expound on that?"

Bianca shrugged. "It is what it is. If he goes to New York, it'll probably be over between us. I can't imagine a coast-to-coast relationship. I'd never want to live in New York, have no desire to live another day in cold weather. The East Coast snowstorms alone are daunting. I grew up there just like you did. Hartford winters were a bear."

Kennedy nodded. "I know what you mean. I suggest you play it by ear if you want to hang in there. If you don't, perhaps you should be the one to end it. But let's just wait and see what he decides about moving before making any rash decisions."

"Yeah, good advice. And that works better for me than him ending it. Who wants to be dumped?"

Kennedy felt for Bianca. She looked very sad and had never mentioned any of this stuff before now. "Did you see him as a good catch in the beginning? What about him were you most attracted to?"

"At a glance, the man's chiseled body is enough to leave a woman gasping for air. I don't know who has the best body between him and Martina's Mitchel."

Kennedy wished she knew if Torrance truly cared enough for Bianca to go exclusive, but she didn't feel it her place to find out. He'd always seemed attentive. If he wasn't interested in a serious relationship with the lady, he obviously didn't know what he'd miss out on. Bianca was a wonderful person, possessing bountiful energy and an amazing spirit. It was now a matter of wait and see. Kennedy was definitely on board for whatever was in Bianca's best interest.

Xavier was already on his third clothing change for this modeling session. No sooner had he stripped out of the Rizzoli black and white silk houndstooth sports jacket, than he was already draping his sexy body in a rare white, three-button jacket tuxedo, with a double-sided vest, styled in a super 120's wool blend. The lightweight material was perfect for all year round. Complemented by unusual ivory snakeskin shoes, he looked superb from head to toe.

Numerous designer labels were used in this high-end fashion catalog. From casual attire to the top of the line in formal wear, Xavier wore everything so well. He knew how to work the lens on the camera, knew how to make every moment in front of it count. Every seductive pose he struck was sure to go over very well with the ladies.

As Xavier's penetrating eyes expressed every emotion imaginable, his full, sultry mouth appeared as if it were begging to be kissed. He worked with several female photographers. Although they kept a professional decorum it was often a hard gig for the ladies to get through. On the hot chart, Xavier was number one.

Once the shoot was over, Xavier quickly changed back into his own street clothing, said his farewells and promptly hit the exit. Getting back to Kennedy was all he'd been able to think about. He'd never missed anyone like this, nor had he ever in his life craved another human being. It was as if he was addicted to her.

Lifting Kennedy off her feet, Xavier crushed her against his body, taking liberty with her sweet lips. "I missed you, babe. Did you miss me?"

Kennedy's passionate kiss not only let Xavier know she missed him, but also how much. "I've been thinking about you all day. How'd your gig go?"

He put her down, making sure she was steady on her feet. "Everything went smooth as silk. The entire session was a piece of cake."

"I'm glad. I love it when things go well—and I hate it when things are messy."

"I guess that goes for all models. I need something cold to drink. What you got?"

"I made a pitcher of cherry Kool-Aid earlier. Want a glass?"

As Xavier thought about how much he'd loved Kool-Aid as a kid, he laughed. "I can't tell you the last time I had that stuff. Mom always kept a pitcherful in the refrigerator. Cherry was my favorite flavor. Grape came in second."

"I think everyone loved cherry. Come on out to the kitchen with me."

Pulling Kennedy to him again, he kissed her thoroughly. "I love Kool-Aid, but I love kissing you more."

Kennedy blushed. "I know the feeling." Placing her hands on both sides of his face, she gently pulled his head down and kissed him passionately.

After pouring two tall glasses of the cold drink, cherry indeed, Kennedy sat down opposite Xavier at the table. "Are you hungry?"

He shook his head. "Not even a little bit. I'm still hyped up from the shoot. I just need to sit here and relax." His expression turned thoughtful before he focused in on her. "Kirsten called today. Looks like I have to be on the set of *L,L&L* tomorrow morning. I guess we both know what that means."

Knowing exactly what it meant, hating the thought of him being around Tiaja Rae and Serita, she nodded. "I hope you're not nervous. You'll do just fine." Though she was sure she hadn't pulled it off, she had purposely tried to avoid the obvious. His being around her nemeses was almost more than she could stand.

"Come to the set with me? I could definitely use your support."

Kennedy knew what Xavier was trying to do—and she appreciated it. However, she was a big girl. And big girls always handled whatever devious women threw their way. "I won't be able to make it."

Just as Kennedy was aware of his purpose, he also knew her intent. Allowing her to maintain her dignity was a must. He didn't want her to go anywhere she'd feel uncomfortable. This gig was only temporary and he wouldn't have to be around Tiaja Rae for a long time. Kennedy wasn't the only person she made feel uncomfortable. Xavier figured she'd try to make it difficult for him also.

The program only required them to be on a judging panel together, not embroiled in some passionate love scene. He was sure Tiaja Rae wasn't romantically interested in him. It was more about her agitating and goading Kennedy than anything else.

With eyes as bright as the sun, Kennedy looked up at Xavier. "I think I *will* come to the set. That is, if you don't think I'll be a distraction. Don't want that."

Xavier appeared pleased and excited. "You'll be anything but an interruption. Having your support will be great. I'll arrange for a guest pass. When's good for you?"

"I don't want to come to the set on your first day, but I can try and squeeze it in any day after that. Let's go for Friday. Since that may be the last shoot, I already know I have some free time."

Xavier's eyes danced with the delight he felt. "I'll work on the pass tomorrow, before they start shooting. In fact, I'll go in early to handle it."

"Okay." Kennedy's mind immediately went to why she had changed her mind.

Backing away from a challenge wasn't Kennedy's thing. She had to prove to herself she could deal with Tiaja Rae and Serita in and out of the show setting. Xavier had invited her to the set and it'd be silly of her not to go because of women who had it in for her. She was probably more confident than either of them could imagine.

No one would run Kennedy away or keep her apart from the man she adored. This relationship only had two people in it: her and Xavier. There was no room in their love affair for any other party.

Chapter 10

Kennedy couldn't help missing Xavier. They'd been together practically every evening for the last few months, but now he was in Orlando, Florida. She hadn't been able to make the trip with him. This was the first day he hadn't called. While she was a bit concerned over the absence of a phone call, she wasn't overly worried.

The type of life models led on the road was harrowing. There were times when all Kennedy could do after a day's work was fall right into bed. People saw the glamour side of the job and hardly ever realized the hard labor put into it. It was mostly a labor of love for her, but it wasn't always so. Females could be testy by nature. When a bunch of them were packed together in one area it wasn't always pretty.

As Kennedy thought about her last evening out with Xavier, she frowned heavily. Just as they'd exited the restaurant that particular night, the paparazzi were there to greet them with flashbulbs and shouts for them to pose together. She'd had her fair share of photographers' attention before she began dating Xavier, but it had increased. They were now viewed by the press as a world-renowned supermodel couple.

Kennedy reached over to the nightstand and picked up the latest tabloids Martina had brought over to her earlier. Xavier's and her pictures were splashed all over the front covers. It had started to look like photographers had been everywhere they'd gone from their first date up until the last one. Several of the pictures were beautiful, but the rag sheets printing them weren't the least bit flattering.

This recent media blitz was more about Xavier than Kennedy. She felt that way because also featured in the sheets were pictures of him with numerous other women at various social functions in the past, before they started dating. There wasn't a single picture of her with another man. She was used to being in front of the camera when working, but this was something altogether different. These were nothing but gossip sheets. This was the kind of dark publicity she and Xavier could do without.

Can I stand the heat?

Kennedy was positive about one thing: how she felt about Xavier. The Tiaja Raes and the Seritas of the world wanted nothing more than to see their relationship fail. Kennedy could only hope these envious ladies were in for a rude awakening. Her strength was being tested, but she was stronger than she was given credit for. Kennedy hoped none of the ladies ever witnessed her powerful wrath.

A glance at the clock revealed the time as eight-thirty, three hours earlier than it was in Florida. She felt disappointed an entire day might go by without her hearing from Xavier. She tried hard not to think something may've happened to him, but trying to convince herself he was just too busy to call wasn't getting the job done, either.

It finally dawned on Kennedy that she didn't have to wait for Xavier to call her. She could phone him just as easily. But coming off as desperate wasn't for her even if she suddenly felt that way. Being patient wasn't working that well for her, either—and the loneliness was starting to drive her up the wall.

The phone rang right as Kennedy reached for it to call Martina. Without looking at the caller ID, she picked up the receiver. A silent prayer of thanks went up the second she heard Xavier's voice on the other end.

"Hey, babe, how are you?"

"Good. Are you okay?" That Xavier didn't sound too hot had her concerned.

"I wish."

Kennedy looked worried. "What does that mean?"

"I've obviously come down with something. My throat is killing me. As soon as I was through with work, around six, I came back to the hotel and got right into bed. My temperature is higher than normal and I'm sweating a lot."

"Sweating out the fever is good for you. Are you feeling any better now?"

"Somewhat. I can't believe I slept this long. It's close to midnight down here. I just woke up. I wasn't trying to go back to sleep without hearing your voice. I miss you."

Kennedy smiled inwardly. "The feeling is mutual." She wasn't going to admit to Xavier that she'd been worried and that she felt relieved he'd finally called.

"How was your day, K.B.?"

"Pretty calm," Kennedy responded. "Earlier this morning I did print ads for a brand-new jewelry line at Tiffany. Opulent chunky necklaces, brooches and watches. Folks act as if there aren't already enough jewelry companies on the market."

"I've done a lot of print work for Tag Heuer. And with your beauty modeling their pieces, they should do extremely well. I have a late-afternoon flight back to L.A. Can we get together after I get in?"

"Sure, but I think we should see how you're feeling first. Maybe you need to rest once you get back home."

"Can't I rest at your place as well as I can mine?"

"I'm not sure about that. You know what happens every time we get together."

"Yeah, I do, but that's not the reason I want to come there. Now that we've grown so close it's hard not being around you. You are sorely missed."

"Keep pouring it on thick."

"You've said that before, making it seem as if I'm being insincere. I'm not."

"I know that. You do whatever your body tells you it can handle. At least you'll gain time coming west. Call me when you land. You can let me know your plans then."

"I'm letting you know them now. I'm coming home to you as fast as I can."

Kennedy wanted Xavier to come home to her as much as he seemed to want the same. "I'll be waiting for you, anxiously."

"That's all I needed to hear you say. Good night, Kennedy."

"Feel better, Xavier."

Xavier got out of bed and trudged into the bathroom. After rifling through his aftershave kit, he came up with a bottle of Excedrin and a packet of multiple vitamins. His head was pounding. He had yet to take his daily dose of vitamins, which he normally took first thing in the morning. Once he filled a glass with water from the sink, he tossed the pills into his mouth, washing them all down at one time.

Before climbing back into bed, Xavier picked up from the nightstand the framed, color picture of Kennedy he traveled with. As his forefinger outlined her full lips, he had to smile. This was the one and only woman who'd ever made him feel like he was coming, going and spinning around in circles, all at the same time. She had constant control of his thoughts. No matter how busy he got, she still occupied his mind.

He had relived over and over again the last night he and Kennedy had spent together in Jamaica. Once they were back at home, he still couldn't believe how things had gotten even hotter between them. It was hard for him to sleep alone now. He'd be at her side every night if she wanted him there. After kissing the picture, he put it back in place. As he turned off the bedside lamp, he hoped to fall right back to sleep.

* * *

Kennedy couldn't believe her two brothers Gregory and Scott were standing at her front door. As she flung herself into Gregory's arms, the eldest of the three siblings, she felt moisture forming in her eyes. She hadn't seen these handsome guys in over three months. After embracing Scott in the same loving manner she'd greeted Gregory, she ushered her two brothers into the family room where they could sit and chat. Before Gregory took a seat, he also gave Kennedy a hug and kiss from their parents.

Both men had athletic builds, standing right at six feet. One brother was milk-chocolate complexioned and the other was a slight shade darker. Both guys were clean shaven and had heads full of thick, black hair. Women were drawn to their long lashes and ebony eyes. Anyone could tell they were siblings.

As Gregory was seated closest to Kennedy, she reached for his hand. "What brings you guys west from our beloved Philly—and why didn't you call to let me know your plans? You know I like to prepare for company."

Scott nodded. "That's exactly the reason we *didn't* call. You would've worked your fingers to the bone, thinking your place had to be spotless. We're here on business, scheduled to meet with a few corporate bigwigs. We hope to land some major accounts."

"You will. You two CPAs always accomplish your goals. Is anyone hungry?"

Gregory raised his hand. "Ravenous! The airlines don't offer much in the way of food these days. Higher ticket prices and less in amenities. I don't know about Scott, but I could get over with just a sandwich. I'll fix it myself."

"Come on out into the kitchen so you guys can see what I have on hand."

The two men followed their baby sister out to her warm, cozy kitchen. Family-friendly was how Scott referred to one of his favorite rooms in the houses of all his family members. He could sit at the kitchen table or the breakfast bar for hours on end, drinking coffee and working on his laptop.

Kennedy opened the refrigerator to show the types of luncheon meats she had stored in the clear meat bin. Since she didn't eat bread on a regular basis, she pulled a couple of packets of two from the freezer, which she kept on hand for occasions just like this one. It'd only take a couple of seconds for the wheat slices to thaw out in the toaster.

Grilled cheese came to Gregory's mind. Spotting the plastic tub of individually wrapped white American cheeses, he helped himself to two slices and also pulled out the tub of Blue Bonnet home-style whipped margarine. Next he rumbled through the lower cabinets to locate a small skillet.

Scott sat at the breakfast bar, rustling through the entertainment section of the *L.A. Times* to see what he and Gregory could get into during the visit. He loved visiting L.A. There were countless things to do. The social and entertainment venues were endless. Neither he nor Gregory was a big club-goer. They didn't mind hanging out there occasionally, though, especially when they felt like dancing and meeting new people, preferably the opposite sex. Neither brother was currently in a committed relationship.

After looking at the clock, Kennedy yelped, seeing at how much time had already ticked off the clock. "Guys, I've got to run within the next fifteen minutes or so. I don't want to be late getting to the mall to meet up with Bianca. We're returning some lingerie she purchased as a gift to me. How long are you guys in town?"

"Maybe until next Tuesday," Gregory responded. "We might have to stay longer, but we're just not sure right now."

The mention of Bianca's name had caused a stirring deep within Gregory. He'd had a huge crush on her since the first and only time they'd met. He loved her warm personality and great sense of humor, wondering if she was romantically involved.

"That's plenty of time for us to catch up on things. We have so much to talk about. At least, I do. A lot of good things have happened to me, fantastic stuff. I'll tell you all about my guy, Xavier De Marco."

Scott turned down his mouth. "Isn't he a male supermodel?"

"That he is. A great model—fabulous-looking in everything he wears." And even more of a dynamic vision when wearing absolutely nothing, she added in her thoughts. "Hey, why don't you guys come to the mall with me. I won't be long."

Glad about an opportunity to see Bianca again, Gregory nodded in the affirmative. "I'm up for it."

Scott had a strange look on his face. "I'm definitely okay with it. I need to pick up a few things I forgot to bring along." He snickered. "Like a few changes of clean underwear. I can't believe I left home without packing any."

Kennedy and Gregory cracked up.

"Thank your lucky stars you didn't leave home without your American Express card. If not, I can loan you a few pairs of my bikinis," she joked.

"Cute," Scott said, smirking at his sister. "You're always full of jokes."

"That's me," she said on a chuckle, "the best darn comedienne around. Now let's get this show on the road."

Kennedy had just made it out the front door when her cell rang. The illuminating smile on her face was as bright as the sun. "I'm good, Xavier. How are you feeling now?"

"I feel exhilarated…kind of hyper, too, but my throat still hurts a little. I'm glad to be back. I'm on my way to the house to unpack and shower. What're you into?"

Kennedy bounced up and down like a schoolkid. "Hanging out with my brothers. Gregory and Scott just surprised me! I opened the front door and they were standing right there, close enough for me to kiss."

Taking a minute to pause, Kennedy pressed her lips together. She wanted to ask Xavier to come meet her siblings, but she quickly decided the suggestion should come from him. Perhaps it was too soon for such a meeting. The fact that it was her family members had her backing off the idea.

"Will I get to meet them?" Xavier asked.

Kennedy covered her heart with her hand. "Do you want to?"

Xavier frowned. "Of course I do. When do you want me to drop by?"

"I'll leave it up to you."

Xavier looked down at his watch. "I can get there in about an hour and a half. Is the timing good for you?"

"We'll be back home by then."

"Where are you now?" Xavier queried.

"Right outside the house." So happy to hear from him, she trilled off a throaty laugh. "We're about to drop by Town Center Mall."

"Buying anything interesting?"

Feeling heat stealing into her cheeks, Kennedy giggled. "Just exchanging some intimates for another size. But you'd think what I bought recently was very interesting." She went on to tell him about the sexy items she'd purchased from Burning Flames, a specialty lingerie boutique. "They're hot enough to get a mighty fire started."

"Can hardly wait to see you in them! I've already conjured up a vivid image."

"That won't happen while the guys are here, not unless I slip over to your place for a romantic rendezvous." She loved flirting with him.

He was a bit disappointed to not have the type of homecoming he'd been dreaming of, but he understood. "Girl, you're turning me on. I can definitely be a party to that. Be careful what you suggest. Do you want to take your brothers out to dinner this evening?" He'd quickly changed gears because the thought of Kennedy wearing the unmentionables had already started to drive him nuts.

"Haven't thought that far ahead yet, but I guess I should. Once I figure it out, I'll let you in on the plans. Bianca and I are meeting."

"Please tell everyone I said hello."

"Will do, sweetness."

Kennedy felt so closely connected to Xavier. Even though they'd spent lots of time together and talking a lot on the phone, the types of deep conversations they had was one of the things that had drawn them closer.

"You go and meet Bianca and I'll see you around six or seven."

"Six," she said, not wanting to wait until seven. *Silly of me,* she mused.

Pleased by her comment, Xavier grinned from ear to ear. "Six it is."

Kennedy had decided that an impromptu dinner party would give her brothers a chance to socialize with Xavier and her other friends in a more relaxed setting. The guys were only familiar with a few people on the guest list: Bianca, Martina and Mitchel.

After introducing her brothers to Xavier, Kennedy stood back to discreetly observe their interaction. Of course, it was too soon to see if they'd get along well, but she knew Gregory and Scott would never embarrass her, even if they ended up not liking Xavier. They'd always been fair with her dates. However, there'd been a couple of guys who'd disappeared altogether, without warning, after a chat with her sometimes formidable siblings.

Before Kennedy and the others could clear the doorway, Jonathan and Janine popped up. Martina and Mitchel were also expected. Bianca and Torrance were invited, too. Bianca had said Torrance couldn't make it, but she still planned to show up.

Within the next thirty minutes all of Kennedy's expected guests had arrived. She was always pleased when her friends visited. She recalled a time when half the people she'd ask over wouldn't show or even bother to let her know their intent one way or the other. Those were acquaintances, rather than close friends. She couldn't be one hundred percent sure, but she felt that Martina and Bianca were lifetime friends, as opposed to seasonal ones.

Some friends stopped by for only a season. After accomplishing the deed they'd been sent there for, they'd disappear. She often wondered if Xavier was there for a season or a lifetime. She hoped for the latter.

All through dinner Kennedy's and Xavier's eyes wildly flirted. The exchange of smiles was every bit as flirtatious. Had he been seated closer to her, she was sure a game of footsies would've ensued under the table. Although it wouldn't happen for a while she couldn't wait to be alone with him again. The man excited her in ways she'd never thought possible. Without uttering a single word, the way he looked at her often conveyed his deepest thoughts, especially the torrid ones.

"How long will you guys be in town?" Bianca asked Gregory and Scott.

"Tuesday or perhaps longer," Gregory said, since she was looking right at him.

"Are you here on business or just a visit with your sister?" Jonathan queried.

"Both," Scott replied. "We have a few business meetings lined up."

"What lines of work are you in?" Janine asked.

Gregory chuckled. "From all these questions it sounds like our baby sister never talks about us. But to answer your question, we're both CPAs and have our own private accounting firm. We're looking to open a West Coast office. We seek out large corporations to bring on board as clients. We're small but we service some pretty heavy players."

"Service! Now that's an interesting word for you," Bianca joked.

"Don't even go there," Kennedy warned Bianca, her tone playful.

A host of compliments were given to the Bassett chefs over the Teriyaki chicken. The brothers were gracious in accepting the kind comments.

The open flirting going on between Gregory and Bianca was quite evident to Kennedy. She didn't know whether to be happy about it or worried. Bianca using her brother to get over Torrance wasn't something she'd sanction. One person getting hurt was enough.

The last thing her brother needed was to be used by Bianca. He liked her too much to have that happen. Rebounding probably wouldn't help her out like she thought it would. If she wasn't interested in him for who he was, Kennedy would have no compunction about telling her to lay off her sibling. Gregory was a really good guy and he needed a woman who wasn't jaded by a broken heart or one on the rebound.

Kennedy served dessert before the group went back into the family room to sit and talk, giving the delicious food a chance to properly digest. She immediately noticed Gregory and Bianca seated next to each other on the smaller of the two leather couches. Whatever was the topic of conversation, they appeared deeply engrossed. Every now and then peals of laughter rang out. Both parties had a great sense of humor so they'd have no problem drawing laughter from each other, Kennedy knew.

Scott, Janine and Jonathan also seemed to have a good conversation going. Those three folks were all about business. The middle Bassett child always had a phone up to his ear. He could talk business 24/7 if he had an audience. His dates often became agitated because they rarely had his undivided attention. The man was a talker.

"Is it okay if I fix a pot of coffee?" Janine asked the hostess.

Kennedy jumped to her feet. "Forgive me. I'll take care of it. I had planned to ask if anyone wanted coffee or tea. Just hadn't gotten around to it. How many want coffee?" Every hand in the room went up so she saw she was the only one doing tea.

Xavier followed Kennedy out to the kitchen, where he instantly took her into his arms, his lips immediately planting butterfly kisses on her neck and ears. "Girl, you sent me all sorts of sexy signals from across the table. I'm really enchanted with the flirty side of you. Our eyes were talking plenty of trash. The conversation was fascinating. Now when do we get around to taking care of all the intimate stuff?"

A stream of cheery laughter came from Kennedy. "In due time, sweetie. My brothers don't plan to leave until Tuesday or possibly later. As I said earlier, I can try to arrange to slip over to your place for a rendezvous."

"You can slip over to my house anytime you like. The door is always open to you." Starving from his desire for the taste of her, his mouth closed hungrily over hers, kissing her with wild abandon. "You are so sweet and hot," he whispered into her ear.

She playfully pushed him away. "Let me do what I came in here for. You make me hot enough to lose my mind. I darn near forgot why I am in here."

"Coffee, my dear, sweet Kennedy, you came in here to make coffee."

Laughing, she swatted Xavier's arm. "I know what I'm supposed to be doing. I was just checking you out to see if you knew."

"Yeah, right," he teased, tenderly kissing the back of her neck.

Wanting more of Xavier's hot kisses, Kennedy turned around and aligned her mouth with his. This man was the best kisser ever. If her toes weren't curling, it certainly felt like it. He also had the softest lips hers had ever connected with. If she didn't have guests, she knew where they'd end up. Gently, she pushed him away again, but he was compelled to help himself to one more passionate kiss.

Kennedy and Xavier started brewing the drinks. Before Kennedy could get the hot drinks out to her visitors, they filed into the kitchen, taking seats at the table and breakfast bar.

"Was I taking too long?" Kennedy asked Janine.

"Not really. We just came out here to see what was up."

Kennedy laughed. "Nosiness is what I suspect. The coffee is just about ready."

"Don't worry about it, Kennedy. Everyone is cool," Janine assured her hostess.

Scott walked up behind Kennedy and posted his chin on her shoulder. "Now for the truth. Everyone thought you two had gotten lost, lost in each other. In case you're interested in knowing, I like him. So does Greg. Xavier seems to care a lot about you."

"He really does care. Thanks for letting me know what you both think. It's important to me that my brothers like the man I'm in love with," she whispered softly.

Scott nodded. "Love! So, it's gone that far. We'll talk later. Whispering is rude."

"Yeah, my parents taught me the same manners your mama and daddy taught you," she teased Scott, laughing. "Mama and Daddy are proud of us all."

"They are that," Gregory chimed in.

Kennedy gave her brothers the thumbs-up sign. 'We're proud of them, too. Coffee is ready, everybody."

Kennedy began filling the coffee cups and Xavier was only too happy to help her serve. Without any prompting on her part, he jumped right in to assist her in the hosting duties. She was pleased by his willingness to roll up his sleeves and chip in and help out. A man who wasn't afraid of a little domestic work was just the sort of man she liked.

Everyone enjoyed their coffee as Kennedy sipped on her tea. Out of the blue Xavier asked Gregory and Scott if they'd like to join their sister as his special guests for the soap-opera taping. "I'd love to have you guys come. I'm sure Kennedy would too."

Xavier was worried about what Tiaja Rae and Serita might do to try to make his lady feel awkward about being on the set. Should anything like that occur, though he hoped it wouldn't, he thought it'd be nice if her brothers were there for her.

Scott nodded with enthusiasm. "That'd be great, man. I'm in. What about you, bro? Are you coming with us?" he asked Gregory.

"Absolutely! I wouldn't miss it. I'm excited," Gregory said.

"All right! Isn't that the show Tiaja Rae Montgomery will be featured on?"

Xavier reluctantly nodded his response to Scott's question.

"Oh, my goodness," Scott exclaimed, slapping his hand against his forehead. "I can't believe I might get to meet her. The girl is smoking hot. Have you seen her Calvin Klein jeans ads? They're everywhere!"

"Boy, have I. She scorched a three-alarm fire in those jeans," Jonathan said, without flinching. He and Janine had a good relationship. Neither of them took it personal when one or the other made a melodramatic fuss over a member of the opposite sex.

Xavier saw the crestfallen look on Kennedy's face. He'd never dreamed her brothers would've mentioned Tiaja Rae. He hadn't seen that one coming. She had flinched at the same moment the other model's name was mentioned. He understood her feelings, but he just wished she wasn't so affected. Tiaja Rae couldn't hold a candle to Kennedy. The two ladies were total opposites in every way possible.

Kennedy made a mental note to share details of their feud with her brothers. She'd never wanted to bother them with such annoyances in the past, but now the stakes were high.

"I'm sure Xavier will try to arrange a special meeting for you to meet the cast. If nothing else, autographed pictures may be possible," Kennedy stated calmly.

"They'll get to meet the cast. I hear it's done all the time," Xavier explained. "I'll find out the process and take it from there."

The brothers once again thanked Xavier for the invite, telling him how excited they were for the opportunity to meet the cast of *L,L&L*. They had grown up with their mother and grandmother and aunts watching the soap and sometimes got caught up in the occasional episode.

Bianca looked as though she'd been left out. "I want to come, too. Can I?"

Xavier grinned broadly. "I'm sure I can work something out."

"If you can't, I'll understand," said Bianca.

"We'll see what happens, Bianca. I'll let Kennedy know one way or the other," Xavier assured her.

The tenseness Kennedy had felt when her nemesis's name had been called had her regretful. She had to be the bigger person in this matter simply because she was. She didn't want Xavier to think she was intimidated.

Xavier reached for Kennedy's hand, wanting to let her know he understood any bad feelings she might have toward Tiaja Rae. With Serita also working on the set, he wondered if she felt the deck was stacked against her.

Kennedy was now alone with Xavier, loving every second of it. Still, she hated to see such a beautiful evening come to an end. All her guests had had a great time. Everything had been relaxing, until the group began discussing politics. Suddenly everyone was talking over each other. Conversations had become very spirited.

Gregory and Scott had turned in immediately after everyone had left. The time difference had gotten to them. Kennedy also suspected her brothers of allowing her and Xavier some private time.

Even though leaving was the last thing Xavier wanted to do, he knew it was time. Both he and Kennedy had had full days. He'd like nothing more than to fall asleep in the same bed with her, in her arms, but that wasn't happening tonight. He respected her and her brothers too much to even suggest he stay over and slip out early in the morning. Yet the very idea had run through his head a few times.

Standing at the front door, Xavier couldn't stop kissing Kennedy. This woman had him burning white-hot. Her tongue mingling with his had the man way past excited. His lower anatomy had expanded considerably, to the point of discomfort. He had her molded closely to him, hip to hip…thigh to thigh, and he wanted to hold her like this forever. "Do you have any idea how you affect me? I love being with you."

Kennedy wasn't in any hurry for Xavier to leave her. "You affect me the same way. My days are so much brighter now than before I met you. I wish our nights together never had to end. You're a good man and I love it when we hang out together. I think we have a good start to a really beautiful thing."

"A great start. If you ever feel yourself starting to doubt me, please don't. I can't get any more real with you. I can't always adequately express my feelings verbally, but if you look into my eyes you'll see everything I'm feeling." His lips lightly grazed her forehead, moving downward to her lips, where the kiss deepened. "Goodnight, sweetheart. You'll be the last thought on my mind before I fall asleep and the first thought when I wake up."

Xavier's comments had Kennedy's insides melting like butter. His remarks had been sincere enough, causing her to feel them deep inside her heart. He was just as honest as she. The relationship had so much potential…and she could hardly wait to explore all its possibilities. Kennedy knew that pleasure awaited them around every corner.

Chapter 11

Greg and Scott had surprised Kennedy by having breakfast ready when she got out of bed. Now that she'd eaten everything on her plate, she felt full and satisfied, ready to lie down another hour or two. She felt very much loved by her brothers and she was thrilled with the pampering. Their visits were always special.

The brothers had spoiled their little sister rotten, making her the center of their attention when growing up. Kennedy made them laugh and they had loved taking care of her when called upon to do so. They had cooked for her and had even washed her hair on a regular basis. Washing and ironing her clothes had also been a frequent occurrence.

Although their parents had told Gregory and Scott to look very carefully after their baby sister, no one had told them they had to delight in it. But they had. The brothers were like proud parents, thrilled silly when she'd taken her first step. Gregory was ten and a half years her senior and Scott was eight years older.

Now that the kitchen had been restored to its original state, the brothers went to seek out their sister.

Trying to figure out how to discreetly get more personal information on Bianca, Gregory stretched out at the bottom of Kennedy's bed. The girl was a tiny beauty and she seemed so nice and sweet. She'd been very flirtatious with him last evening so he had reason to think they carried a mutual attraction.

"Your big bro is infatuated with your girl Bianca. Is she in a serious relationship or what?" Scott asked before Gregory could inquire.

Kennedy dragged her finger back and forth across her lower lip. "There's a little trouble in paradise. Her male friend, Torrance, is talking about moving to New York to work for another network. He's a television cameraman."

Gregory stoked his chin. "Is she in love with him?"

"Some people fall in love at first sight, but I don't think that's the case with them. I try not to pry into my friends' personal business." She couldn't help thinking of how quickly she and Xavier had fallen hard for each other.

"I'm interested in getting to know Bianca," Gregory said, as a matter of fact. "She's sweet and her personality is captivating. What are my chances with her?"

Kennedy's eyebrows shot up a quarter of an inch. "Have you forgotten you live in Philly, all the way across the country? That's the dilemma she's already faced with in her relationship with Torrance. She can't see herself living in New York or in any other cold climate. So that leaves both you and Philadelphia out."

"I wouldn't be so sure about that," Scott remarked. "We're looking to open a West Coast office, too. Wouldn't you love to have us around a lot more?"

Shooting straight up in the bed, screeching like a banshee, Kennedy could hardly believe her ears. "Are you guys kidding me? That'd be fantastic, if you're not pulling my leg. How do Mom and Dad feel about it?"

"They're all for it," Gregory remarked. "Mom and Dad are also kind of tired of living in subzero climates. You might just have your entire family around."

"Bring it on," Kennedy enthused, her eyes bright with joy. "Why hasn't anyone mentioned this to me before now?"

"Because nothing is etched in stone yet," Gregory said. "We have meetings arranged with a few corporate bigwigs, the real decision makers. We're also scouting out another office. It won't come together in the twinkling of an eye. We anticipate the entire process taking at least a couple of months once we land a lease."

Kennedy looked astonished. "You guys are really serious, aren't you? This is amazing! I can't believe my brothers are actually considering opening an office in L.A."

Scott poked at her toes through the blanket. "Believe it. We're dead serious about owning bicoastal offices. We've been thinking about this for a long time."

"More so since the last time we visited you," Gregory confirmed. "California has gotten into our blood. The weather is the main attraction, not to mention the endless entertainment venues. Now back to Bianca. Do I stand a ghost of a chance with her?"

The phone rang, cutting into their conversation. Without Kennedy having to ask, the two men quickly vacated the room so she could talk in private. The sound of Xavier's voice did what it always did to her, driving her wild, making her desire him like crazy. He had the deepest, sexiest voice she'd ever heard. "Good morning back at you! I slept great. How about you?"

"Couldn't sleep the first part of the night for thinking of you." Xavier had been worried about Kennedy, somewhat disturbed by her demeanor after the unanticipated mention of Tiaja Rae's name. "I've given this subject a lot of thought before deciding to bring it up. If you're not comfortable coming to the set, I'll understand. I know how rude Tiaja Rae and Serita are. Please don't think you have to do this for me. I want you to visit the set, but I need you to be comfortable."

Kennedy was touched by Xavier's thoughtfulness and his deep concern for her feelings. Tiaja Rae continuously acted horribly rude, but her evil disposition wouldn't change whether Kennedy stayed away from the set or not.

"You'll see me later. I'm fine. I try not to allow anyone to control me, Xavier. I'll be there. Okay?"

"That's good enough for me. See you later. Call Bianca and tell her it's a go. Hit me on my cell when you get on the lot." Xavier then gave her the instructions and procedures for entering the television studio. She already knew how to get to the location.

"Can't wait to see you and I promise to use discretion," Kennedy remarked.

'That's not necessary. There's no such practice between us. Well, maybe in some instances. But I'll take the lead on this one. Oh, by the way, don't make plans for lunch. If you don't mind craft provisions, we can all eat together."

"Lunch on the set is fine. I've eaten my share of craft foods. Bye, baby."

"Later, Kennedy." He made kissing sounds into the phone.

Kennedy tossed her head back on the pillow, immediately conjuring up Xavier's image. She didn't want to push anything, but she wondered where all this wonderfulness was heading. They both had great careers and each traveled extensively throughout the world. She couldn't imagine giving that up, at least not right now. She was at the top of her game, had worked extremely hard to get there. The man she knew as Xavier wouldn't want her to give up her career or her hopes and dreams. He allowed her to be as independent as she chose. She afforded him the same freedoms.

Kennedy saw her and Xavier as perfect partners for each other, yet she had a few niggling doubts. What would happen when she was in Milan and he had to be in Athens? His few days away in Orlando had taken a huge toll on her. Being away from him for long periods of time might make her uncomfortable. It was already hard being separated from him for a few hours. She was away from him right now, but she'd see him in a couple of hours. With that in mind, Kennedy closed her eyes and began to drift back off to sleep.

Kennedy penned her name on the sign-in log and handed the pen to Gregory, who wrote down his name, Scott's and Bianca's. The security guard's search on the ladies' purses would hardly qualify as thorough, since he'd only glanced at the contents. Once the foursome finished with the security measures, they headed toward the green room, where they'd been instructed to wait for Xavier.

Catching up to his guests, Xavier greeted everyone cheerfully, shaking hands with the fellows. He then tilted his head and had his way with his lady's luscious lips. As he kissed Kennedy's mouth with gentle but firm pressure, he felt his blood pressure rise. Kissing her was always an awesome experience.

Kennedy looked up into Xavier eyes. "I like the way you take the lead."

A wide grin spread across his mouth. "You don't forget anything, do you?"

Kennedy briefly laid her hand against the side of his face. "Not much, especially when it comes to you. Is everything falling into place?"

"It's getting there." He put his lips close to her ear. "Between you and me, everything to do with the show is chaotic. But let's not concern ourselves. I'm here to escort you to your seats. *L,L&L* is normally a closed set but occasionally they make exceptions."

"I'm so excited!"

As usual, Xavier was impeccably dressed. His navy slacks were perfectly creased and pressed. The collar on the deep pink Ralph Lauren shirt was crisp enough to pop. Fabulous-looking navy-blue Italian loafers didn't appear as if they'd seen much wear. This man was the consummate package.

And he's all mine, Kennedy mused with giddy satisfaction.

Xavier held out both his arms. "Ladies, grab a wing."

Kennedy and Bianca giggled, as they each looped an arm through his. Xavier instantly regretted his monopoly of the women. Gregory's attraction to Bianca hadn't been lost on him. He hoped the guys didn't feel snubbed, because it wasn't his intent, yet he felt like he had to make it up to them.

Only a very small portion of the vast studio audience was made available for visitors. The majority of the sections were roped off. It appeared seats *were* at a premium. Kennedy had thought of putting off the visit, but Xavier had told her there was no guarantee of another day on the set for him. His segment could actually wrap today if they got it picture-perfect.

Once Xavier saw his guests comfortably seated, he kissed Kennedy goodbye, promising to see her as soon as possible. "Stay right here until we wrap for lunch. I'll come back for you." He waved farewell as he left the area.

Bianca nudged Kennedy. "You've got a rare gem in Xavier. He's so personable. I don't know anyone as successful who's that down-to-earth."

Kennedy gave Bianca a sideways glance.

"Oh, besides you, that is." Bianca had quickly realized Kennedy's obvious exception to the remark.

"Nice recovery," Kennedy teased. "Count yourself in among the earth dwellers. You're successful, personable and your feet are firmly planted. You positively own the runways in the petite modeling world."

Bianca blew on her fingertips and brushed them off on her shoulder. "I do, don't I?" Bianca fell out laughing at her silly antics and her pitiful attempt at arrogance.

Kennedy could see that Gregory had been drawn in by Bianca's laughter and effervescent personality. The expression on his face was priceless. He looked as if he'd just discovered he'd fallen head over heels in love. While Bianca wasn't in love with Kennedy's brother, she wasn't in love with Torrance, either. She'd revealed that much to Kennedy last evening. Bianca had also confessed to having a crush on Gregory.

There was a ton of crew and cameras around. Watching Xavier seated at a long table of modeling judges thrilled Kennedy. Not so awe-inspiring for her was seeing Tiaja Rae seated right next to him. She constantly touched his arm and hand in an intimate way. Her periodic leaning her head in close to his to whisper something to him grated on Kennedy's nerves. *The lady should learn to keep her hands and her whispered secrets to herself,* she thought churlishly.

As if Tiaja Rae wasn't enough for Xavier to contend with, Serita Devlin also had to make her presence known to him. Kennedy didn't know what she had leaned over and whispered into his ear—and she really didn't want to imagine.

If only the ladies knew how foolish they looked and what idiots they continued to make of themselves. It was quite obvious that Xavier didn't desire either woman. He appeared merely tolerant of them.

Although Xavier didn't appear comfortable with the touchy-feely episodes from both women he hadn't done anything to thwart it. Kennedy thought that moving his hand away might send a strong signal. They'd probably ignore his attempt to rid himself of their unwanted company.

The director yelled, "Action!" Unhappy with her sudden negative thinking, Kennedy rapidly refocused her attention on the stunning model taking the runway.

The smartly dressed brunette, standing in at six-one, was fascinating to watch. The white gauzy pants outfit designed by Burberry draped her long frame beautifully. Navy and bright yellow accessories caused the clothing to explode with color. She had good control of her entire body, moving it all about in an exciting way. The flurry of twists and turns sizzled the flooring beneath her feet. She knew how to electrify.

As the mocha-complexioned model strutted her stuff before the judges, she stopped, looked down at Xavier, lifting his chin with two fingers. The smile she gave him was scorching. She pursed her lips, as though she intended to kiss him. Instead of lowering her head to capture his mouth, in one quick motion she glided back down the runway.

Kennedy thought it had been a bold move on the model's part to touch one of the judges, period, let alone in an intimate manner. From the loud, animated reactions of the other judges it had gone over quite well. Kennedy had to admit it was original. As a big fan of the various modeling shows on television, she hadn't seen anything like it. And she certainly didn't like how it felt.

The next three models weren't nearly as exciting as the flirty brunette. The clothes worn were nothing short of fabulous, however. Numerous designers were represented in the show: Dior, Lauren, Prada, Baby Phat, DKNY, Calvin Klein, to name a few.

Right as the judges put their heads together to discuss the performances, Tiaja Rae suddenly yelled loudly at Serita, telling her she needed to keep her opinions to herself and to lay off her. An ugly argument ensued between the ladies for several minutes.

The rest of the panel members looked embarrassed by the boisterous display of tempers. Kennedy couldn't help noticing Xavier shaking his head in disgust. She didn't know what had caused the eruption of tempers, but she hoped it had nothing to do with Xavier, who seemed terribly uncomfortable caught up between Tiaja Rae and Serita. The director yelled cut and they did the scene again.

Kennedy half filled her plate with salad, lightly dousing it with raspberry vinaigrette dressing. The grilled salmon looked tempting, but she'd already had seafood twice this week. Steamed vegetables were the best alternative and bottled water was her drink of choice. Satisfied with everything on her tray, she walked over to the reserved table and sat down. Even though Kennedy thought it best to take the seat across from Xavier, he quickly moved right over next to her, kissing her lightly on the mouth.

Xavier gently squeezed her hand. "How'd you enjoy what you've seen so far?"

Kennedy nodded her approval. "Really nice. You look great up there! Not that I expected any less from you."

"Thanks for the vote of confidence, babe, but all I did was sit there and try to look charming. I'm glad you're here."

"You succeeded. You *were* a barrel of charm." Kennedy smiled beautifully. "Thanks for inviting us. Glad I came."

The rest of the group came to the table and took seats. While Bianca hardly had enough on her plate to feed a bird, the Bassett brothers' plates were filled to capacity.

Once everyone was settled in, Scott led the group in a blessing of thanks.

"Well, well, well, what do we have here?" Tiaja Rae wore a mocking smile.

Without waiting for an invitation, she took the empty spot next to Scott, extending her hand to him. "I'm Tiaja Rae Montgomery. And just who the heck are you, handsome?"

Scott looked as if he couldn't believe who was seated right next to him. "Scott Bassett, visiting from Philly. I'm a real big fan of yours. Nice to meet you!"

"Bassett," Tiaja Rae remarked, as if the name had left a bad taste in her mouth. "Please don't tell my you're related to…" Purposely stopping short of saying Kennedy's name, she gave off her little derisive laugh, the one that made Kennedy's skin crawl. "I guess I can't hold it against you. You're too fine for that." She then cozied up to Scott, as if they were in a committed relationship.

Scott didn't like Tiaja Rae's veiled reference to his sister and he scowled. "I'm not sure what you mean by that, but I'm very much related to Kennedy Bassett." He pointed at his brother. "She is our baby sister. We all three carry the last name Bassett."

"I'm sorry." Tiaja Rae's apology to Scott had been barely audible, and it had a ring of insincerity, but he felt compelled to take her at her word. Besides, this wasn't the time or place to argue the point.

Kennedy's discomfort and embarrassment was obvious. She was mortified, vehemently disliking Tiaja Rae's attempt to make a fool out of her brother. If Scott didn't know how to handle himself with the opposite sex, she'd be worried. It wasn't her brother she feared getting into something he couldn't handle. The lady just might be biting off more than she could chew, Kennedy easily assessed. Scott was a ladies' man.

Kennedy did her best to eat her lunch, but she had lost her appetite the moment her nemesis had appeared. She was aware that this might happen, but she'd prayed fervently for mercy. Xavier squeezing her hand, trying to invoke the calm within her, wasn't helping. The agitation she'd initially felt had now turned to burning anger.

Kennedy had to wonder how many times she should allow Tiaja Rae to upstage her.

From all indications, the other incidents were just the tip of the iceberg. Had the dousing of Tiaja Rae with wine only made her more determined to get under Kennedy's skin? It certainly seemed so, Xavier thought, mentally cursing this situation.

Tiaja Rae spent the next ten minutes softly whispering her comments, as she conversed with Scott, pretending to be the perfect lady.

Kennedy saw that Scott seemed intent on everything the model said, but she also noticed he hadn't voiced much. Perhaps he couldn't get in a word edgewise. It wouldn't surprise her one bit since Tiaja Rae was all about Tiaja Rae.

Xavier nudged Kennedy with his shoulder. "Have you checked into going to Paris with me? I'm due to leave shortly."

"I can only go if Chase finds something for me. He's already looking into a project for me to work on at the same time you're there. I'll know something soon."

"That'd be super." Xavier was also trying to get his shoot to include her, just as she'd done on the Jamaica project. He had yet to hear a response from Kirsten.

Right after the lunch hour Xavier reclaimed his seat on the panel. The production wasn't nearly as exciting as he had hoped. There was still the possibility of him landing a recurring guest spot on the show, but he really didn't care about that outcome one way or the other. He liked structure in his jobs. Everything on the show had gone helter-skelter before the production had officially begun.

Besides the disorganization Xavier really didn't want to work with Tiaja Rae. She represented total chaos in her deep desire to sabotage his relationship with Kennedy. She seemed hell-bent on making his lady uncomfortable and he didn't care for that at all. All the touching and feeling wasn't necessary and he'd done nothing to encourage it.

The money Xavier made off this gig didn't compare to what he made as a supermodel. He wasn't in this for the money. He had to like the job he was asked to perform before he even considered the pay. There was nothing to draw him on the side of taking seriously this job or any future ones in television. It had disappointed him so far.

Kennedy knew she'd stepped into the lion's den the moment the bathroom door shut behind her. Seeing Tiaja Rae and Serita in the same spot immediately unnerved her. Since their voices were raised, they were possibly still having a difference of opinion.

"You don't need to be telling me what to do, Serita. I'm my own woman."

"Maybe you've forgotten how you got this job. You asked for a favor and I got it done. Some people are never grateful. I don't know who has less gratitude, you or Xavier…" Serita stopped talking now that she'd spotted Kennedy.

Kennedy avoided eye contact with either woman as she made her way to where the stalls were located.

"Don't you speak to people?" Serita shouted after Kennedy.

"Hello, Serita," Kennedy said calmly, still not making eye contact with her.

Serita narrowed her eyes. "I see you're not so mouthy when your man's not around. You sure have a lot to say when he's with you."

As Kennedy tried to move on to her destination, Serita ran over and grabbed her by the arm. "I know you hear me talking to you."

Kennedy aggressively snatched her arm back. "Maybe I could hear you if you were saying something worthwhile. What gives with you, anyway?"

Serita stretched her neck. "You're kind of bold, aren't you?" She pointed at Tiaja Rae, who seemed to be enjoying the confrontation. "There are two of us and only one of you. Neither one of us can stand your behind. We could beat you black and blue by the time you're missed out there. Sure you want to tangle with us?"

Tiaja Rae laughed derisively. "I don't think she has any fight in her."

"Don't be too sure about that," Kennedy countered. Standing up to these two bullies was a must if she was going to walk out of there in one piece. If they thought she feared them, no telling what might happen. "Worried that you can't take me one-on-one? I'm not into fighting, but I will defend myself."

Serita came over and got right up in Kennedy's face and stared her down.

Kennedy didn't flinch, but she sure was praying hard, hoping she didn't have to fight her way out of there. Besides, she really had to go to the bathroom. And she did just that, leaving Serita surprised by her quick retreat. The dirty name she was called by Tiaja Rae reached Kennedy's ears just as she shut the stall. She shook her head in dismay.

"You can't hide from us forever," Tiaja Rae shouted. "You will see us again. Maybe you should remember to carry your boxing gloves around with you." Tiaja Rae strolled over and kicked the stall Kennedy was in. Then the two women laughed loudly.

At that moment Xavier stuck his head into the door and called out to Kennedy. When she didn't answer, he came all the way in, wondering if she was sick. When he saw the two she-devils, he knew she'd run into trouble. "Kennedy, where are you?"

Kennedy rushed out and ran right into his arms. "Boy am I glad to see you! I thought I was going to have to fight my way out of here."

Xavier glared at Tiaja Rae and Serita. "If there's any fighting going on in here, I'll be the one doing it." He pointed at the two women. "Let me tell you something. I've had enough of you both. If you come near Kennedy again, we're getting the police involved and restraining orders will be filed against you. Grow up. There's nothing more unattractive than back-biting, gossipy, jealous women."

Seeing the rage in Xavier's eyes had the two ladies running for the door. Neither of them had had a single word to say since he'd come into the room.

He put his arm around Kennedy. "You ready to go?"

"Soon as I wash my hands." Kennedy's hands trembled as she turned on the water. As she lathered the soap on her hands, she broke down.

Xavier pulled her into his arms, holding her close. "This is over. I can promise you that. Everything will be okay." He knew he really should get back to the set, but until she was composed he wasn't leaving her side. However, he did escort her outside the ladies' room since he was in forbidden territory for men.

* * *

Taking his eyes off Kennedy was hard for Xavier. She had been unusually quiet ever since they'd first entered his home. The rest of the group had gone back to her place. Despite his desire to have some time alone with her, he had asked the others to join them. Sensing that they needed some time alone, Gregory had been the one to speak for everyone, saying they'd just go back to Kennedy's place and relax. No one had minded them going off together to spend time alone.

Xavier briefly touched Kennedy's hand. "Are you okay?"

She looked at him and smiled gently. "I'm fine. Why do you ask?"

He gulped hard, figuring they were about to embark on a serious conversation. "I'm worried about you. You've been so quiet. What's going on inside your pretty head?"

She shrugged. "Nothing of great importance, I can assure you of that. I've been thinking of some of the things I need to get done within the next couple of days."

Xavier raised an eyebrow of interest. "Like what?"

"Like taking a few items to the cleaners and restocking my kitchen pantry." She laughed. "Like I said before, nothing of great importance."

Xavier nodded his understanding. "What are your feelings about the show?"

"Thought it went well, but it wasn't as organized as I'd imagined." Kennedy used her hands to demonstrate the chaos she had witnessed. "Including the director, no one seemed to be on the same page."

"That's because we weren't. I agree with everything you've said. Things didn't exactly run smoothly. It wasn't a great experience, either, at least, not for me."

Not wanting them to waste their time alone on rehashing earlier, Kennedy leaned over and kissed Xavier full on the mouth. As he responded ardently, pulling her onto his lap, the kiss blossomed with intense passion. She was hungry for the taste and feel of him. He felt the same as she did.

Lifting her up from the sofa, he carried her through the house and into the master bedroom, carefully laying her down on the mattress. Slowly but surely, Xavier and Kennedy began to disrobe each other, touching and kissing places they thought would bring the most pleasure. Her soft purring and his deep moans let both know when they'd hit just the right spots.

With the upper portion of his body now bared, Xavier slowly lowered himself onto Kennedy's fully undressed body. She felt so soft and pliable and deliciously warm. His full lips first sought out her nipples. Both peaks were hard and erect, and he laved and suckled each, feeling himself rapidly losing control.

The intimate contact made Kennedy squirm about uncontrollably beneath Xavier's sizzling touch. It had taken her a couple of minutes, but she'd finally worked his pants over his hips, down his legs and off his feet. Wanting him had her heart throbbing hard, nearly as hard as his lower anatomy felt. As his manhood strained against the entry gate to her womanhood, she could hardly wait for him to come inside.

Xavier was an artist, one who took his time in painting his masterpiece. Never would he be so thoughtless as to rush through the art of tender lovemaking. Never had he put his pleasures first. Protecting them and fulfilling the physical needs and desires of his woman came before everything else. He prided himself on bringing untold bliss to the woman he loved.

Kennedy was the one and only woman Xavier loved and desired to complete.

As Xavier's fingers tenderly explored the soft flesh around the opening to her delicate flower, Kennedy began to grow impatient. Her desire for him had now grown to a desperate state, but she'd never let him know it, verbally or otherwise. However, she had no problem showing him how much she needed him by taking over the reins.

Kennedy continued to mesh her mouth against Xavier's as she rolled him off her. Once she had him flat on his back, she straddled him, keeping their mouths locked together. Then, as she lowered herself down onto his protected manhood, she heard the rushing sound of his breath. She smiled, knowing she had surprised the heck out of him, rendering him speechless. Moving around on him was almost more than she could bear. Each time he raised up to delve deeper into her pulsating sex, she nearly came unglued.

Her desire to climax was strong. Although she wanted to prove to Xavier she had just as much staying power as him, she wasn't sure she could hang on as long as he normally did. Instead of entering into a stupid contest, she began to solely concentrate on making wild, passionate love to the man she craved manically.

The not-so-subtle grinding of Kennedy's hips against Xavier's had him calling out her name, causing her to increase the uninhibited gyrations. As their body temperatures continued to rise above normal, the dripping sweat from their bodies mingled.

Kennedy felt extremely sexy tonight. Even though she hadn't brought along the intimate apparel she'd told him about it did nothing to diminish her sex appeal. Skimpy nightclothes were sexy and arousing but nothing compared to sheer nudity. The coming together of naked bodies was exciting and beyond erotic.

Ready to retake control of their sexual encounter, Xavier flipped Kennedy over on her back in one rapid motion. As he entered her with all the tenderness he was capable of, he heard her sharp intake of breath. Moments after burying his lips in the soft folds of her neck, he began sprinkling her throat with soft, butterfly kisses.

Knowing he couldn't hold on much longer didn't upset Xavier because he knew Kennedy was also ready to explode. He felt her readiness to detonate. Her flower was overflowing with moisture and her jerky motions beneath let him know it was time.

Several more deep thrusts caused her to untrap her desires.

Then, as Kennedy's body began to quiver uncontrollably, Xavier became overly excited by her desperate moans and the clawing of his back. Feeling the passion and intensity mounting far beyond his control, he thrust his manhood deeper and deeper into her moisture-filled canal. As each of them toppled over the edge, soaring into ecstasy, they confessed the heartfelt love possessing them.

Xavier rolled over and brought Kennedy down on top of him. As he held her tightly against him, he spread kisses all over her face and into her hair. He felt content, utterly fulfilled. He could feel how labored her breathing still was, hoping she knew she'd left him just as breathless.

With Kennedy's brothers visiting her, Xavier was pretty sure she wouldn't spend the night. God only knew how much he wanted that to happen. Having her in his bed all night long would put him on top of the world.

Kennedy raised herself on one elbow and looked down at Xavier. "Is it okay if I spend the night? I don't think my brothers will mind. They understand I'm an adult with adult needs. And they definitely know how we feel about each other."

"Your question is an answer to my prayer. I want you here all night with me, babe, but I don't want to cause a problem between you and your family. You sure they'll be okay with it?"

Kennedy shrugged. "They really don't have much of a choice, but I'll call and let the guys know I'm staying here. It'll be fine."

He pulled her head down and kissed her thoroughly. "Whatever you feel is best. I'm for what Kennedy wants and needs. Don't ever doubt that you come first with me."

"Appreciate it." She kissed the tip of his nose before reaching over to the nightstand and picking up the phone.

As soon as Kennedy began talking on the phone to her family, Xavier got out of bed and went into the bathroom, where he turned on the water. Once he'd achieved the preferred water temperature, he added soothing bath salts and lit several votives. He wanted each of the nights they spent together to be memorable. Keeping Kennedy constantly thinking about him, as he did her, was his objective.

Before leaving the bathroom, he made sure to hang an extra bathrobe on the back of the door. Drying her off and wrapping her up warmly and cuddly was one of his favorite things to do. She loved the pampering and he loved to pamper her.

Striding over to the bed, Xavier reached down and scooped Kennedy up into his arms. She knew what to expect and was always eager for them to shower or bathe in the tub together. He made it difficult for her to take her mind off him. He did so many special things that she couldn't forget if she wanted to.

Before settling Kennedy down into the water, he kissed her passionately. "I love you so much."

Kennedy hungrily returned his kiss, looking forward to more sizzling pleasures. "I love you, too."

With the issues that seemed to face them almost daily, Kennedy couldn't help wondering if love would be enough to get them through the tumultuous days ahead. Although she'd like to believe their relationship would run smoothly from now on in, she wasn't one to kid herself. All relationships had problems, but with the number of women she had already encountered, she wasn't sure how many more she could stomach.

Chapter 12

Kennedy was all smiles as she drove toward Xavier's house to discuss traveling plans for their Paris rendezvous. She'd landed a couple of lucrative modeling jobs in the fabulous "city of light" so she'd called to tell him not to worry about trying to land the gig he had hoped to include her in. They'd been discussing this for a couple of weeks.

The one thing Kennedy had thought about all day long was how they'd repeatedly made love. She and Xavier weren't able to get enough of each other. By the time they'd finally fell off to sleep, in the wee hours of the morning, they both were exhausted but completely satisfied, physically and mentally.

Instead of pulling her car into the driveway, Kennedy parked on the street. As she gathered her belongings, before exiting the vehicle, she spotted movement.

Unable to believe her eyes, she stared at the two entwined figures on the front porch. Xavier and Tiaja Rae had each other wrapped up in what Kennedy considered a compromising embrace. After the stunning model kissed Xavier on the mouth, she made her way down his walkway and strolled the few yards to her late-model Corvette.

As though Kennedy thought she could somehow ease the excruciating pain, she clutched at her heart, massaging it briskly. For someone who professed not to like someone, it didn't look to Kennedy as if Xavier had any dislike for Tiaja Rae. If there *was* an explanation for what she'd witnessed, she couldn't imagine what it'd be. No matter how fleeting the kiss may've been, it shouldn't have occurred, not if Xavier De Marco was in love with her.

Kennedy wondered if she should confront what she'd seen or just walk away from the man she loved and her arch enemy. She certainly felt betrayed by Xavier. The last person she would've expected to see him share an intimate moment with was Tiaja Rae. And what had happened between them inside the house, before she'd ever gotten there?

As sick as it made Kennedy feel inside, she dared to wonder, *Had their love affair been too good to be true?*

Nestling her head back against the seat's headrest, Kennedy closed her eyes to ponder the troubling situation. Her agent had already lined up a couple of jobs for her in Paris and it wouldn't look good for her to back out.

Kennedy finally made the decision to drive away unnoticed. It'd be better for her to think everything through before facing Xavier. She felt rabid with anger. This was a dark time for her, a time when she wasn't sure she'd ever see the light of day. After a quick turn of the ignition, the automobile roared to life. Feeling pain and deep regret, Kennedy drove away from Xavier's home, worried that this was an issue they might fail to work out.

The tears had begun to fall before Kennedy had actually pulled the car away from the curb and were still cascading down her cheeks. As she entered her home, she hoped she could get into the master bathroom and repair her makeup before she had to face Gregory and Scott.

A sigh of relief escaped Kennedy the moment she closed the bedroom door behind her. Dashing into the bathroom, she went right to the sink, washed her face and reapplied makeup.

Kennedy took off her outfit and slipped into lounging attire.

As she glanced at the clock-radio, she figured it was time to think about what to prepare for dinner. Eating wasn't at all appealing to her. Finding out why Tiaja Rae was at her man's house was the only thing that whet her appetite.

The female laughter coming from the front of the house had Kennedy downright puzzled. Even though Bianca and Gregory were supposed to have lunch today, the laughter wasn't very familiar. As she followed the cheerful sounds, she tried to figure out who else was in the house besides her siblings.

Just before entering the family room, Kennedy stopped dead in her tracks. Seeing Tiaja Rae seated on her sofa had her in shock, which quickly turned to rage. This woman had her nerve coming into her house like this, especially after she'd just left Xavier's home! Instead of saying what was on her mind, which definitely would've been offensive, Kennedy turned on her heels and headed back toward her bedroom.

Before Kennedy could close the door, Scott kept it from shutting by jamming his foot in the track at the bottom. "Please let me explain. I can see how upset you are. We need to talk. She offered to pick me up…and I agreed to her plan because I'd thought we'd be long gone before you made it back home."

"How could you have her come here after the way she treated me at the television studio? Or doesn't her horrible behavior toward me mean anything to you?"

Scott grabbed hold of Kennedy's hand. "You know better than that, K. She apologized to me and wants to do the same with you. Will you please hear her out?"

"She may be able to sell you a line of bull, but not me. There's not a sincere bone in her body. Get her out of my house or I won't be responsible for my actions."

Scott frowned. "Kennedy, this is so unlike you. What's really going on?"

"Just get her far away from me, Scott. She's not welcome here."

Scott frowned. "I'm sorry. I didn't use my head in making this call."

"You used your head all right, it's just a matter of which one," Kennedy shot back, her expression full of sarcasm.

Scott acknowledged his sister's churlish, unfair response with a nod. "I wonder why it always comes down to that." Before his anger got the best of him, without uttering another challenging word, he walked off. After all, this *was* Kennedy's home—and she had every right to say who was or wasn't welcome in her personal space.

Looking after Scott with tears in her eyes, wishing she hadn't hurt him like that, Kennedy couldn't help wondering if she would've reacted so horribly had she not seen Tiaja Rae and Xavier holding each other close. The kiss her rival had given the man she was in love with still had her blood past boiling.

No matter how much Kennedy regretted her bad behavior with her brother it couldn't be erased. She owed Scott a big apology and she'd see to it that he got a sincere one. But all she wanted right now was for him to get Tiaja Rae out of her home. Now was hardly the appropriate time for the two women to begin any sort of dialogue between them. The very nerve of her coming to her home rankled Kennedy. Tiaja Rae had been nasty to her from the very first day they'd ever shared a runway.

Kennedy would never forget how nastily she'd been treated that day.

Back in her bedroom Kennedy threw herself across the bed. At the same time, her cell phone rang. She leaped up from the mattress and dashed across the room, scrambling around in her purse for her phone. The caller ID revealed Xavier's number. She had a strong urge to throw the phone across the room, yet managed to refrain.

Once the voice-mail feature clicked on, Kennedy laid the

phone down on the nightstand. She would listen to the message later. There was nothing Xavier could say to her to make her feel any better, at least, not at the moment. He also had a lot of explaining to do, but she wasn't in the mood to hear a single one of his remarks, either. Seeing him with Tiaja Rae was more than enough for her to deal with right now. Burying her face into the pillow, she released the stinging tears.

Kennedy awakened to insistent knocking on the bedroom door. Looking over at the clock produced quite a shock to her system. It was after 7:00 p.m. and she'd come into her room in the late afternoon. Sleep had come upon her not long after her head had hit the pillow. *I must've been exhausted,* she mentally reasoned. After pulling herself up in bed, positioning her back against the headboard, she called out to whoever was on the other side of the door.

Surprised to see Gregory standing there, as opposed to Scott, the smile she tossed her brother was weak and ineffective. And she instantly knew she'd failed miserably at putting her brother at ease. "What's up, big brother?"

"Maybe you should answer that one." He crossed the room and stretched out at the bottom of the mattress. "Scott told me what happened earlier. How're you feeling?"

"Lousy. I was downright unfair to him. Is he still here?"

"He's in the guest room. He felt so bad about what occurred that he canceled their outing and sent Tiaja Rae home. Scott hates that he upset you so badly."

"The feeling is mutual. I was wrong. I let my emotions win out over common sense. I've been able to keep my cool around her up until now. Well," she said, "there was the horrific little incident that called for a wine bath some time ago."

"I don't blame you for how you reacted. Neither does Scott. He blames himself for what happened. He's upset that you might believe he hurt you intentionally."

Kennedy sucked her teeth. "Of course I don't believe that. Scott would never hurt me on purpose. He just used poor judgment where Tiaja Rae is concerned."

"He likes this girl, Kennedy. And she seems to like him, a lot."

"Tiaja Rae is just using him to get at me. For someone who's all over Xavier every chance she gets, I find it hard to believe she's that interested in Scott."

"What, I don't measure up to your supermodel boyfriend?" Looking none too pleased with what he'd heard, Scott stood in the doorway, leaning against the jamb.

Kennedy whirled around to face Scott. "This has nothing to do with you measuring up to anyone. You stand in a class all your own. Tiaja Rae is simply not who you think she is."

"Can you be absolutely sure of that?" Scott asked.

"No, but neither can you be so sure of her. Look, if you still want to see her after you witnessed how she treated me, you go right ahead. Just don't court her in my house."

"I'll move into a hotel right away." Scott turned on his heels and left.

Kennedy and Gregory exchanged bewildered glances.

"Is he serious?" Kennedy asked her oldest brother.

"Afraid so. Now he's hurt. You two need to work this situation out. It's not worth losing the loving relationship you've always reveled in. Are you going to let that happen? Are you willing to let your flesh-and-blood brother go over some woman you don't like?"

Without answering the question, Kennedy dashed out of the room and ran toward the bedroom Scott occupied. She went right inside and threw herself into his arms. "Please don't go. I'm sorry I upset you. Tiaja Rae is my problem, not yours, and I shouldn't try to make you take issue with her because I don't like her. Will you stay?"

Scott gathered his baby sister into his strong arms. "I never wanted to go, but I thought it might be better for me to leave. I want to stay right here with you. We're family, Kennedy. Think we can get past all this?"

Kennedy slipped her hand into Scott's. "I know we can."

Scott looked her dead in the eye. "Even if I continue to see Tiaja Rae?"

Kennedy tried to ignore the dagger-sharp pain she felt inside her chest. "No matter what you do or who you do it with. It's your life. I just want you happy."

He kissed her forehead. "I want the same for you, Kennedy. I'd never do anything to intentionally hurt you. I promise to keep Tiaja Rae out of your sight."

Kennedy wrinkled her nose. "That's probably for the best. I wish you well."

The two loving siblings embraced warmly and then Kennedy left the room, bumping into Gregory on her way out. The two exchanged endearing smiles but she didn't stop to talk to her brother. Scott and Tiaja Rae as a couple didn't sit well with her, but like she'd told her brother it was his life. Maybe he'd have a positive impact on her antagonist. Scott was sweet and had a bubbly personality, so it could rub off on Tiaja Rae.

Kennedy wasn't about to give up her brother for anyone so she decided she'd have to sit back and watch things unfold. If Tiaja Rae was concentrating solely on Scott, that could mean she just might take her eyes and hands off Xavier. Only time would tell.

Seeing Tiaja Rae's car parked in front of her house only two days later made Kennedy want to turn around and leave. Thinking that it might cause her brothers to speculate about her true character, she reconsidered her position, not wanting them to think she couldn't be the bigger person. Kennedy was capable of that…and so much more.

Perhaps getting this face-to-face meeting with Tiaja Rae in her rearview mirror was best for everyone concerned, Kennedy thought. She owed it to Scott to at least make an attempt at civility toward the model who'd had it in for her for a long time now. As Kennedy pulled into her driveway, she noticed Bianca's midnight-blue Porsche, which was parked across the street from Tiaja Rae's Corvette.

After Kennedy had pulled her car into the garage, she quickly exited the automobile and hurried through the door leading inside.

Putting on her game face wasn't as easy for Kennedy as she'd hoped. The second she saw her brothers and the two women seated in the family room she began to pray for courage. Gregory and Scott had clearly made themselves at home, but she wasn't sure the women they appeared at such ease with had their best interests at heart. She still believed Bianca was on the rebound even though she claimed to have cut all ties with Torrance. Tiaja Rae's actual agenda with Scott wasn't the least bit transparent.

Tiaja Rae practically leaped out of her seat. "Hi, Kennedy," she said, shuffling her feet nervously.

It was still hard for Kennedy to be in the presence of Tiaja Rae, yet the two were nearly standing toe to toe in her home. She would only hear her out because of Scott. Her brother had gone completely off the deep end over the stunning supermodel.

Tiaja Rae once again made direct eye contact with Kennedy. This meeting with Scott's sister was every bit as hard for her. She'd had a hard time talking him into letting her come there to do this. "I know you find my sudden change of heart toward you hard to believe. If it makes you feel any better, I'm having a hard time with the change in myself." She looked down at her beautifully manicured fingernails before looking back up at Kennedy.

Kennedy closely studied the woman she still considered her enemy. "The change in you is hard to accept. I'm not convinced anyone can change that quickly. But what is even harder for me to believe is how you went on the attack against me from day one. You've been downright vicious to me."

Tiaja Rae was clearly aware Kennedy had spoken nothing but the truth about her nastiness. Her bad treatment of Scott's sister had cost the other model dearly, causing her to flinch at the raw pain visible in Kennedy's eyes. Something that had occurred a lot lately, Tiaja Rae's expression had softened and was darn near wistful. "You have yet to learn what it means or how it feels to be dethroned. I hope you never find out."

Tiaja Rae held nothing back. She didn't blink an eye as she told Kennedy that her sudden appearance in a world she saw as exclusively hers had caused her insecurities to flare up in the light of day and act as a neon sign in the darkness of night.

"I was the top black model, possessing top billing, when you blasted onto the scene, gorgeous, fresh faced and full of vitality. My position as an African-American supermodel was unrivaled until you came along, thinking you could steal my thunder. No way was I turning my crown and jeweled scepter over to you. You had to earn them and I simply didn't think you capable of stepping into my shoes, let alone following along in my zealous strides. I was the queen. In my eyesight you weren't even fit to be crowned princess. Obviously, I was dead wrong."

Kennedy frowned. "What I don't get is why you suddenly realize you were wrong. There is nothing right about the callous way you treated me. I was young and on fire for the fashion world. I didn't come into this business to dethrone you. I simply love modeling. I *was* proud of you and I would've been honored to walk in your footsteps, though walking beside you was my preference. I don't see how you can change your attitude toward me this quickly. You've been acting up with me for years now."

Tiaja Rae lowered her lashes. "It's called envy. Because of you I saw me growing old, though I'm hardly long in the tooth. Suddenly the eyes of the world were all on you. I couldn't handle it. So I made scene after scene, refusing to work a job if they kept you on. For a good while my tantrums worked. Then one day, my bad behavior was no longer tolerated. I was told I could leave the job if I couldn't work with you, but that you were staying. I saw myself beginning to lose job after job to you, not to mention the numerous endorsements you began winning out over me. That's it in a nutshell."

"That's quite a lot to fit into a mere nutshell. So now you want me to believe you've changed because you're romantically interested in my brother. Is that really a good enough reason to change your cache of evil ways?"

"It is if you believe a man is capable of bringing out the softer side in you. I've kept my heart and my emotions packed solidly away from the world my entire life. No one was ever privileged to see my vulnerabilities, yet innocence and vulnerability worked so well for you. I tried to wipe the brilliant shine off your character, to unmask the ugly tarnish beneath—mission still not accomplished."

Tiaja Rae surprised Kennedy by saying she'd found no tarnish on her person or inside her. She then stated she saw the need for her to make drastic changes because she didn't think Scott could ever be with the kind of woman she'd intentionally led the world to believe she was. It had been much easier for her to mask her countless insecurities.

"Scott's far more deserving of a woman much better than Tiaja Rae Montgomery, the nasty-tempered supermodel the world has come to know me as. I'm changing because I've finally found someone worth altering my behavior for. Your brother deserves the best Tiaja Rae I can offer him. The genuine lady, the one my parents raised me to be, is hiding in here somewhere," she said, jabbing softly at her heart.

Kennedy was astounded, yet she remained reserved. This could all be just a game to Tiaja Rae, a game that she wouldn't put past her to indulge in to get what she wanted. On the other hand, Kennedy desperately wanted to believe the woman, if for no other reason than her brother, who was interested in her, and was still in L.A. because of her.

"I sincerely apologize. I also ask for your forgiveness, though I know none of it will come in a hurry. I promise to earn your forgiveness so I can become deserving of your respect. Caring for someone comes with its share of demands. My feelings for Scott are demanding me to change and to become a better human being. I owe it to myself first and to Scott second. We both know it won't work if I'm doing it just for him."

Anxiety gripped Kennedy. This moment was downright alien and beyond bizarre in nature. Not only was she ill at ease, the whole scenario felt extremely uncomfortable. Kennedy found it difficult to crack so much as a smile, but she managed to soften her stern expression a tad.

"I have behaved badly," Tiaja Rae continued. "I'm very much aware of the awful things I've said and done to you. I'd like you to give me a shot at making it all up to you, no matter how hard it might be. My apology is heartfelt." Tiaja Rae extended her hand to Kennedy. "I'd love for us to call a truce."

Although Kennedy wasn't exactly feeling Tiaja Rae's sentiments she considered forgiveness by taking hold of her hand and shaking it firmly. "I only hope you mean it. If you're just doing this to get next to Scott, the chances of it working out are nil and none. On the other hand, if you genuinely care for my brother, I'm the last person who'd stand in the way. I'm willing to give you the shot you've requested. I never got a chance to tell you this, but I had admired you for a long time. I *was* a big fan."

Scott had noticed the emphasis Kennedy had put on the word *was*. He understood her. He knew she'd been a huge fan of Tiaja Rae's before all the nastiness had begun. All he could do was hope that Tiaja Rae stood on her word. If she didn't, he had a pretty good idea there'd be hell for her to pay from Kennedy. His sister wouldn't stand idly by and let her brother get hurt by anyone. And he wouldn't dare be with anyone who wanted to hurt Kennedy. It wouldn't take Scott long to find out if Tiaja Rae was sincere or not. Two weeks wasn't enough time for her to change completely.

"I have something else to say, too," Kennedy expressed, making direct eye contact with Tiaja Rae. "I didn't want to go here, but I have to. If you're so interested in my brother why did I see you in an intimate embrace with Xavier a few days ago?"

Scott's eyes immediately fell on the woman he'd gone to bat for against his sister, believing she was making positive changes. He didn't know all the history between his sister and Tiaja Rae, but Kennedy had laid out a few ugly instances for him. He was every bit as eager to hear the answer to his sister's pointed question.

Tiaja Rae sighed with impatience. "That was innocent."

"It didn't look innocent to me. It certainly didn't feel that way, either. You are very deceptive. This isn't the first time you've shown an interest in the man I'm dating. What about your hands all over him after the modeling show, the evening Xavier and I had our first date? What about how you conducted yourself on the set of the soap?"

Surprised by the kissing revelation, Scott raised an eyebrow.

"Didn't you hear anything I've said, Kennedy? Everything I did to you was out of jealousy, including flirting with Xavier. You're going to feel this way one day, too. Believe me. Just wait until the next young sister bubbling with energy comes behind you, stealing away jobs that you could always count on."

As Kennedy slapped Tiaja Rae hard across the face, she saw red. She had stunned the other model, but good, causing her to quickly step out of the line of fire, shielding her face, as if she expected to be assaulted again. "How dare you continue to insult me! I've never come after you once. Every job I landed I competed for it fairly or I was requested by the designer," Kennedy raged. "Are you really that damn insecure?"

Scott was shocked by his sister's act of violence. He'd never seen her anger out of control. On the other hand, he wasn't too happy with what he'd learned from Tiaja Rae, either. He didn't care for her self-serving responses, but he felt bad for the slap that would probably leave a bruise. "I'd really like to hear you give Kennedy a straight answer for a change," Scott weighed in, worried that his sister could be arrested.

Refusing to show the raw fear she felt inside, Tiaja Rae shrugged, staying true to her coldhearted form. "That's as straight as I can get, Scott. Do you think it's easy for me to stand here and confess jealousy and insecurity? It's not." She made sure to stay out of Kennedy's reach. She had no idea that she was capable of this kind of retaliation.

"So you are insecure," Kennedy shot back, her hands shaking. "Glad you can finally admit it. What I don't understand is why? You're a beautiful, talented woman."

"Beauty doesn't always go hand in hand with honor and kindheartedness. I acted dishonorably. I've apologized and I don't know what else I can do."

Scott looked over at Tiaja Rae. "I'm astounded by your cavalier attitude about this whole issue. Believing you could change, I feel like I betrayed my sister. I'm unsure if you're still not getting back at her by trying to use me against her. It won't work. My sister means the world to me. I don't demand that the girl I'm with has to love my family, but they have to show respect. I think we should let things between us cool down and perhaps revisit our issue later. This matter has gotten way out of hand."

Tiaja Rae looked as if she'd been hit again, this time by a ton of bricks. Besides Xavier, she was normally irresistible to men. Yet another rude awakening did nothing to uplift her spirit. She really felt bad and she didn't know how to express it with sincerity. This whole mess she'd created bothered her, but it upset her more to have Scott turn away from her. For the first time in a very long while she had actually felt hope for a serious romance. "I see your point. Is it okay if we remain friends?" she asked Scott.

"Friends also have to respect each other. I'll give you a call when I figure this all out. Is that okay with you?"

"It has to be if I want to salvage what I thought we could have." She turned to Kennedy again. "I am sorry. I just don't know how to express it. I'm not used to apologizing to anyone. That's how we got here. I hope you can one day forgive me."

Kennedy was surprised that she didn't feel an ounce of regret for tagging Tiaja Rae, wishing she'd slugged her a couple of times. It was dead wrong to attack another human being. This rage had been building up inside her for a long time and it had simply finally boiled over.

Sure that Kennedy didn't have anything left to say to Tiaja Rae, Scott believed it was his duty to see her out since he'd allowed her to come in the first place. He'd been so sure Kennedy would've been more forgiving, yet he knew why she felt such rage.

Bianca came over and stood next to Kennedy. "I have something to say, too. I know you think I'm on the rebound, but I'm definitely not." She smiled broadly at Gregory, blushing in the process. "I really like this sweet guy. He's given me a renewal of hope. Something I haven't felt in a while. I need a chance, too, a chance to prove I only want to enhance Gregory's happiness. You taught me a long time ago I can't make anyone happy, that joy comes from within. Now that I know what I want, I think I've finally gotten it."

Everyone laughed at that. Kennedy hugged Bianca.

"I think I need a drink," Gregory said, taking Bianca's hand. "Come out to the kitchen with me. By the way, I like you, too, a whole bunch."

Bianca kissed Gregory on the cheek. "I'm glad we like each other."

Scott came back into the room and slipped his arm around Kennedy's shoulders. She needed his support right now and he felt it in spades. She had a daunting task before her in accepting Tiaja Rae's apology. He believed if anyone could pull it off

Kennedy would manage it. She was a fair person, though Tiaja Rae had treated her grossly unfairly and with utter contempt. If he was a gambling man, his money would be placed on Kennedy.

Chapter 13

Kennedy held her breath in anticipation of Xavier taking the runway. The moment he appeared, she released her pent-up breath. *Oh, my goodness, he keeps getting finer. Every time I see him he looks more handsome than before.*

Xavier was in complete command of his performance, reveling in his element. No woman who claimed not to be even slightly attracted to a man could pass him by without stopping and staring. The ones who didn't stop and gawk had to be legally blind. A woman madly in love with another man wouldn't be able to control the desire to give him the thrice-over. A once- or twice-over wasn't enough.

The stylish Dior pinstriped tuxedo, making its runway debut, looked as if it had been designed right on Xavier's sexy body. Kennedy's eyes left his gorgeous face and went straight to his strong, sturdy thighs, thighs she had imagined her body trapped beneath at least a hundred times since they'd first made love. She rarely had a problem conjuring up erotic images of them in compromising positions.

Xavier pushed his hands through his hair in dramatic fashion, thrilling Kennedy no end, causing her to darn near bounce up and down in her seat. As he strutted his magnificent physique up and down the runway, her eyes followed his every move. It was almost hard to believe she had been romantically involved with this magnificent creature. Men didn't come any more sensitive and attentive than Xavier had been with her.

As the exquisite female model Carlita Richardson, draped in a seductive white, tiered bohemian-style gown, joined Xavier, their eyes met in what appeared as a hot, passionate coupling. Her tongue slowly roved the end of her finger in a provocative way before she rested her fingernail on the very tip of her tongue. Eyeing him from head to toe, looking as if she wanted to devour him, Carlita circled him, her hips moving with rapid, fluid smoothness, as she checked him out from every angle.

The arrogant smirk, along with the sultry come-hither look Xavier gave to his lovely feminine counterpart, received a rousing cheer from the audience. It was almost like a cat-and-mouse game—and everyone appeared eager to see who would win. Most of the women would've already swooned at his patent-leather-shod feet by now, Kennedy guessed, including her. No one would mind getting caught by this sexy hunter.

Once several more exciting poses were flamboyantly executed, the two models came together in a brief caress, their eyes expressing fiery desire for each other. Seconds later, the stunning couple left the runway in the same pompous way they'd entered.

Kennedy was still in a confused state of mind because she hadn't seen or talked to Xavier since spotting him with Tiaja Rae over two weeks ago. She didn't know whether to slip out without speaking to him or at least let him know she'd dropped in to see him perform.

Everything about their relationship was up in the air for Kennedy, except for the fact of her loving Xavier. She loved him deeply. There was no doubt in her mind about her feelings for him. However, his hugging and kissing her archenemy had hurt her deeply. Although he'd called her repeatedly, leaving numerous messages over the past two weeks, she hadn't returned a single phone call.

According to her brothers, Xavier had even stopped by the house after he couldn't reach her by phone, but Kennedy had been out. He had also asked her brothers if they knew why their sister wasn't returning his calls, but neither sibling thought they should get into her personal affairs. They knew their sister well enough to stay out of her business, unless she asked for their advice; she hadn't. Kennedy had told them she'd needed more time to figure it all out.

Wanting desperately to see Xavier had gotten the best of Kennedy. If she wasn't ready for an up-close-and-personal meeting, watching him on the runway was the next best thing, yet it had hardly fulfilled her emotional and physical needs for him. She had to act fast since he normally left the venue right after he completed his assignment.

To talk to him or not to talk to him was the million-dollar question in her mind.

As Kennedy made her way up the steps to reach the lobby, the question was answered for her. Xavier stood at the top of the stairs, looking down upon her. A sudden case of nerves went on the attack inside her stomach, yet she felt giddy at the same time. God, he looked wonderful. He was so beautiful and manly. Then she noticed the formidable expression of his face. He didn't appear happy to see her.

Xavier extended his hand to Kennedy before she cleared the last step. Hesitantly, she slipped her hand into his. She immediately felt the electrical current shoot through her entire being. "How are you?" She hated that her voice had sounded weak and crackly.

Xavier eyed her curiously. "I'm fine, but I need to know how you are."

Xavier ushered Kennedy into the lobby, where several red velvet wingback chairs were strategically positioned. He quickly led her over to one of the seating arrangements that didn't have a table in between the two chairs. He wanted to be as close to her as possible, hoping she'd fully explain her sudden absence from his life.

Kennedy nervously peered at him. "How'd you know I was in the audience?"

"I definitely felt you, but that's not the only way I knew. Apparently Scott told Tiaja Rae about your plans and she later called and told me."

Kennedy failed to keep herself from tensing up. "Why would she do that?"

"Because she knows how I feel about you."

"And how would she know that?" Kennedy had grown impatient.

"I told her I'm in love with you. Everyone but you seems sure of it."

"You have no clue why you haven't heard from me?"

"I didn't, not until Tiaja Rae found out from you you'd seen her at my house. I had every intention of telling you she'd come to see me, and why, but you refused to take my calls or see me. Please tell me what's bothering you."

"I think you already know. I'm not into game playing, Xavier."

As Kennedy got up from her seat, Xavier jumped up and stood right in front of her. "Please don't go. I can't figure out what went wrong if you don't tell me."

Kennedy stared him down, breathing rapidly. "I saw you two in an intimate embrace. She even kissed you. You didn't object to her affectionate displays."

"There was no reason for me to protest. If you'll please sit back down, I'll explain everything to you."

"Explain it or lie to me about it?"

"Have I ever lied to you?"

Kennedy responded to Xavier's question by reclaiming her seat. The expression on her face let him know she was ready to hear him out. He hadn't lied to her thus far.

"Tiaja Rae came to my house to call a truce. She's sorry about her behavior toward you and she wanted me to know that." He then explained to Kennedy that Tiaja Rae had planned to apologize to her when she'd come over to her house to see Scott. "I believe she's sincere in wanting to make amends with you."

"Oh, this is just too rich! Why all of a sudden is she having regrets? She's only been treating me with disdain since the first day we met."

"I know, babe. But people *can* change. Do you believe that can happen?"

"Some people do change, but not everyone does. Tiaja Rae doesn't have a compassionate bone in her body. Why would she suddenly change her attitude with me?"

"According to her, she has fallen hard for Scott. She doesn't see a future for them if she's at odds with his only sister."

Kennedy looked as if she'd been Tasered with an electrical shock. Trying to assimilate what Xavier had said to her was difficult. That Tiaja Rae cared enough about Scott to stop being so mean and nasty to his sister was still shocking to Kennedy. Since Xavier had heard it, too, perhaps it was really true. Still, was this the kind of woman she wanted her brother involved with? She knew it wasn't up to her.

"Maybe Scott has touched something deep inside her. How do we know why she acts the way she does? Her actions are certainly those of an insecure woman. I know that much. Perhaps she's been heartbroken before. Scott's a good man so maybe she's able to recognize his great character and wants to see where things can go."

Kennedy was impressed that Tiaja Rae had informed Xavier of how she felt. It was time for her to let him know she'd spoken with the lady in question, but it seemed he already knew. "She told me as much and she's apologized. The jury is still out on her change of heart, but I'm going to try real hard to accept things. Scott is trying, too."

"It's possible Scott is also changing. They may've found something in each other that's causing a definite impact on how they might've viewed love before."

As Kennedy was about to respond to his take on things, Xavier moved out of the chair and knelt down before her. Without him uttering another word, his mouth covered hers in a kiss that nearly made her heart stop. "None of what's going on with them has anything to do with us." He kissed her again. "We love each other and there has to be trust between us."

Xavier's mouth possessed Kennedy's again, kissing her deeper and longer. "What you saw happening with Tiaja Rae and me was merely my acceptance of her truce. My heart belongs to you, Kennedy Bassett, no one but you. Please tell me you believe me."

Kennedy found it hard not to believe Xavier. His eyes showed his sincerity as well as the tone of his voice. She could continue to act silly or fly into this man's arms and surrender her heart to him once again. The thought of being made a fool of caused her a bit of hesitancy. Then, throwing caution to the wind, she threw her arms around his neck, kissing him back as passionately as he'd kissed her.

Kennedy kissed him several more times before allowing them both to come up for air. "I believe you, Xavier."

Xavier closed his eyes, relieved she'd said the words he'd longed to hear. "You can believe *in* me, too. I won't hurt you or let you down. We're so good together. I don't want to lose you, not ever. I've been miserable without you."

Kennedy captured Xavier's face between her two hands. "We definitely have that in common. I didn't know I could be so despondent. I don't ever want to feel that way again. I love you so much."

Xavier didn't even bother to wipe the tears from his face. "I love you, too."

It was just about time for Kennedy to know just how much he loved her.

The majestic Eiffel Tower gleamed in the sunshine, appearing to dwarf all the other magnificent structures in the vicinity.

Kennedy loved to visit the popular landmark whenever she came to the City of Light. It didn't matter how many times she'd visited there, she had never once failed to make the tower a stop on her route of travel.

In fact, Kennedy loved everything about Paris, one of the most renowned fashion metropolises in the entire world. She always brought an empty suitcase along with her so she could shop until her finances ran low. This time was no different. On frequent visits to numerous Parisian fashion houses, she rarely left one empty-handed. The lingerie was to die for. Lucky for her, one of her modeling jobs was exclusively for intimate apparel. She loved to feel the delicious sensations of satin and lace against her skin.

As Kennedy sipped on a cool drink outdoors at one of the sidewalk cafés, she couldn't help stealing covert glances at Xavier every chance she got. He fit into this city like a hand to a glove, loving Paris as much as she did. She was genuinely thrilled about reexploring Paris with him at her side. She'd been in France less than twenty-four hours, yet she already dreaded the time of her departure. Leaving Paris was never easy for her.

Xavier had landed in Paris several days prior to Kennedy's arrival. The scheduled modeling assignments she'd had at home all had to be handled before she'd flown out. Gregory and Scott were back in Philly now, but they planned to return to California in the next month or so. The Bassett brothers had found the perfect office space with more than adequate square footage. They'd happily signed a three-year lease, having negotiated a great and equitable deal on the prime rental property.

Xavier reached over and covered Kennedy's hand with his own. "What are you thinking? You seem preoccupied."

"Just thinking of how much I love this magnificent city. My brothers have also crossed my mind. I'm thrilled they're moving to L.A. My parents are also coming out west to help Gregory and Scott move in. My uncle will manage the Philly office."

"Sounds like quite a family affair. I can't wait to meet the rest of your family. How much have you told your parents about us?"

Kennedy smiled brightly. "Everything there is to know."

Xavier angled high an eyebrow. "Everything?"

"Barring the intimate details of our relationship, I've shared a lot of our history with them. Mom and Dad are eager to meet you, but they feel they know you already. They also know of our recent problems. I'm sorry I didn't believe in you. And I need you to know I'm no longer insecure about the women that flirt with you. It took me a lot of time to recognize that a lot of the problems were with me."

"Being my girl is a tough gig. Don't think for a second that I don't know what you've been up against. You are not at fault. Back to your parents, I'm looking forward to having a serious chat with them, especially your dad. I've kind of been rehearsing some of the things I plan to say to him."

Kennedy appeared intrigued by his comments. "Like what?"

"Oh, like asking him for your hand in marriage," he said with nonchalance, feeling everything but indifference.

As moisture formed at the corners of her eyes, her pupils brightened considerably. "Would…you mind…repeating that?"

Xavier got out of his seat and came over and knelt before her, taking her hand in his. "I love you unconditionally. Will you marry me, Kennedy Darryl Bassett, for richer or poorer and in sickness and in health? Will you become my bride, my soul mate forever?"

Tears spilled from Kennedy's eyes. She only fleetingly wondered how long Xavier had been toying with the idea of asking her to marry him. With her arms thrown about his neck, she willingly accepted his kisses.

Xavier wanted to marry her. *Hallelujah! Would wonders never cease?* With her heart overflowing with love, Kennedy looked into Xavier's eyes. "I'd love to be your soul mate for the rest of our natural lives. I accept your proposal of marriage, absolutely and unconditionally. I can't wait to become Mrs.

Xavier De Marco. Wow, what a resounding ring that has to it! Kennedy Darryl Bassett-De Marco is a powerful moniker. I hope I can live up to it."

"I know you will—and then some. I'm positively thrilled about you carrying my last name for the rest of our lives. So, what in the world do you think your dad's answer will be to my proposal of marriage?"

Kennedy's heart was filled to the brim, making it hard for her to converse with him. "I'm sure he'll give you his blessings, but I've already accepted your proposal, regardless of his response. My parents will come to love you as much as I do. Gregory and Scott already think the world of you. I can't tell you how many times they've said to me how they think you'd be an awesome in-law."

"I want to be more than in-law. I want to become a son to your parents and a brother to your brothers. You'll have the same importance to my family. My parents haven't met you yet, but they already adore you. I've told them how you fill me with joy and light up my world. That's enough for Mom and Dad."

"There's nothing that'd give me greater pleasure than becoming your bride, Xavier De Marco, my husband-to-be. I am so excited, way past joyful."

"Let's do a Jamaican wedding-honeymoon on the anniversary of our first date."

Kennedy gave Xavier a staggering kiss to show her enthusiastic agreement, nearly toppling him over. As he returned her thrilling kisses, his jack-hammering heart overflowed with the deep love he felt for her.

The Paris runway was designed with an arched trellis, fully decorated with fresh white roses and dainty bunches of baby's breath. A shimmering white carpet covered the flooring under the romantic archway. As the wedding march softly strummed the air, the bride appeared. A beautiful harpist dressed in a silvery sequined dress accompanied the four tuxedo-clad male violinists.

A group of six lovely bridesmaids and handsome grooms-men entered from the right side of the stage. The ladies wore simple strapless gowns in buttercup yellow, fashioned with beautiful bows streaming down the low-cut backs. The men were dressed in traditional two-button black tuxedos by Perry Ellis. The group was right at home on the runway as the professional worldwide models showed off what they had to offer.

Gasps of pleasure rent the air as Kennedy took center stage, looking like royalty draped in a strapless ivory gown, created from luxurious matte duchess bridal satin, adorned with crystal beading and a wraplike waist. The full pick-up skirt had diamond-cut floral embellishments in the center of each one. The corset-style back was elegantly designed, with matching material-covered buttons. On her feet she wore graceful satin slippers with the same crystal beading as the gown. With her hair piled high in dozens and dozens of silky ringlets, the sophisticated style was accented with bugle beading.

Kennedy's makeup was flawlessly applied, She held her shoulder-length-veiled head up, stepping high, lively and grace-fully, her tantalizing movements followed by all eyes in the audience. Twisting and turning her body, affecting gentle poses befitting a bride, she was in full command of her performance. She felt relaxed as she made a last full turn before standing perfectly still to wait for the next model to take the runway.

Xavier was the quintessential groom. He looked every bit the part of a man about to marry the woman he loved. As he made his way down the runway, he showcased his endless finesse. He was the consummate professional, dressed in a fabulous Joseph Abboud tuxedo, with single-breasted notch collar, non-vented coat and suspender buttons.

Single pleated pants with on-seam pockets, featuring zip fly with extended tab closure and elegant satin side braid were a perfect fit for Xavier. A white tuxedo shirt with French cuffs, wing collar and a 1/2" pleat in one hundred percent cotton highlighted his broad chest. Black star diopside cuff links with silver trim helped to round out his formal look, along with the patent-leather shoes.

Kennedy waited patiently for Xavier to come and meet up with her, her eyes riveted to his sexy body, a body that she would sleep next to every night, a body to pleasure hers as often as they both desired. Even though this was a fashion show featuring wedding attire, she couldn't help but fantasize about their upcoming wedding. She managed to keep the threatening tears from coming. This was the happiest she'd ever been in her entire life. They had truly enhanced each other's infinite joy.

Xavier stopped right in front of her, beneath the flowery trellis, extending his arm out for her to take, his eyes conveying to her how much he loved her. After looping her arm with his, they covered the entire runway, showing off their beautiful attire and fabulous bodies in premier fashion. The other models came together and paired off, following right after the enchanting bride and groom.

The loud shouts of bravo had the couple beaming from head to toe. This Paris audience, people who weren't always easy to please, approved of them in a huge way. Just before leaving the stage, Xavier took Kennedy into his arms. As he kissed her thoroughly, passionately, the crowd went wild. Holding hands, they took one more stroll down the runway, smiling at the loudly cheering audience.

Xavier looked deeply into Kennedy's eyes. "Talk about romancing the runway," he whispered. "This is a fashion show but a day very much like this one will soon become our reality. I can hardly wait. I love you."

Kennedy didn't try to hold back her tears. "I love you, too."

**When you can't trust anyone, the only thing
you can do is trust your heart....**

Essence Bestselling Author

GWYNNE FORSTER

PRIVATE LIVES

Following a bitter divorce, Allison Sawyer seeks seclusion at
a rustic mountain retreat. Though attracted to her neighbor,
Brock Lightner, she's wary and keeps her distance. Intrigued
by Allison, Brock wonders who she's running from—and how
he can convince her he'll do anything to protect her.

"A delightful book romance lovers will enjoy."
—*Romantic Times BOOKreviews*
on *Love Me or Leave Me*

*Coming the first week of March 2009
wherever books are sold.*

KIMANI™
ROMANCE

**www.kimanipress.com
www.myspace.com/kimanipress**   KPGFi040309

Welcome to Temptation Island…

Fan Favorite Author

Michelle Monkou

Only in PARADISE

For teacher Athena Crawford, the career opportunity of a
lifetime is set on an idyllic Caribbean island. But then she
and her project's administrator, Collin Winslow, start locking
horns—and sharing kisses. Can their delicate relationship
weather the storms about to break?

"Sweet Surrender (4 stars)…is an engaging love story."
—*Romantic Times BOOKreviews*

Coming the first week of March 2009 wherever books are sold.

KIMANI™
ROMANCE

www.kimanipress.com
www.myspace.com/kimanipress